The Rock 'n' Roll Kids

The
Rock 'n' Roll Kids

Liam G Clancy

Matador
Unit E2 Airfield Business Park,
Harrison Road, Market Harborough,
Leicestershire. LE16 7UL
Tel: 0116 2792299
Email: books@troubador.co.uk
Web: www.troubador.co.uk/matador
Twitter: @matadorbooks

ISBN 978 1803131 306

British Library Cataloguing in Publication Data.
A catalogue record for this book is available from the British Library.

Printed and bound in Great Britain by 4edge Limited
Typeset in 11pt Adobe Garamond Pro by Troubador Publishing Ltd, Leicester, UK

Matador is an imprint of Troubador Publishing Ltd

Chapter 1

Piper Jim's Incredible Meeting

'Good God, man! Why the hell are you laughing? This is not a laughing matter, Rockingham! The target is to be disposed of. Destroyed! The decision is to waste this bastard! We break our competitors by destroying their character. In the ranks I want total control and obedience. I am not going to suffer ambitious fantasists. Elimination, that is the goal. Understand?'

Two hours earlier, Pipe Sergeant Jim Rockingham was summoned to a North Dublin mansion. Dressed in a new civilian suit, he rushed by taxi from Ormond Square, where he lives in a rented council house, in the unkempt, inner-city Fish and Vegetable Market area. Piper Jim's visits to this impressive mansion were reasonably frequent. Relationships with his host were typically formal but also cordial. His highly influential friend always supported him enormously, both personally and financially. When times were tough, Jim was fast-tracked into several well-paid positions overseas with the United Nations and European Union. Jim, in return, was an established provider of valuable insider information. He regularly reported on the overall mood of army personnel but, more importantly, on the activities of certain targeted individuals.

Recent months saw him involved in a mysterious, highly planned undercover operation. He obediently followed certain strange instructions that emanated from the office of his influential friend. Increasingly, however, the Pipe Sergeant began to experience significant worry because he had absolutely no idea where all this intrigue was leading. He hopes that this meeting is now set to clarify everything.

'Let's get straight down to business. Your son, Rocky, is soon to be working in McKee Barracks officers' mess bar, serving army headquarters' VIP visitors.'

'Correct, sir. There is a token interview, but I've arranged it so that there is no other candidate.'

'Fine. The young lad takes after his dad, I hope. Will he do precisely what we tell him?'

Jim nods and forces a fake smile. It is vital for him to hide the ongoing intense confrontation and hostility that currently characterises the father-son relationship.

'Of course, sir. Young Rocky is a chip off the old block and always carries out my exact instructions. I am the sergeant; he is the soldier. You order. We deliver. Just ask.'

'That coloured boy you were having trouble with. He's out of your way now. We had him transferred out of Dublin.'

'Thank God he is gone. He was a bad influence. You know, since my wife Maria died, those two boys together were a handful. They had all kinds of crazy childish notions about becoming long-haired, beatnik, pop stars like The

Beatles, Fleetwood Mac and Thin Lizzy. I blame my late wife for encouraging it. I've put a stop to it. With the two of them separated, I'm sure that I can now convince Rocky to settle for a disciplined long-term army career.'

'Good. Now, what I need, Jim, are eyes and ears on the ground in McKee officers' mess. You and Rocky are going to become important informants, with your son as our key asset. We have a few problem people who are advancing in rank and building their reputation too fast for our liking. I need a flow of information about these people. We all know that barmen hear a lot when customers' tongues become loosened by a few pints.'

'Ha! Ha! You're right on that one, sir.'

'We love to exploit the "demon drink". All around the villages of Ireland, our cabal of bartenders keep us informed with stories picked up while standing behind the counter. We give them people to target and, being in the perfect position to overhear all the intrigues of a community, they oblige. Your son Rocky will have the same task. We need to get something negative on a rival. You know the drill.'

Jim nods and leans forward in expectation of finally receiving detailed clarifying information.

'Jim, our cabal system operates on a "need to know" basis. Every case is different. You often will not know the reason we need information on a target. So please accept and understand that reality. It's how our entire nationwide network denies information to our rivals. For this new task, all that is required is that you follow exactly my instructions.'

'Okay, sir, business as usual.'

'I can tell you now that your first task will be to help us concoct disparaging stories about a significant young target. The slurs may be just slightly true or totally false, just make sure we can make them stick. Your task will be to source the basic seed information via Rocky and we'll then grow them into a nice juicy humiliation.'

'Young. Hmm! Will my son be working close to this person? How easy is it going to be?'

'Jim, all I can say for now is that your first target is a regular in the VIP bar in McKee Barracks. Your son will be on the lookout for sex, money, drugs and honesty issues. If the target is drinking a lot, let me know and we can set him up with our boys in blue for a drunk-driving rap. We can even contrive a traffic accident. We have many embedded influential people in our blue cabal.'

Jim sucks in a clearly audible short breath as his mouth springs open. He shifts nervously in his seat. This is the type of scenario that he had been worrying about. Dawning on him was the fact that he was, like never before, being trusted with confidential methodology information of questionable legality. Doubts are creeping into his mind which he must conceal by feigning admiration.

'Oh! Wow! A blue cabal. We have the ability to do that… right, I see.'

'Now, if the target is not dating, we often manufacture gay inferences. His male colleagues will abandon his friendship in case they end up in prison or just to avoid getting tarred with the same sexy pink brush. So, think of blue and pink as they are perhaps our most powerful smears. We use them a lot. If the target has a girlfriend or wife, we move to expose unfaithfulness or exaggerate any hints of tension. You're getting the picture? Though your first target is somewhat immature, he is a dangerously rising star. Great CV, wonderful experience, brave, determined and, most worrying, he is an independent thinker. He is also rigidly honest, and so far, we have not managed to compromise

4

him. He is totally unwavering regarding the importance of his army officer commissioning oath of office. One of these believer types. Loyal to the Constitution, and he likes to emphasise his distance from any kind of politics. In fact, he is known to hate any form of politicisation of the green and blue uniforms. Otherwise, we would have gradually induced him into one of our secret cabals. He will soon find out the negative consequences of naive integrity. Laws are there to be broken, Jim.'

The next sentence is spoken with cool, clear intent. 'We are looking at elimination in this case.'

Jim grins broadly, attempting to make light of a horrific unfolding truth. 'Ha! Jaysus, sir. Elimination? He is to be eliminated. Real 007 stuff. Ha! So, I will become Piper Jim Bond. Ha! I love the way you use such tough language. You were never one to pull your punches.'

At this point, the entire atmosphere of the discussion changes. Clenched teeth, together with the sound of an angry fist abruptly pounding the table in front of Piper Jim, heralds the arrival of a shocking new reality.

'Elimination of a young officer? You are serious, sir. You know in all of these years, I've never been included in this kind of operation before.'

'Wrong! Totally wrong! You've played your part in many similar operations, Pipe Sergeant Rockingham.'

Jim immediately notices the use of his formal rank.

'However, I never told you of the consequences of our use of the information and stories you provided. You were not a cabal member. You were not on the inside track. You didn't need to know our techniques. Now I am telling you much more because you must manage the information-gathering of your son. He will be a spy, like you, but at a more sophisticated level.'

Jim is unable to hide a grimace of annoyance as he never considered himself to be a spy. He begins to adopt a defensive, argumentative tone.

'Sir, I was just passing on well-known army gossip. Nothing secret. I never considered myself to be spying on anybody. Now, will my son be protected in some way? The destroyed officer will, surely, immediately know that it is my son who is the source of the scandal we create. At best, he will have a fair idea of the identity of the person who wrecked his life. Now, that worries me.'

'Hold on, Jim, down through the years we never let you down. Did we?'

'Of course not, sir, but—'

'Jim, getting rid of people is how we keep power and control. Now, relax. Our smear warriors are on the ground, all around the country, to give any gossip the necessary legs. What we do is kill off our opponents' relationships with their friends in the community. We attack their social capital. Does that make sense, Jim?'

'Friendships are somehow attacked and destroyed. Is that what you are telling me?'

'Correct, basically, Jim, we drive a wedge between our opponents and their support network of friends and family. We denigrate their good name. To keep it simple, Jim, "poisoning the well" is the term we use. The East Germans Stasi have a great saying… *hassen auf*, which literally means "to put a hate on". We poison the targets' reputation and create hatred. Often even family members abandon them. You know full well that Ireland is a highly networked little island. Gossip in the form of emotional harassment works well. By destroying the vital warmth of human company and his support network, a target cannot function meaningfully in this country. We pull the rug out from under his social life, destroy his happiness, wreck his business or career. We break him mentally. People turn their back on him when they see him entering the local pub. The girls he is chasing in the dance hall disappear when they see him around. Unsmiling staff in his village shop serve him silently.'

'So, we copy the Stasi tactics? Were they not the hated and feared communist secret police?'

'Correct.'

Piper Jim's face flushes a bright red. His mouth momentarily falls open as he sucks in a tiny sharp breath. He shakes his head disapprovingly. 'Suicide. That must be a risk in the case of sensitive people. I do not want my son Rocky blamed if the target kills himself. If that happened, he might crack up as well.'

'Naw! Have no worries. Only a small minority actually do commit suicide.'

Piper Jim's eyeballs almost pop from their sockets as he becomes increasingly troubled. His mouth falls open.

'What? Suicide, only… *a small minority!*'

There is no immediate reply to Jim's exasperated exclamation. He stares downwards at the floor between his ankles. His momentary silence is followed by a further stern probing question. 'Then what about nervous breakdown? What about their loved ones? The innocent family members… their children. Kids hear a lot at school. Do any of the children commit suicide or have a nervous breakdown when they get bullied because of our smear?'

'Calm down, Jim. Yes, many targets go to the very edge emotionally. With lifelong friends and family rejecting them, they are devastated.'

He shrugs and continues. 'But that's how it works. Jim, the great thing is that nobody knows who is behind the stories, which is why it is so effective. We claim total ignorance.

No allegations of human rights abuses to contend with. No need for torture. No civil liberties bullshit. No wankers like Amnesty International to contend with. No media coverage. It's ingenious. We can be as oppressive and brutal as Nicolae Ceausescu or Stalin but, unlike those dictators, we have clean hands. So, we stay in the shadows while the hostility of a disgusted community does our work for us. Our famous Irish gossip culture provides us with many people who relish in smear. They do our bidding and inflict the torment. They have no idea that they're just being used.'

Jim shakes his head and responds in a very timid voice. 'Oh Jeez… so that's where the popular Irish greeting "any scandal?" comes from.'

'So have no worries, Jim. We are hidden in the background while the community enthusiastically dishes out the harassment. Far more effective than giving the person a beating. If you batter them, you could go to jail. But this is totally legal. Look, Jim, most targets just suffer from severe depression. That's all. Many just leave this little island. That is what I mean by elimination. We are rid of them. They are rid of us.'

'Hmm, "native cunning". I've seen this type of subtle, redneck, intimidation so many times.'

'Many foreign cities are full of the Irish who fled from our smears. I was over in Boston last year and found people in Dorchester who will never come home. They know we will be waiting for them with even more defamation. Ha! Ha! Yes, it's tough. I met quite a few Irish, mentally broken and alcoholics. However, I also found that many do well and start a new life. The opponents we fear most are the clever ones. Their competence is a serious threat. They're a challenge to our dominance. Guilty of holding strong critical opinions. Guilty of having influence and brazen talent. Guilty of posing too many embarrassing questions about us for their own safety.'

Piper Jim is, by now, decidedly dismayed. He had no idea, until today, of the nature of the frightful mission that lay ahead for both himself and Rocky. He reminds himself to appear relaxed until the entire meeting is over. He must not lose the confidence of this incredibly dangerous friend. He draws in a deep breath to calm his nerves. He hopes that some form of incentive or reward might emerge late in the meeting.

'Yeah, I'm beginning to see your point of view. I have no respect either, sir, for smart-arse people showing off.'

'Exactly. Jim, we usually have no trouble with simpletons here in Ireland who, largely, are unquestioning and do what they're told. They are self-serving and obedient enough to realise what's good for themselves. In fact, our policy is to select compromised, mildly corrupt simpletons for many top jobs. Being compromised is very important. We have something nasty on them, so they unquestioningly follow our orders. No intellectual arguments. I am sure you know what I am talking about. Jim, the message is that people should not be too smart with us if they want to survive. They follow orders, even the ones they don't agree with. Right? Do you understand what I am saying, Pipe Sergeant Rockingham?'

Jim shifts uncomfortably in his chair, discerning the emergence of an apparently threatening manoeuvre from his influential friend. A tense silence fills the room while the dazed, compromised simpleton comes to terms with what is being implied.

'Just to say again, sir, I really never ever knew that anything like this happened in Ireland. I never knew you used the gossip I... eh... innocently provided you as a means of eliminating people.'

'Well, now you know, my good man. It's the deep state, Jim. Totally unseen. It is not just in East Germany, China or Romania that it exists. I am sure you realise that it's very much in your best interest to help us. We are your loyal friends... now. I really mean that, Jim. I hope we remain friends for many years to come.'

Jim again shifts uncomfortably in his seat, fear quietly gripping him. Gazing into his imperfect past, he knows that he is trapped.

'Hey, Jim, here is a really funny story. I once asked this greenhorn reporter to help me spread a little bit of scandal. He sat there... yeah, in that very chair you are in now. I gave him an exclusive story. A beautiful scandal. He promised me the sun, the moon and the stars. But then, nothing happened. I was furious. But we caught him on a night he was drinking alone in a quiet country bar. We had his drink spiked with a date rape drug. Then we dragged him into the pub back yard and, with a Polaroid Land Camera, we took some very sexually compromising pictures. We stole his clothes, threw photos on the ground beside him and kept a few for ourselves. When he woke up, he was so shocked that he left Ireland the next day on a flight to New York. Ha! Ha! Never even packed a case apparently. That was four years ago. Total wimp.'

Piper Jim swallows forcefully. 'Look! Sorry I am hesitating a little. Getting my teenage son involved is a new departure for me. It's lucky that his mother is dead because she would go crazy if she heard what we're planning.'

'Jim, it's time now to look at the positive side. Let's examine your son's future. Soon he will be able to gather massive information flows from behind the VIP bar in McKee Barracks. All going well, my plan is to have him selected for an officers course. How does that sound?'

Piper Jim gasps and manages a nervous half smile.

'What? That would be amazing. But there's always thousands of applicants for just a few positions. Most of the people selected for officer cadetship are culchies. I'm not sure why. Seems to me that Dubs need not apply.'

'Jim, what did I say? Injecting our people into important positions is a key to our success in maintaining total control. We call it seeding, like in farming. Of course, the key first step in seeding is recruitment. So, I am pleased to tell you that we can make your son an officer regardless of how many thousands apply for the job.'

Jim looks totally bewildered.

'Remember, right through Rocky's many years in the army, we will manage his career. After seeding, he grows to become our mature plant. Plant! Get it? He will quietly do well in promotion. He will be selected for the more financially lucrative and exciting overseas missions. We will build his CV so that he smoothly glides into the top ranks. Remember, Jim, we have looked after you, with many overseas trips, in similar fashion.'

'Yeah, it has been wonderful for me, sir.'

'Jim, I am offering you a superb life for young Rocky. Yes, he might have to, sometimes, on demand, deceive his friends and colleagues—'

Jim interrupts and plucks up his courage, pleading for understanding as to what makes the army tick.

'But! But... sir! I am sure you know that deception is very difficult in the army. We massively rely on esprit de corps. It is your comrade who covers your back in a dangerous war zone. He's expected to risk his own life to protect you. In the army, our bond of mutual trust is vital for survival. At times it's a very dangerous job.'

'Bull feckin' shit! Now, Jim, cop yourself on! I am fed up hearing the talk of naive infantile army believers. I find that you soldiers are totally brainwashed. Now forget it. In my new army, life will increasingly be about competition. Your traditional comradely army is finished. Trust, team spirit and devotion to colleagues… yes… lip service only. Jim, be politically clever and *look after number one*. Look after your son and forget about that army "esprit de *crap*"!'

Jim finds himself grinding his teeth, certain that he strongly disagrees. However, the personal power difference between the two men is so massive that he cannot take this argument any further. His bravado evaporates without a whimper.

'Okay, sir.'

'You know the strategy we drill into the minds of our cabal members?'

Jim shakes his head and timidly prepares himself for yet another ugly revelation. 'No… no, sir. I don't.'

'You first praise your target. You befriend him and feign admiration. You make him feel that you hold him in deep respect. Show him love… lots and lots of love. Do little favours. Eventually, the target reciprocates and comes to really like you. Once you have gained his confidence, it's easy to fool and trick him. He drops his guard and confides in you. He tells you his secrets. Then you have him by the balls. That is how we operate.'

Jim responds tactfully, now erring on the side of self-preservation. He takes a deep breath and swallows before engaging in naked deception.

'I think I understand, sir. I can train Rocky. He's a fast learner and hungry for success.'

'That's good for you Jim, because it's payback time. We want the services of your son and that is a good thing. It's a lovely payback. Like all spies, he will receive terrific rewards. Rocky will become an officer. He will have free university on

12

full pay and a government-guaranteed brown pay envelope every month for his entire life. He will be financially secure. You know an accountant told me that a career in the public service could be worth more than two to four million over a lifetime.'

Jim gasps. 'Wow, people would kill for that kind of money.'

'Exactly. Every person has his price. We pay well. Rocky will drive a beautiful car and live in a modern, leafy, suburban neighbourhood. He will spy for us, and nobody will be any the wiser. His family will dress impressively, attend church, sit in the front row, take communion and he will be considered a bastion of respectability.'

'Yeah, it will be great, sir. Away from the stinking inner-city fish market.'

'Jim, when your friends and neighbours hear that your son is an officer, it will be the proudest moment of your life. Nobody will know how you swung it. It will be our secret.'

Jim nods. For a father from a rough part of Dublin, this is a stunning offer. 'One last question, sir. Do many targeted people fight back and take their battle to the courts?'

'Oh, yeah, some do… but smart judicial selection can tilt the balance from an evidence-based verdict to a politically pragmatic one.'

'Oh!' The bewildered Pipe Sergeant has no idea what any of this means.

'Jim, a well-crafted accusation alone is enough to destroy a person. The average man on the street tends to immediately assume that the accused is guilty. Our targets find themselves massively out of pocket for legal fees even though they are eventually found innocent. We get to financially destroy them. Justice is the preserve of the super wealthy and powerful.'

The meeting is coming to an end. They stand up and proceed to the hall door of the mansion. Jim's eyes are full of the brooding one might expect from a seriously depressed person. But now there is more good news.

'Oh, by the way, Jim, you are now on the inside track. I consider you to be one of our warriors.'

Jim again tactically equivocates. 'Well, I am delighted and honoured to be, at last, considered a full warrior.'

'Oh, Jim! I meant to mention something to you earlier. We are hearing that there may be more positions coming up at *Palais des Nations*, United Nations, Geneva. They will be hiring security guards next year. Well paid in Swiss Francs, easy hours, low tax, free quarters in a lovely apartment, subsidised dining facilities. It would be a great retirement job for somebody like yourself. If you are interested, let me know when we meet next time.'

Jim's eyes open wide. 'What? Switzerland! Me? I can tell you straight away, today, sir, I am interested.'

'Yes, but now I need performance, Jim. I will send you the name of your first target shortly.' The tone of Jim's influential friend's voice again becomes emphatic and demanding. 'Be ready to aggressively kick arse. Let me repeat, this is *payback* time.' He pokes Jim's chest firmly with his index finger. 'Not to be screwed up under any circumstances.'

Chapter 2

The Sweet Barley Pub for a Pint

Piper Jim draws in yet another deep breath as he walks down the stone driveway of the mansion towards a set of heavy gates. The meeting had been more profound than he had, even in his wildest dreams, expected. Though elated by the opportunities presented, he is nevertheless burdened by what has emerged. He is still flushed in the face and uneasy. A taxi pulls up on the lonely, dark road. He opens the rear door of the vehicle with a trembling hand and gets into the back seat. He tells himself to calmly gather his thoughts. He decides that he should go for a quiet pint to a city-centre pub where he is not well known. His mind is racing, and he is certain that he would be unable to cope with neighbourly small talk in his usual local. Equally, he decides that he could not handle a meeting with his son, Rocky. Piper Jim feels that his own demeanour is just too tense for normal social or family conversation. It is best to arrive home late and after Rocky has retired to bed.

'Taxi, can you take me into the city centre? Drop me anywhere near the Sweet Barley pub on the quay… around O'Connell Bridge.'

The taxi driver pauses while studying Jim in the car rear-view mirror.

'No problem, mister! Are you all right there? Mister! You are not sick or anything? Here is a plastic bag. I'll put on the heater. You are shivering a bit.'

'No worries. Thanks. I'm just a bit flustered after a tough business meeting.'

'I know exactly. You know, a lot of people come out of that house trembling. I see the comings and goings every other night. Not nice by all accounts. Rich, influential but a terrible bleedin' bastard at the same time. I always used to say that decency and honesty is more important than power. But now Ireland is gradually going down the tubes. Oh! Hey, mister, listen – here is one good man. His last day in office as president.'

The taxi driver turns up the volume on the car radio so that they can both hear extracts of the final address to the nation of the retiring president, Theobald O'Toole.

…Ireland's most important role in the international community is that of peacekeeping. Our neutrality is neither for barter or for sale. Our staunch determination not to become involved in arms manufacture or civilian, undercover military activity is of crucial importance.

Our army, navy, air corps, police and judges must always hold themselves above factional party politics. They must serve the Constitution and whatever government the people elect. These security forces are there to defend the Irish people and never to spy on the citizen for the benefit of foreign interests.

Finally, let me emphasise that in this Republic, a strict self-discipline is imposed by the taking of an oath. Never forget that oaths of office are fundamental to our thriving as a people of integrity.

Having listened to the idealistic words of the president, Piper Jim becomes even more concerned about the morality of his own prospective task.

The Sweet Barley pub is subtly lit and most of the patrons are either professionals or tourists. Piper Jim is confident that he would be unlikely to meet anybody he knows there. He sinks into a dark corner seat. He pulls out a pen and pocket notebook with a view to scribbling a few notes on the night's events. His first pint of black, creamy porter is swallowed in seconds. He immediately orders another.

Piper Jim has been six months working on positioning his son Rocky, including coercing the unwilling boy into joining the army. Jim has aggressively engineered the break-up of Rocky's emerging and highly talented pop band. The band's lead guitarist, Jim's coloured stepson, was also persuaded to join the army and was then immediately transferred to a barracks outside of Dublin. This manoeuvring was achieved to create geographic distance between the, usually, inseparable boys.

Today, the meeting delivered overwhelmingly more than he had anticipated. But what he must now accomplish is both immense, rotten and risky. Jim is now, somehow, in the big league. He admits to himself that he is frightened. *Now, Jim, it's sink or swim time.*

Jim quietly examines the events and relationships of the past few years and realises that he probably slithered into the current situation incrementally. Small favour after small favour. Indiscretion after indiscretion. He trusted them with a lot of personal information. They know everything. Things were so gradual. He had not noticed that he was heading into, the equivalent of, a dangerous cesspool. Now, he has a growing fear that he might be totally out of his depth. Never had it been demanded that he reciprocate to such an enormous level of payback. He takes a slug of his pint. *Phew!*

On the positive side is the possibility of a big breakthrough. He knows of nobody, from the inner-city tough working neighbourhoods, whose son has made it into the officer or cadet ranks of the army. He, himself, always wanted to be an officer, and now a golden possibility for his son is staring him in the face. Jim sees himself as an excellent, respected and superior non-commissioned officer. Now he will gain personal elevation through the rapid advancement of his son. He comforts himself through encouraging self-talk.

If we play our cards right, young Rocky and I can greatly enhance our family reputation. It really is a lottery win… worth millions… yeah. Now, I must realise that there is nothing for free in this world. I must regain my calm and self-control. Today was, in fact, a great day. My eyes have been opened after all these years. Now I am an inner-circle warrior. Nothing to be afraid of. So, this is the "deep state" that journalists often talk about. I now know, for the first time, how the top people in Ireland operate. Feckin' ruthless. Yeah, real bastards. The taxi driver was right. But they are my bastards. Got to keep it that way.

Piper Jim quietly speculates on why this entire chain of influence in Ireland is rarely spoken or written about.

I suspect that journalists are too scared to print revealing truths. Printing dumbed-down comforting lies probably sells more newspapers and is safer. It's a dangerous profession. So many journalists around the world face intimidation and many are murdered.

He scribbles the word "Rocky" in his notebook followed by "got to improve relations" and "not likely to willingly co-operate". He then writes "apply immediately – Geneva".

Great retirement... wow... working in Switzerland – beautiful. A massive win on my last throw of the public-sector dice.

Jim visualises his son, the handsome Second Lieutenant Rockingham, wearing a superfine uniform, peak cap and spit-polished Sam Browne leather belt.

I'll be so proud when he comes to visit me in Switzerland. I'll get him to wear full uniform and introduce him to all my new Swiss and United Nations colleagues. I can even have a party in my luxury apartment to impress everybody. Rocky can sing and play guitar. I will play the pipes. My UN colleagues will be amazed by the talent at our party.

After his third pint, Piper Jim begins to feel reasonably composed. It's almost an hour after midnight and he is feeling calm enough to consider heading home. He knows that there is a pint bottle of porter in the kitchen fridge of his house in Ormond Square. He is sure he will need it as a final relaxing sedative.

As Piper Jim walks down the north bank of the River

Liffey, he suddenly feels a severe chest tightness as well as shortness of breath and a racing heartbeat. He immediately suspects that he is suffering a reaction to the tension experienced during and since the meeting. He grips and massages his chest while leaning over the riverbank wall. He stares into the dark waters of the River Liffey, waiting for his condition to improve. His racing mind tirelessly continues its self-dialogue.

Maria would be so angry with me if she was alive. I know that I am getting too old for this sneaky spying shit. This new task means that I will have to try to change Rocky's entire personality. Like his mother, he is strong-minded and spiritual. He visits the church and lights candles all the time. Always smiling. I love my fun-loving, energetic son. How the hell am I going to achieve such a massive transformation in him? But I must get that final mission overseas in Switzerland. I need to get him fixed up, as well, with a top job. It will then be fantastic to happily retire abroad into a UN position in gorgeous Geneva. They might leave me alone in peace there. A retired snake in the grass.

After a short period, Jim's condition somewhat improves. His racing heartbeat subsides. He realises that he is going to have to lose a lot of weight.

On arrival home, he pulls the waiting bottle of black porter from the kitchen fridge and quietly sneaks up the stairs to bed, being careful not to wake Rocky.

Chapter 3

The New Barman

It's interview time at the army headquarters officers' mess in McKee Barracks, Dublin.

'Okay, take a seat. You are Gunner Tony Rockingham I understand. Is that correct?'

'Yes, sir.'

'Have you just finished some physical training?'

Young Rockingham is freshly showered, radiating the distinctive aroma of Imperial Leather soap. He rubs a bead of sweat from the side of his forehead and grins.

'The entire regiment has just completed a five-mile artillery gun push exercise in the Phoenix Park, sir. Sorry if I am still perspiring a little.'

'Okay, that's not a problem. Well, I am Captain Paul Gilmore, the Mess Manager, and this is Sergeant Tom Gormley, the Mess Sergeant. You are probably aware that we are interviewing this morning for the position of Barman. I can tell you straight away that you come highly recommended. The sergeant major feels that you would be perfect for the job. So, can you tell me something about yourself?'

Rockingham answers fluently and with confidence. 'I am nearly six months in the army, sir. I have completed my training here in Dublin and in the Glen of Imaal, County Wicklow. I have enjoyed the tough army discipline. I am currently on the duty list doing armed escorts of cash and gelignite. I have already gained Border experience. Last month, when things looked bad in the north, I was selected for a three-week stint in Aiken Barracks, Dundalk. Things were very tense after all of those bombing atrocities between Belfast and the Border.'

'Yeah, things have been very difficult in the north but, thankfully, it's calming down.'

'We were sent to reinforce the security of the Border area, doing twenty-four-hour checkpoints on the mountains of the Cooley Peninsula.'

'Sounds like it was an exhausting assignment.'

Rockingham is delighted to enlarge on a dynamic military experience of which he is visibly proud. 'You know, sir, the Cooley Peninsula is a beautiful place. It is very vulnerable if there is trouble north of the Border. We dominated all the mountain roads, and everybody felt highly motivated. The local people loved us.'

'Yes, the town of Dundalk would have been bombed again but for the professional approach taken by the troops from the regiment. But, okay, let's talk now about the officers' mess. Today, Rockingham, you face a new challenge. It is important that you fully understand that working in a VIP bar will be a totally different task.'

'You know, sir, I am really just trying to gain as much military experience as I can. I know that it would be nice to be picked to work here in the officers' mess, but I still have so much to learn about the real army. I love my life as a soldier in the regiment. But sir, thank you for considering me… anyway.'

Captain Gilmore totally ignores Rockingham's hint that his preference is to continue operational security duties. The captain knows that he needs the best staff he can find. Rockingham looks presentable, with all the features of a person who has just completed an intensive, physically demanding period of outdoor operational military service. He is probably just about five feet ten inches tall with a lean, muscular frame. His sculpted, sharp facial features are deeply tanned by wind and sun. His sandy-coloured hair is tightly crew cut into an army short back and sides. Captain Gilmore immediately recognises that this soldier is, what Irish military slang would be described as "gildy". A soldier of superior grooming, pleasant, well-spoken and one who is sure to impress wherever he is assigned.

'Well, Rockingham, it's the army. They train you intensively for one job and then put you working at something totally different. Take me for example. I am a highly experienced instructor in internal security, counterinsurgency and peacekeeping. Unfortunately, we all must do short stints in catering establishments like this. For you, I see it as a growth opportunity.'

Rockingham draws in a breath, purses his lips, while vaguely shrugging his shoulders. He stares directly into the officer's eyes, unable to hide his concern. Captain Gilmore again chooses to deliberately ignore the body language. Instead, the tone of his voice becomes business-like and demanding.

'Gunner, let's get straight to the point. The army now needs somebody of your calibre for this serious job. You will do six months here in the most important catering establishment in the entire Irish Defence Forces. All going well, Rockingham, you will then be selected for United Nations peacekeeping duty in Lebanon. I promise that. The sergeant major tells me that you are already high on the overseas list. If you do well here, you will not lose out on the chance of an overseas tour of duty. In fact, I will be pushing your case for selection. How does that sound?'

'You must be reading my mind, sir. I was worried that if I was away from the regiment, I might be forgotten. I really want that United Nations trip and to travel with the lads who I did my recruit training with. It looks like we will all be going out to Lebanon together. So, I would like to say that, now, I am enthusiastic to do the job here.'

'Great, let's move on to talk about cash management and basic maths. Sergeant Gormley, this is your area.'

"Okay, Gunner Rockingham, as Mess Sergeant, I am responsible for bookkeeping. You have a good education standard I am told.'

'I will have no problem keeping the books right, Sarge. I got a good mark in maths in my Leaving Certificate last year.'

'Okay, Leaving Cert. Hmm! So, before you joined the army, had you considered doing any further education?'

'I had enough points to do a degree in Business Studies at Trinity College, but I really had enough of school. Then, I got the call-up as part of the big army recruitment drive.'

'Unusual, the army was your first choice, not university?'

'Neither! Sergeant Gormley, my first love is music. I really wanted to go on the road with my band and try to become a success on the pop music scene. I have had to put that on hold for now. My dad was very insistent that I join the army.'

'Okay, so, for your dad, the army was the less risky alternative.'

'You are right, sir. In the inner city, times are tough. The army offers a guaranteed career, not easily found elsewhere. My dad is serving as a pipe sergeant in Cathal Brugha Barracks in the south city. They call him Piper Jim. Also, we have a big army history. My grandfather was awarded a Victoria Cross. In the last century, our family moved to Ireland with the British Army when Ireland was under the Crown. I am an authentic "jackeen"[1].'

'Hmm! So, I am talking to a Dublin "jackeen" with a Victoria Cross at home to prove it.'

'Yes, Sergeant, I love this city. I am a Dub and proud of my family history.'

'Right, so, the music was pushed into second place. Any regrets?'

There is a pregnant pause while the young soldier searches for words. He inhales deeply as stern facial features emerge and his eyes appear to water. 'Devastated... yeah, it hurt... badly... just for a while. It was a terrible time in my life. Breaking up my band was a massive decision. We were doing well and making great money.'

Sergeant Gormley immediately realises that he has stumbled upon a highly sensitive subject. Rockingham quickly recovers his composure. 'Anyway, I got over it.' He inhales deeply. 'Now I am really proud to be an artilleryman here in McKee Barracks. The training was so intense... awesome... best thing that I have ever done in my life. I

---

1. Modern usage mostly sporting. A mildly derogatory term to describe a Dubliner who has historic British leanings. "Jack" refers to the Union Jack flag and "een" comes from the Irish language designation for small.

have also gained friends for life. Artillery gunners all look after each other like brothers. For the first time, I learned about the importance of comradeship and teamwork.'

Gilmore is warming to Rockingham's openness. He takes over the questioning. 'So, your dad is actually a serving pipe sergeant?'

'Yes, sir. He is a dedicated soldier with seven peacekeeping trips overseas with the United Nations. He has been to Sinai, Cyprus and Lebanon. He also worked for a year in European Union Logistics based in Brussels. He is famous for entertaining the troops overseas with folklore, storytelling and traditional pipe music.'

'So, long-term, what about the music? Do you plan to eventually follow your dad into the pipe band?'

Rockingham's upper cheeks flush red. Now, he totally loses his formal interview poise, almost shrieking.

'Jeez! No, sir. Please don't say that! Not the pipe band. You know, at school, we were constantly slagged about our dad. We were the only ones whose dad wore a skirt.'

'A piper's kilt, you mean, surely. That uniform looks great.'

'Yeah, sir. He was always wearing it walking around the neighbourhood. When we were young, he used to walk with us to the school playground wearing the kilt. The kids joked that I had two mammies. When we arrived in the school playground, they would all start chanting "Mammy Bear! Mammy Bear!". It wasn't the kilt so much as his bony, hairy legs.'

Sergeant Tom Gormley intervenes.

'I was overseas with Piper Jim Rockingham, sir. He had a brilliant show that had all the UN contingents clamouring for him to visit them.'

'Thanks, Sergeant, I am totally different to my father. I can sing, write music and lyrics, play keyboards and guitar. We did a lot of gigs in the SFX. We called ourselves RRK.'

'Slow down, Rockingham. What do all of those letters stand for?'

'SFX is the tiny venue where Ireland's greatest rock band, Thin Lizzy, started. It's the St Francis Xavier Hall near Mountjoy Square. RRK evolved from our first band name. When we started the band in school, everybody called us "Rock 'n' Roll Kids". It sounded like Rockingham, and we were so young. As we got older, we wanted to drop the "kids" part of the name. So, we used the initials and became more comfortable with the name "RRK". We played a lot of music at school parties. I became known as Rocky. That's my stage name as the lead singer in the band.'

Gilmore is impressed. 'I see… Rocky… hmm. That is a really good stage name.'

Rocky is cheeky enough now to jokingly propose a casual affiliation to the officer. He smiles, knowing that he is being somewhat impertinent. 'I don't mind if the officers in the mess call me Rocky.'

Gilmore sharply looks up, surprised. He scolds, immediately tackling Rockingham's attempt at overfamiliarity. 'In the officers' mess we are very formal. I expect you to introduce yourself as Gunner Rockingham, nothing else. No first names, no nicknames. Understood?'

Rockingham fights hard to hold back a mischievous grin. 'Yes, understood, sir.'

'Anyway. The music. So, is it rock or pop?'

'Sir, I personally love Latino rock music like Santana. But as young kids the band was also hugely inspired by the harmonies of the Everly Brothers. Then, everybody at school worshipped Thin Lizzy and Phil Lynott.'

The sergeant major had briefed Gilmore in detail about Rockingham earlier. Gilmore told the sergeant major about the uncanny history that mismanaged army bars had for ending officers' career aspirations. Gilmore saw staff selection as that vital pre-emptive step in self-preservation. He squints in the direction of Sergeant Gormley for a sign of approval. 'Rockingham should be perfect, sir.'

'Well, Gunner Rockingham, you will have an opportunity to impress the right people, including the minister for defence and army chief of staff. Now, I want you to go to our tailor, down in Manor Street. Pick up two red waistcoats, a few white shirts and black pants. I need you to have that uniform by Monday.'

'Okay, sir.'

'Oh, Rockingham, one last thing. In military bars, during wars, there is often a sign in big print hanging on the wall. The sign says, "Remember the barman is listening". We are at peace here in the south of Ireland so you will not find that sign anywhere in the mess. Still, you have recent first-hand experience of the ongoing security problems on the Border and in the north of Ireland. I want to advise you to act as if the sign is hanging up there behind the bar. Be polite and do not overly engage in conversations with your customers.'

'I understand, sir.' Rockingham immediately realises that he is receiving his first formal pep talk as a member of staff.

'Do not compromise yourself by finding that a situation arises where you overhear sensitive information. When not serving, you must be in the barman's little room out of earshot, away from the counter. Advise the customers to ring the bell when they need you. You are not the customer's pal. Yes, be friendly, smile, but always retain the appropriate military distance and protocol. Behind the bar I do not want a talker, a gossip or a joker. Do I make myself clear, Gunner Rockingham?'

'Absolutely, sir.'

With the pep talk over, Gilmore finishes, stands up and shakes Rockingham's hand with a broad, welcoming smile on his face. 'Now, save all of the usual jackeen jokes for me... and Sergeant Gormley. All the staff regularly enjoy a laugh behind the scenes. Right?'

Rockingham grins, somewhat relieved by the final friendly conclusion to the interview. 'You bet, sir.'

Chapter 4

Father and Son

Gunner Rockingham leaves the officers' mess deep in thought and feeling reasonably happy with himself. Captain Gilmore comes across as a little rigid, but at least he seems to be able to enjoy a bit of banter and fun. A straight-down-the-middle, cool, reserved type of officer with no hidden agendas. Rockingham feels that very clear, distinct direction will not be in short supply. This he likes. He knows that his performance will need to be top class to keep the captain and mess sergeant happy. He is pleased with his selection for the new appointment. *Wait till I tell Dad. He will be proud of me.*

Today was Rocky's first time in an officers' mess and he found the decor to be as dazzling as he had ever seen before. Yet, surprisingly, the selection interview was not, at all, intense. He felt that he got through it with ease. He must thank the sergeant major for recommending him and advancing his career. Now that he will not, apparently, lose out on United Nations Peacekeeping service, he is excited about this new-found opportunity. Being selected from all the 150 gunners in the regiment represents welcome recognition. *Yeah, this arrangement could work really well.*

He is deep in thought as he walks down Blackhorse Avenue to catch his double-decker bus home. *The sergeant major says I will be rostered to work in the bar seven days and nights continuously and, unfortunately, I will have to sleep in that freezing-cold F Block billet in the barracks. That's not great, but I can cope. Seven days on, seven days off. Not bad. Loads of free time.*

He knows a few pubs and restaurants where he might even pick up a few impromptu musical gigs. That means he will earn some extra money, as well as stay in touch with his contacts in the music industry. *This could be just ideal, in fact.*

His thoughts are full of optimism as he jumps on the bus and climbs to the top deck. He sits back, reflecting on his fast-changing life.

I am now glad I did what Dad demanded and joined the army. I must really tell him tonight what a wise old man he is. I must try to reduce that terrible tension between us.

Despite his desire for reconciliation, Rocky continues to be wounded by the manner of his father's arrogant diktat, compelling him to join the forces. His band, RRK, had been doing well, pulling in lots of offers of gigs and beginning to make very serious money. They had even got their first quarter-page review in the highly influential UK magazine, *NME*, the *New Musical Express*. The article described them as an "exciting young Irish band emerging on the Dublin scene, following on the musical coat-tails of Thin Lizzy and Rory Gallagher".

In the lead-up to him joining the army, there had been many heated discussions and quarrels in their Ormond Square home. While sitting on the bus, memories of those quarrels return to haunt him:

'Dad, is the army really a good idea for me? Dad, stop pressurising me! I am not sure about the army if it takes me away from the career that I really love. Dad! What I want is music! I am a singer, songwriter and musician. That's me. It's who I am. I am not interested in following in your footsteps. I am not interested in your dreams. I want my dreams and my future is music.'

The legendary Piper Jim is dogged as a father figure. Memories return of frequent forceful pointing of an index finger jabbing Rocky's chest:

'Look, son! I am considering what's best for you. There are too many one-hit wonder bands out there who quickly get forgotten and end up on skid row. It's not glamorous at all. Crooked agents, illegal drugs, disgusting long hair, dirty whores, pox and drunkenness. Need I say any more. I want a clean, well-groomed, disciplined son. On that topic, your hair is too long. Cut it by Monday like a good man!'

He recalls Piper Jim's tendency to slow down his sentences and attempt to control his emotions as things became more heated. Other times, his father would lose control, his purple spider veins and red face signalling a fearsome passion for command and control. As an army sergeant, Piper Jim was not used to people arguing back at him, shouting and being aggressively insubordinate. He would lean forward, hiss his words while almost foaming at the mouth. At times, the tension in the home was almost unbearable.

'Now, listen carefully, son. *Just listen.*'

Piper Jim had a standard line of attack as the arguments continued, night after night and week after week.

'Okay! I have spoken to a few senior officers who are very close friends of mine. They admire me. I played the pipes for their platoons in the United Nations missions when they were young lieutenants. Officers respect me and I am seen as a steady, solid, dependable and loyal sergeant. Soon there is to be a big intake of recruits. The north of Ireland is still tense. The government also must do something to sort out the unemployment in this country. The politicians know that in the inner city they must give young people a chance of a job and take them away from crime and drugs. What I want for you is a good, solid government job, self-discipline, foreign travel and a long-term career. All of that is there for you now. *On a feckin' plate!* Do I make myself clear?'

Rocky lost his cool on that occasion:

'Dad, just hold on a minute. What you are saying is that you are rejecting my interests in life. Whose *feckin'* life is it? Yours or mine? Mother had it all planned. She understood how important the band was to me. You have not got a clue how to be a proper father... not a clue.'

'*Listen* to me, you little pup! Do not dare square up to me like that. I will not tolerate your backchat in this house! Very soon, I expect to see your dependable government wage packet coming in that letterbox every Friday. A government harp on the centre of that lovely brown envelope! Get it?'

'Dad, I am making good money already. You know where you can stuff your bleedin' harp and brown envelope. I am sick of this constant pressure. Why don't you feck off overseas again. We were always so happy when you were abroad.'

'Son, I am not for turning. Now, you save your breath.'

When things reached this level of rage, Rocky usually walked out of the house, feeling dejected and totally humiliated. He could not understand why his father was so determined to rubbish the career path he wanted in life.

Piper Jim's next line of attack was to start playing a sly, mischievous game, suggesting to Rocky that the economy was on the verge of collapse.

'I see two more restaurants and a pub have closed down on Abbey Street. Tourists are afraid to come because of the violence in Northern Ireland. I am really scared that this country is facing serious difficulties and massive unemployment.'

Piper Jim's destructive mind games began to create a sense of worry and questioning as he slowly chipped away at Rocky's self-confidence. The power of negativity heightened Rocky's awareness of a struggling Dublin entertainment sector. He noticed that the attendance at gigs seemed slightly down… or was that just his silly perception? Rocky's youthful immaturity meant that he had no experience of what a recession might be like. So, even though gig requests and money kept rolling in, Rocky began to allow doubt enter his mind. For the first time in his life, he became alert to the fact that Dublin's north inner city was becoming devastated by unemployment. He avidly began reading newspapers as they reported a plague of gangland crime and drug dealing in the streets around his home. As Rocky increasingly lost his cheeky self-confidence, parental rejection of his career plans took its toll. He finally found himself being sheepishly led by his father to the local barber's shop and then the army recruiting office. It was the loss of his much-admired, long, sandy hair that signalled to Rocky his total capitulation and defeat. His happy days as a successful bandleader were over.

That was more than half a year ago. As his bus yanks and stutters to a halt at his final stop in O'Connell Street, Rocky's thoughts cause him to quietly grind his teeth with anxiety. *I was elected school captain. I am a natural leader. But none of my little achievements matter to my dad. He never acknowledges my talent or successes. He always wants me to make him feel good. I have had to leave behind everything that I worked for. If I were left to my own devices, I would already have made a big impact on the music world. My father has screwed up my musical career big time.*

Rocky punches the palm of his hand while walking down O'Connell Street, still angrily ruminating. *Dad has no interest in risk. Service in the army has been good for him, but it is all he knows. It is what he is comfortable with. In terrible economic times, it represents a sure thing. A steady, safe job. Still, I suppose, in this dreadful recession, most outsiders would not blame him. But I do. My father is the one who totally derailed my dream.*

Rocky passes a record shop and hears the familiar tones of Cat Stevens' album "Tea for the Tillerman". This music triggers further intense thought. He diverts onto the centre of O'Connell Bridge and leans on the wall facing westwards towards the river and setting sun. *Cat Stevens. Yeah. Will I ever forget?*

Recollections of his first night in the army pour into his head. He shivers as he recalls sleeping in the freezing-cold billet in F Block, McKee Barracks. He remembers that for new recruits, getting security clearance to join the army was an exceedingly slow process because of the crisis in Northern Ireland. Nevertheless, sons of serving soldiers were fast-tracked as low security risk. Rocky ended up sharing a huge accommodation wing, for two weeks, with just one other recruit. He remembers that this lad was an officer's son called Barry. Barry had brought a record player with him and kept it in his locker in the billet. Even though singing was forbidden in F Block, there was no mention of record players.

The two new recruits waited until the barrack orderly sergeant called lights out. Then it was down from the bunk beds and the record player was plugged in. Rocky produced two flagons of Bulmers Cider. Barry pulled from his kit bag an LP record with a beautifully animated colourful sleeve. He placed the shining black LP on the rotating turntable.

'Hey okay, it's track five on side two… here we go… Rocky, this is my favourite album. I want you to hear a song which should be the anthem of army sons for the entire recruit training course. Listen to this. It must be about us. The two of us. Army pups with bossy fathers.'

Rocky was momentarily unnerved by the accuracy of this statement from a recruit he had just met. 'You too? Jeez, I hope we don't turn out like them.'

'I don't know about you, Rocky, but I won't. Anyway, let's enjoy. I bought the album after I read this review. Listen, I will read it to you. "Father and Son" is the most deep and haunting track on the album. The father cannot understand the son's desire to break away and shape a new life. The son knows that it is time for him to seek his own destiny.'

'Wow, it looks like we are two of a kind.'

For Rocky, this review was shockingly close to the bone. He would never forget that night. It was a milestone in his life. Living away from home in a strange place. His first night sleeping in an army billet. A night anointed by the perfect musical backdrop of the song "Father and Son" from Cat Stevens.

The story of the song was all too familiar and, for Rocky, it was like his dad had pursued him to the billet to again give him a lecture. Barry gently placed the needle on the album and selected the speed of thirty-three rotations per minute. The turntable revolved and the built-in mono speaker crackled before the song began.

Cat Stevens sung of a man looking back at a lost dream which was spoiled by a conventional father. In the song, the son is constantly order by his father to listen, but he finally decides that he must abandon everything his father demanded and find a new life. Rocky recalls the agony of the blunt fact that he might be around in the army for many years but that his youthful dream of a musical career would soon fade away. It was impossible to be a soldier and a bandleader at the same time. He was now signed on for three years' service in the army. There was no turning back. Rocky wondered if he, like in the song, would end up running away from home to escape his dad's coercive influence. He remembers being scared by that thought.

Siren city! A noisy ambulance screams across O'Connell Bridge and startles him, bringing his thoughts back into the present moment. He wonders what his dad will be doing for the weekend. Rocky, half a year later, is now a fully trained artillery gunner and those early fears and doubts about army life are now just a memory. Much to his surprise, he has come to love everything he has learned during his military training. Best of all has been the friendships, which he has really come to value. He is certain that it was the military bonding that sustained him during those dark, horrible, physically demanding early recruit training days.

It has been a tough time for Dad since Mam's death, so I need to patch things up between us. I can lift his spirits by telling him, truthfully, how well the army is going for me. I never told him how much I really enjoyed the intensity of the military training. It was all worth while. Now, those desired pay packets in brown envelopes are coming into the house every Friday. Dad looks less stressed even though he has put on a little weight. He has now achieved just what he wanted. An end to financial worries. We cannot keep fighting. I will praise him this evening. I think he might join me for a few pints tonight to celebrate my elevation with the move to army HQ officers' mess bar. I am dying to see the look on his face when I tell him that I will soon be serving the minister for defence and chief of staff.

Chapter 5

Family Tension at Ormond Square

Rocky slowly strolls down the north bank of the River Liffey and crosses the road at the Ormond Hotel. Hidden away from the noisy traffic, behind the hotel, is a quiet red-and-yellow-brick residential enclave called Ormond Square. The Rockingham family live in a two-bedroom, two-story terraced house. This has been the family home for Rocky's entire life. As he arrives on the square, he immediately notices that the downstairs lights are on. He guesses that his dad must be home already. He opens the freshly decorated hall door. The aroma of gloss paint still lingers but, in all his years living there, he never remembers the house looking so well.

'Hi, Dad! Hi, Dad, I'm home! Hello, anybody home?'

Piper Jim plods from the kitchen to meet him. He hugs Rocky. 'Hi, son, how was your day?'

'Great, Dad, I met more people today who know you. It's tough on me being the son of the legendary Piper Jim. They are all so disappointed when I tell them I cannot play the pipes.'

'Ha! Ha! I have a massive adoring fan club for sure. But at least meeting my devoted admirers is helping you to appreciate me at last. So, how was your day? Any news from McKee Barracks?'

'Yeah, it's the usual. I might have to go as a skivvy, washing dishes in the officers' mess next week.' Rocky baits his father to observe the reaction.

Piper Jim glares out through the kitchen window, into the distance, and seems suddenly troubled. 'What? Skivvy? You?'

Rocky continues laying a trap by embellishing his story. 'Well, I will be starting off peeling spuds. But not to worry, they have a machine and there are just 120 officers dining there every day. So, it's only, say, two hundred spuds. Peeling the vegetables and scrubbing the kitchen floor will be a real pain. I bought kneepads today in a hardware shop on Capel Street. And then there is the hardest job of the lot. Scrubbing the bleedin' ovens. But anyway, it's only for six months. Then I might be going peacekeeping to the Lebanon as a real soldier again. The sergeant major told me to just keep calm and it would all work out.'

'What the hell! No, son, that was never the way it was meant to be. I guarantee you, it's a mistake! I never agreed to that!'

'Oh! What are you talking about, Dad? What do you mean by a mistake? Whose mistake?'

'Eh! Nothing. I mean… what I mean is that you are too smart a lad for that kind of work.'

'Dad, come on. What's going on? What have you been up to? What do you mean that you never agreed?'

'Nothing, nothing. Just leave it, son, let's change the subject. It's not the nicest of jobs… that's what I mean.'

They both sit silently in the kitchen for a few minutes and Piper Jim buries his head in the *Evening Herald* newspaper. Rocky eventually decides to reveal the good news.

'Dad, I also did an interview for barman in the officers' mess. I might be serving the Chief of Staff and Minister for Defence. Yeah, then there are the foreign diplomats… ambassadors… yeah, all those top-brass people. A guy called Captain Gilmore interviewed me. He said that I had come highly recommended.'

Piper Jim continues to hide his face with the newspaper as he needs to conceal the emergence of a telling smirk. 'Yeah, yeah, son, once they heard that I was your dad, the officers in the mess would be very interested in having you work there with the top brass. I am highly regarded.' Piper Jim drops his newspaper and speaks directly to his son. 'Perhaps you might get the bar job, but don't worry if you don't. I never met that Captain Gilmore, but he is supposed to be a nasty piece of work. Very efficiency-oriented apparently. Not a laid-back, friendly type, like the rest of us. It's best to be peeling the spuds, working with nice people, than be under constant intense pressure. Your beautiful mother in heaven is praying for us all and she will protect you.'

'Well, actually, Dad, Captain Gilmore was really cool and very nice to deal with during the interview. I must go to a tailor in Manor Street to get fitted for my bright red Department of Defence barman's waistcoat. I am actually starting work in the VIP bar on Monday.'

Piper Jim loses his composure, throwing his arms into the air like a jubilant football fan celebrating a shock, last-minute, winning goal. He stands up with his burly frame almost smothering Rocky with a euphoric celebratory hug.

'Son, I am so glad. That is great news. It's theeeeee place to be working! The powers-that-be will notice you. I never got that opportunity, or I would be an officer now. I was always a bit too lumpy and out of shape. I was strong, polite but not well scrubbed enough to get the officers' mess. Jeez, now you are in the premier officers' mess in Ireland. Fantastic. You are going places.'

'Dad, take it easy. What are you saying? I did not get that job on my own merits. Did I? That's what it sounds like. Did you pull strings for me with the sergeant major?'

'Son, well it's a small world. I just happen to have bumped into him last week in Old Biddy's Pub in Stoneybatter. He's a dear friend and we had a grand chat about happy days serving together in Cyprus. He remembered that amazing night when I met your mother in a bar in Aya Napa. Ha! Ha! It was great to bump into him again and enjoy a couple of pints together. He was singing your praises. He did mention that barman's job, but I said nothing. I promise. You got it because you did well in training, I think. But you would not have got it if you were out of shape or did not look well. Thank God your mother was so beautiful. You will be spotted as a super talent. Your military career will fly. The lads in the pipe band will be so impressed when I tell them.'

Rocky falls silent. He is suddenly overcome with a sense of dejection. The pride of achievement has suddenly evaporated. He sullenly, silently, ruminates with his head in his hands. *Here we go again. Pull, God-damn pull. I was so proud to have been selected. If only I had got it on my own merits. Dad keeps interfering, prying and snooping. I should have been suspicious when the interview turned out to be a non-event. An utter bleedin' foregone conclusion. Damn it. All set up in advance by my meddling celebrity father. I am disgusted with his interference.*

The exhilarated Piper Jim tries to encourage his son to share in his enthusiasm. But for Rocky, things now get emphatically worse.

'Son, the real test is the next six months. Nobody can help you every day there in the mess, except to give you advice. Perform well and you might be picked for a potential officers course or cadetship. You have great exam results. You speak well. In fact, you speak like an officer. You are a real leader. I pray every day that you will make me proud by becoming a big success as an army lieutenant. My son, work hard and be careful to look after all the officers. Then, they eventually will look after you with promotion after promotion.'

There is a pregnant silence, finally broken by a flabbergasted Rocky shaking his head and staring his father directly in the face. 'I cannot believe what I am hearing. So, I now have to become a lieutenant to make you proud. Is that what you are telling me? You are not proud of me already. You are not proud of what I have achieved in life… my musical success… all the praise heaped on us by the music magazines.'

'Hey, calm down, son.'

'I am not sure about all of this, Dad. We are not really on the same wavelength. I think you are offside, Dad… totally offside. I just wish we could sit down some day in this house and talk about what I want for my life. But… Dad… it never happens. You are rejecting my wishes all the time. I am gutted, just gutted by your constant interference. You are creating havoc in my mind. You are living my life for me, Dad. Because you were never an officers' mess barman, I now, strangely, must become one. You were not picked to be a lieutenant and now you expect me to achieve that goal. What else have you lined up for me? Is this how I am going to have to live my entire life? Is that fair? I must live a false life so that you accept and love me. You are a cold person, always dismissing things I am proud of. Never encouraging, just meddling.'

'Hey, son, I am only trying to help. This is good news. We should celebrate.'

'No, no. Sorry, Dad, not for me. Now I must go upstairs and get an early night. I am sorry, but I cannot listen to any more of this.' Rocky shakes his head and dejectedly trudges up the stairs. He immediately enters the tiny bathroom and runs a piping hot bath for himself. He augments the baths calming propensity with the addition of a cup of Epsom Salts, which his mother Maria frequently used in times of stress. He now firmly decides that he will not go socialising with his father. There is nothing to be happy about. He hopes that the piping hot bath water will exhaust him, calm his mind and, in turn, facilitate a full night of gratifying sleep.

However, it is not to be. After his bath, he lies on his bed, but sleep will not come. He hears his father heading out alone for his habitual Friday night pint. Rocky has not calmed down. Both his father's constant intrusion, as well as this evening's bombshell of newly amplified career demands, has sickened him.

For Rocky, there follows a long night with a continuous period of restlessness. He tosses and turns while pondering on a worry that a trap has been sprung on him. The pressure to make the army a permanent career is now growing into a more specific goal. His father has subtly heightened the tension by defining how his son can make him proud. Now he is required, somehow, to become an army lieutenant. The chances of eventually walking away from the army for a music career have just been dealt a significant blow. Things are getting worse.

Rocky is confident that he will be noticed and be a success working in the officers' mess. It is not in his character to fail. In fact, he has never failed at anything and does not know the meaning of failure. Failure is just not an option to be considered. The desire for perfection is embodied in his consciousness. His zealous ethical make-up is such as to make it unthinkable for him to intentionally disappoint a boss, friend, parent, army colleague or customer. At the same time, he now realises that any high-profile recognition might become another nail in the coffin of his musical ambition.

To make things worse, Rocky fears that his father will be tirelessly prearranging his future, sneaking and lurking around. He detests this behind-the-scenes activity.

Cat Stevens' lyrics keep running through his head all night. In his imagination, the needle of the record player gets stuck in a scratch and keeps playing that line of the song in which the son is ordered to listen. He tosses and turns until he eventually springs up in the bed.

'Ahh! This is all going wrong. My old man is wrecking my head. He is ruining my life. He is destroying me.'

Rocky really misses Maria, his Spanish mother. He remembers that, throughout his childhood, she had been totally dominant when it came to decisions about the family. As a professional singer and dancer, she was the inspiration behind his love of music. Rocky knows that things would be totally different if she was still alive. Piper Jim would probably have disappeared, escaping on yet another overseas United Nations mission. Then Maria would have been left with the freedom, as usual, to call the shots. Maria and Piper Jim always seemed happy to live, mostly, separate lives. Tension between them was always in the air but mostly left unspoken.

Military duty abroad provided the release that permitted the marriage to survive. One memorable year, as soon as

Piper Jim arrived home from UN service, Maria seemed to be, night after night, bathing in Epsom Salts. Suddenly, without warning, she packed the two boys off to granny's house in Cadiz in the south of Spain. There, the three of them spent an entire wonderful summer cooking for granny in her small restaurant, swimming, playing Latino music and learning flamenco. Piper Jim did not visit them at all, not even once. He wrote a few short letters and they learned he was being granted leave of absence by the army so that he could accept a one-year job in warehouse logistics with the European Union. He was already gone, having departed Ireland for the job in Brussels, when they arrived back in Dublin for the autumn school term. As Rocky matured, he realised that he really did not know his father. The house in Ormond Square was always such a happy place, particularly when Piper Jim was overseas.

As the light of dawn peeps through his bedroom window, Rocky realises that he has not really slept. His pillow is wet, and he knows that he is still grieving for his mother. Last night's shenanigans with Piper Jim have made him miss her even more. It has been eighteen months since she departed this life, and Rocky has come to fear that his world will never, ever, be as carefree again. Her joyous, unconditional positive regard, her attention to his needs, her total understanding of his emotions and her uplifting high spirits – all gone and irreplaceable. He remembers her sense of awe when he would master a new song. As he gets out of bed, he resolves that the effervescence he inherited from Maria must never be allowed to drain from his personality.

Despite his poor night's sleep, there is an early morning uplift in Rocky's mood. He smiles into the bathroom mirror as he remembers that today he will be meeting the prostitute's son. *Just great.*

Chapter 6

School Days with the Prostitute's Son

There is a spring in Rocky's step as he strolls down to the nearby Dublin central bus station, Bus Arus, to meet Philip, the prostitute's son. Philip is a year younger than Rocky and is completing his military training eighty miles away in Costume Barracks, Athlone. He is also being trained in Border security operations at Finner Camp in County Donegal. The boys have not seen each other for over six weeks. Philip is getting very little time off as his training is coming to its intensive finale. For years, everybody has called Philip by the nickname Lizzy. Even though Lizzy is a girl's name, Rocky knows that Philip is totally at home with it.

The bus from Athlone is late, and Rocky helps himself to his favourite combination of Earl Grey tea and Club Milk chocolate at the crowded Bus Arus café. His feeling of exhaustion has been replaced now by a state of anticipatory exhilaration. He will be overjoyed to see Lizzy again.

When Lizzy was signing on for his recruit training, he was given the surprise news that some recruits would, due to lack of accommodation, be trained outside of Dublin. Neither of the boys were happy when they were separated. Rocky was worried about Lizzy moving to Athlone. Because he had dark skin, he had been bullied a lot at school and involved in fights on more than one occasion. At that time in Ireland, there were very few coloured people and local Dublin kids often adopted some of the sickening behaviour they saw on imported US television programmes. At the time, the Irish school system had little experience of diverse cultures. From a very young age, Lizzy was vulnerable. Rocky remembers a timid and frightened little person who seemed totally perplexed by his dissimilarity in appearance to other kids living in the neighbourhood.

The Rockingham family, it seems, came to know Lizzy due to their friendship with Mrs Jacinta Denihy. Rocky's earliest memory of Jacinta was of a lovely, pale-faced Dublin woman who lived next door on Ormond Square. She was always warm and welcoming, forever smelling of expensive perfume, usually wearing high heels and the most luxurious of attire. Rocky remembers his worry about her overwhelming red lipstick and the marks left on his cheek and shirt collar when she was greeting him with hugs and kisses. She was a delightful lady who encouraged Rocky to play games in her house with her rather strange-looking dark-skinned child. Rocky was initially scared of this potential new friend as he had never seen a coloured person before, except on TV. However, growing up as an only child, he also had friendship needs. Gradually, a close bond of mutual support emerged between the boys. As the older of the two, Rocky flourished in a leadership role. Lizzy, the loyal follower, seriously lacked confidence and was totally fearful of people's reaction to his foreign looks. In a world of white people, he craved protection and empathy. This flowed in abundance from his comradeship with his confident friend.

Jacinta Denihy was comparatively better off than the Rockinghams, with expensive home furnishings and a kitchen fitted with the most modern of appliances. Rocky knew from an early age that she had a lot of boyfriends, and he was not allowed to visit the house after 6pm. Often, there were bundles of cash lying around the house, and Rocky assumed that his neighbour was "loaded".

A pattern emerged of Rocky's mother Maria collecting the young dark child most evenings in time for him to join them for their evening meal. Maria reared the two boys. Her enthusiasm massively inspired their interest in music and song. The lingo of the home was occasionally English but most often monopolised by a very noisy Spanish, spoken by the boys, in mild jackeen accents. Both boys were fluent in the language and went on to achieve honours in the Leaving Certificate. But it was music that prevailed over everything else in their early lives, and musical instruments were their most important and loved toys. Maria bestowed all the skills she had learned during her career as a professional entertainer. The result was the achievement of consummate vocal and musicianship mastery.

Rocky remembers the warm summer nights when they would sit in Ormond Square playing classical guitar and singing the latest pop hits. Appreciative neighbours from the street, hearing the music, would often gather around and, sitting on old timber boxes, sip beer, enjoy the sessions and sometimes join in. Then the boys would work on their homework together on the kitchen table. On completion of their nightly study, Maria would routinely commence music training. The house would vibrate with the sounds of exuberant loud Latino music accompanied by energetic, playful singing and dancing sessions. More and more frequently, the coloured boy would stay overnight in the Rockingham home, particularly if Jacinta was entertaining boyfriends. Maria even bought bunk beds for Rocky's tiny bedroom so that his friend could stay as often as necessary. Then Rocky remembers Jacinta Denihy's funeral. Lizzy had stayed in their house for weeks on end and was told that Jacinta was in hospital and seriously ill. At the funeral, both Rocky and Lizzy heard the whispered comments of the adults. There were mutterings about failed drug rehabilitation and the all-too-frequent Dublin tragedy of heroin overdose. Piper Jim was on yet another overseas tour of duty when the death occurred.

After the funeral, they all came home in a taxi with the dark-skinned boy crying and trembling with fear and shock. The uncertainty concerning his future, as well as his tragic loss, threatened to destroy his already fragile nature. After the funeral, he spent a week in bed absorbing the bereavement and worrying about what terrifying future was in store for him. He had often read in the newspapers about the cruelty people had to endure in institutions. He was afraid that he would be sent to some faraway country and adopted. Maria could easily comprehend what was going on in his traumatised mind. After the funeral, she stayed with him for hours on end. Rocky remembers her regularly visiting Lizzy in the top bunk, even during the night. For a full week, she talked repeatedly of great days ahead. When she had to leave the house on chores, Rocky was under instruction never to leave Lizzy alone. Rocky knew that his mother was spending many evenings in McKee Barracks, using the satellite link to the Sinai Desert in Egypt where Piper Jim was stationed. She had returned late from McKee Barracks on quite a few nights, and he could hear her intense crying in the bedroom next door. He was not sure what was wrong. Then Maria came home from the barracks one evening with a smile on her face and a spring in her step. She immediately called the boys together. All three of them sat around the kitchen table and, first, Maria led them in reciting a few prayers. This was very unusual, so the boys were prepared for some big announcement. Maria then asked Lizzy if he was willing to become a full member of the family. Without waiting for an answer, she asked Rocky if he could cope with a new stepbrother. The two positive answers were a foregone conclusion. The crisis was over as agreement was reached with much hugging and laughter. The hall phone rang, and it was Piper Jim being patched through on a special satellite link from the Sinai Desert. He welcomed Lizzy to the family and said he would be home very soon to celebrate.

Everything happened with great speed. Maria, it seemed, moved quickly with whatever paperwork was involved, and Piper Jim flew home for a week. Lizzy and Rocky resumed their lives as inseparables and the newly constituted family spent a lump sum of Piper Jim's UN wages on a posh celebratory meal in the Gresham Hotel in O'Connell Street. Maria was the one to give a short piece of advice at the end of the meal.

'In this family, we are trend-setters. We are a unique multiracial Irish family. Dad and I have decided that from now, we want you boys to pick out and then deeply focus on the things you love. I hope you choose music and dance.'

Rocky remembers how Lizzy began to have a total change of personality once he took onboard the feeling of unconditional family acceptance. He and Maria also began to talk about the importance of focus and his enjoyment of life. A few days after receiving Maria's advice, Lizzy went to the nearby Walton's Music Shop in North Frederick Street where an electric guitar was purchased. He then signed up for an intensive course of lessons. He began to smile and laugh a lot, increasingly cheerful and often playing tricks on Rocky. It was evident that the new experience of full family love was treasured to the extent of giving him a massively increased sense of self-worth. Rocky remembers that, surprisingly, Lizzy seemed to quickly become taller, rolling back his shoulders more and adopting a self-assured, upright posture.

As well as the death of Jacinta, several other landmark events changed life for Lizzy and occurred in their early teens. Rocky remembers that Lizzy began to experience a new enthusiasm for school. Wounding comments from his school mates, apparently, became less frequent as it emerged that he was nearing the top of his class academically. Rocky remembers one particular happy conversation:

'Hey, Rocky, they are not abusing me anymore. Two weeks ago, the teacher announced that I had come first in the maths exam. Somehow, that seems to have ended all the hassle and nasty remarks. Now they are all crowding around me in panic before class, begging me to help them with their unsolved, half-finished homework problems.'

But an even bigger, unexpected, positive situation for Lizzy began to emerge as he acquired his nickname. It was also around this time that a hard rock version of an Irish ballad exploded onto the music scene, taking Ireland, Europe, and even as far away as Australia, by storm. Controversy raged. The traditionalists were horrified that the modern generation was intent on despoiling Irish folk music. The song was called "Whiskey in the Jar" and almost every kid in Dublin knew the words of this old, popular ballad. Nobody had dared transform a traditional Irish song into a rock anthem before. That was until the handsome, Afro-haired, coloured guy, with a sweet jackeen accent, called Phil Lynott came along with his band Thin Lizzy.

Rocky remembers his stepbrother becoming totally fascinated that somebody with the same colour skin as he had could become a success in Ireland. As "Whiskey in the Jar" moved up to number one in the Irish charts, the kids at school were quick to notice that they had a classmate who looked not unlike the controversial celebrity. Very quickly, his real name, Philip, was cast aside, and his stepbrother began to exude a new confidence due to his new school nickname, Lizzy. When the song moved into the UK Top 10 and Phil Lynott appeared on the celebrated BBC television show, *Top of the Pops*, interest in this new interpretation of Irish music reached fever pitch. Then the song broke through into the 208 Radio Luxembourg charts. On board the *Mi Amigo*, disc jockeys from the pirate station Radio Caroline repeatedly blasted the song into homes across the UK and Ireland by "power playing" it every hour. Suddenly, traditional Irish music was emerging with a new, exciting modern interpretation lead by a coloured lad, who grew up in the hardy Dublin neighbourhood of Crumlin.

Maria was initially alarmed and worried when she heard that Philip was being called a girl's name. She was perturbed that this represented renewed harassment and cruelty. However, she soon came to understand the origin of the nickname as the fame of the band Thin Lizzy grew. Then she saw a TV news clip of a grinning Phil Lynott, being mobbed by frenzied fans, mostly young girls, while walking down Grafton Street in Dublin. Now she quickly understood why Philip was so delighted by his new nickname. She realised that this was an unexpected golden opportunity to enhance the boy's self-image dramatically. A coloured Irish superstar as a role model. Absolutely perfect. The self-belief of Philip, aka Lizzy, soared with the appearance of his lookalike hero on even more popular music programmes on television. Suddenly, the electric guitar lessons gained a new urgency, with Lizzy spending hour after hour in practice. Then began a self-grooming phase as he attempted to grow a wispy Lynott-style moustache. Visits to the barbers were abandoned in favour of a specialist hairdresser who gradually created a rock-star-like Afro hairstyle.

To crown all these changes, there was the school talent competition, a few months later, with all the parents invited along to the big assembly hall. It was Maria's first time to see the boys perform on stage, and they were all a little nervous. This event saw Lizzy and Rocky launch their new band "Rock 'n' Roll Kids". Lizzy, now, not only had a full, massive Afro hairstyle, but on stage, he decided to wear the exact same clothes as he had seen Phil Lynott wearing on *Top of The Pops*. Rocky, not to be outdone, also got in on the act as lead singer, wearing a long, blond wig closely resembling another Thin Lizzy star, the American, Scott Gorham.

Each contestant was allowed perform one song. Despite the demanding requirements of the music, the choice of song for the Rock 'n' Roll Kids was "Whiskey in the Jar". When Lizzy fluently played the explosive opening electric guitar introduction, the school hall erupted. Maria thought there was going to be a riot as the kids jumped up to stand on their seats, screaming and dancing with excitement. There could only be one winner after that. Maria was in tears of joy when they were called back onto the stage to collect their prize. All her years of musical coaching was finally paying dividends. Her boys were maturing and emerging into incredibly talented young performers.

Chapter 7

Together Again. The Boys are Back in Town

At last, the bus from Athlone pulls in and a tall, skinny, dark young man with tight, almost skinhead, haircut emerges. He has a small Cadiz Football Club rucksack hanging loosely from his shoulders. Rocky immediately spots this gift which he knows Lizzy had been given by Granny. From a distance, Rocky immediately notices a change in his stepbrother. Lizzy is thinner and even darker tanned than usual. The weather over the past month has been glorious, and Rocky immediately guesses that Lizzy must have spent considerable time out in the open air on physically demanding military tactical exercises. His tan enhances his sparkling white smile, which announces his delight on spotting Rocky. The lads embrace and there is the usual exchange of upbeat laughter and jackeen banter.

'Jeez, you are as skinny as I have ever seen ya. Is there no food down in that bleedin' redneck barracks? Now we can all really call you thin Lizzy! But you look outstanding, my little bro, so athletic and muscular. Hey! You are the same height as me now. Stand up straight till I measure ya.'

Rocky could see, from the broad smile on his face, that the reunion and brotherly slagging exhilarated Lizzy. Lizzy also loved being referred to as "bro", being short for brother. It was a mutual term of endearment used by both. As they walk out of Bus Arus, Lizzy is standing tall, portraying confidence and exhibiting all the features of rude health. Rocky can read Lizzy like an open book, and he immediately knows that things are going well for him down in Athlone.

'Hey, Rocky. I need a pint and, for some reason, I'm really longing for a sandwich. Creamy porter and ham sandwiches? Does that ring a bell? Hint, hint! I am dying to talk to you. You only have thirty-six hours to fatten me up before I go back to Athlone.'

'Aha! I know where you want to go. Fresh ham *sambo*s and porter means it must be the Molly Malone Inn on Talbot Street. Jeez, you are a creature of habit when you are hungry. I can read your bleedin' mind, bro.'

'Great, I could eat a horse. They have us running five miles every morning at 6am. Not jogging now. Bleedin' running and with packs on our backs. Then tactics in Carna Range outside the town all day. We have five-a-side soccer at night. Even eleven-a-side sometimes in St Mel's Park. I absolutely love every minute of it. Never felt fitter and healthier in my entire life.'

They reach the pub.

'I was thinking of Molly's because Dad likes it. It's a real old man's type of pub. Where is he? Is he joining us? I thought he might be with you.'

'Yeah, we will meet him later at home.'

Lizzy immediately knows that something is wrong, and the smile momentarily leaves his face.

'Is he okay? He is not sick or anything?'

'No, it's me that is sick, Lizzy. Sick of Dad. Sick of bleedin' celebrity Piper Jim.'

Lizzy bursts into laughter. Some things never change. He knows only too well of the clashes between the two. Poor Piper Jim has an uncanny ability, often seemingly unwittingly, of getting under Rocky's skin. Strangely, Lizzy has never had a similar problem. His stepfather rarely intrudes in his life, usually leaving him to his own devices. In total contrast to Rocky, Lizzy was happy to follow his stepfather's demand that he join the army. Of course, he had expected to do his training in McKee Barracks in Dublin and was really surprised to end up halfway across the country in Athlone. However, in some ways, he is pleased that the unfamiliar location has given him his first taste of adult independence. He is happy to be away from Ormond Square and is enjoying life without parental supervision.

The Molly Malone Inn looks the same as always. Still ancient and unchanging. A great pint, fresh ham sandwiches, old men behind the bar serving mostly old men in front of the bar. Not a woman in sight.

'Two pints of porter and two ham sandwiches, please.'

'With or without mustard?'

'No mustard in either the pints or the sandwiches,' Rocky teases.

'Okay, Rockingham, very funny. I will get Piper Jim to put manners on you.'

Rocky grins, not sure if the elderly barman fully appreciates his joke. The boys find a quiet corner of the bar and sit up on two high stools.

'So, Lizzy, I have a feeling that things are going well in Athlone.'

Lizzy laughs. 'I am the only bleedin' "darkie" in the entire town and there are no Dub accents down there either. Zero. Nobody even says "bleedin'". It's like a different planet. But people are nice to me and there is not one bit of hassle anywhere. The training is savage physically, but I am doing well. Out of the sixty that started, it looks like only thirty-five will pass the course. Twenty-five have been booted out because they could not make the grade.'

'So, how is the platoon? Are they all rednecks? It must be terrible to be surrounded by muck savages.'

'Rocky, I can honestly tell you that I am getting on great with everybody. I am well ahead when it comes to the physical demands of the course. That has been a huge help. You told me during your training how endurance ability earns you respect from the other lads in the platoon. I remember you saying how much you loved your platoon in McKee Barracks. Well, it's the same for me down in Athlone. Friends for life. I will bring you down to meet them when we get a break after the course is over. They are all really civilised, clever guys. No dimwits, no muck savages. In the barracks, they have come to understand me as a real person, not as a coloured bleedin' jackeen.'

Lizzy pauses for a second to take a sup from his pint and a big bite from his ham sandwich. 'You know, the music also helped me to settled down. I pulled together a few musicians from the Western Command Army Band and we did a gig for the troops on a Saturday night in the canteen. It went down a treat. The day after the gig, immediately, I noticed that my relationships around the barracks were transformed. Suddenly, there were lots of knowing smiles. The word had gone out very fast and people came to see me as the entertainer, singer and guitarist. That one gig left a permanent stamp. Life became instantly more pleasant.' Lizzy gazes into the distance, suddenly recalling his early teenage years.

'You know, Rocky, in teaching us to sing, dance and play music, Mam gave us the best set of skills any person can possibly have. You and I can go to any town in the world and very quickly have friends and earn money. It's like this – for me, music has demolished any negative attitudes towards me because of my dark skin. It's brilliant. At the high level we have reached in music, we have a leading edge. Rocky, music has been like a magic wand.'

'You think we are really *that* good?' Rocky smiles teasingly but already knowing the answer.

'Do I what? You know, Rocky, it's not what you and I think. We play music for other people. The audience reveals a lot to us through their reaction to our performance. We draw our energy from the buzz. You know, we are *that* good, bro, because the feedback every time we perform is brilliant. I come off the stage on a bleedin' high. No drug in the world could give me that.'

'You are right, Lizzy. That is why I am annoyed with Dad today.'

It is time for Rocky to dump his frustration on Lizzy. 'Dad is trying to push me forward for a long-term career in the army. All my music training will be lost. That's why I did not bring him down to meet you. I want to talk to you alone.'

'But we are both in the army. What more can he want from you now?'

'We had a sort of father-and-son discussion last night. I found out some of what is going on in his head. I caught him out, Lizzy. Last night he blurted out the next stage of his plot. Now it's not just enough for me to have joined the army. To make him proud, I must become a lieutenant. He says that he has all the contacts to get me a cadetship as a first step. Yet, he knows full well that I want to get back to music after I have completed my military service. Now think about that for a minute and then tell me your reaction.'

The pints of porter are disappearing quickly. Rocky leans over the bar counter to attract the barman's attention while Lizzy absorbs this bombshell in silence. He is perplexed by Rocky's news and is a little ashamed that his initial gut feeling is one of jealousy. What a surprise. Piper Jim will, again, apply unrelenting pressure on Rocky for sure. That fatherly forcefulness worked the last time in coercing Rocky into joining the army. Though Rocky likes to portray himself as tough and unbending, Lizzy knows that Piper Jim is exceptionally cunning.

As a soldier, Lizzy has come to strongly admire the lieutenant in charge of his platoon in Athlone. Becoming an officer seems like a great option for his dashing stepbrother. Lizzy never realised, before this moment, how far they had both come to reach this point. Even talking about Rocky going forward for an officer's course is totally new territory for them. None of their inner-city friends in Ormond Square, The Liberties, Smithfield or Stoneybatter ever even imagined that any of them might have the remotest of chances of becoming an army officer. A thought is triggered in Lizzy's head. He wonders if this possibility might be open to him as well. Would Piper Jim help him too? He knows that he has even better exam marks than Rocky and a high level of physical fitness. But being realistic, Piper Jim has a massive interest in Rocky, his son by birth. Towards his stepson, Piper Jim has simply cold disinterest. Rocky has always been a winner. Lizzy figures that if Rocky accepts this proposal, he must have a good chance of achieving it. Rocky never fails. As Rocky pays the barman for the drinks, Lizzy realises that he needs to quickly discipline his thoughts and suppress those brief initial pangs of envy. He decides to encourage Rocky to give it a try. He chooses his words carefully.

'Rocky, you are going to have to think long and hard before you dismiss your father's idea. He loves you and he never bought into Mam's plan of us forming a band. It's an amazing chance and there is no better man to swing it for you. He has loads of contacts and influence and gets great overseas trips at the drop of a hat. He is chummy with some top politicians. You will be perfect for the job. In school you were a natural leader. In the cadets you can go to uni on full pay.'

Rocky is not buying it. 'Lizzy, I am totally scared about this new pressure he has sprung on me. I hope this is not going to be the beginning of more arguments and tension in the house.'

'Rocky, at times my platoon lieutenant in Athlone reminds me of you. Well spoken, clear ideas and driven by ambition but still good-natured. If you do become an officer, I will be proud of you. When I become a fully trained private or even corporal, I hope you look after me well. Perhaps I might, someday, become an officer too. No matter what happens, I am delighted and shocked that we are even having this conversation.'

'Wow! Lizzy, take it easy. I have my clear plans. I am determined not to be side-tracked even further.'

'Side-tracked? What are you feckin' talking about? We have both been steered away from music. The band days are over. Gone. History. It was fantastic fun at school. But surely, we must now make the best of the army.'

Rocky is stunned and upset as he hears Lizzy, his most treasured confidant, advising him that their long-held boyhood dream should be scrapped. Rocky goes on the attack.

'Hold on now, bro. Five minutes ago, you were telling me how music helped you to be a success down in Athlone. Now don't feckin' break my heart. Cool it, bro. Don't destroy me and don't even think about abandoning our dream. Don't let them change you. I am happy to do my military service, including United Nations peacekeeping. Then I am returning to music. Full stop. You know, Lizzy, I wish Dad would just disappear on another overseas mission. I try to do everything he wants me to do, but he never returns the favour. It's all one-way traffic.'

'Rocky, you are so talented that you have probably too many options. You have the world at your feet. All I can say is that if Piper Jim comes to me with the same proposal, it will be hard for me to dismiss it. I love the army.'

'No! No! No! Lizzy, listen! You are one of the best young electric lead guitarists in Ireland... even in Europe. You are closer to a breakthrough than you realise. I read in last week's *Spotlight Magazine* that Thin Lizzy have just signed a seventeen-year-old young Dub as a substitute guitarist for their next world tour. He is going to be playing backstage most nights learning his trade and gaining experience.'

Rocky puts his hand on Lizzy's shoulder and shakes him. 'That could have been *you, you, you*, bro. You are probably better than that lad they hired. You should have been at that audition in the SFX, but you were down in Athlone. I tried to call you, but they said you were in Roscommon on a three-day tactical exercise.'

Rocky reiterates his hostility to Piper Jim's proposal. 'Look, out of respect to my fat-arse father, I am going to play along with him. The army will send me to Lebanon soon anyway, away from all his scary, snooping interference. It will be great to get away from him. In the meantime, I intend staying significantly active on the music scene. I do not want people to forget that we exist… and Lizzy, I need you to come back to Dublin. Bro, you are a key man. I could become a solo artist but really want your support for the idea of a full band. Remember, we were making fantastic money before we split up. Is there any news on where you will be sent after your training is completed? What are the possibilities of you coming back to Dublin?'

'I spoke with my platoon commander. We have a great relationship. He told me that if I want to go back to Dublin, nobody in Athlone will stand in my way. I am the only Dub in the platoon. The lieutenant will recommend that I be sent to McKee Barracks immediately after my training. We might be back together very soon. I think it's best not to discuss this with Dad. In Athlone I am certain that people will help me. If anybody starts pulling strings, it might upset everything.'

'Hey, that really is good news… but hold on a minute. What are you telling me? You are the only Dub in the platoon in Athlone? Wow! I never knew that before. How the hell did that happen?'

'Now, Rocky, be careful not to jump to conclusions. Say nothing at all to Piper Jim. Now we better think about heading home to say hello to him.'

'Okay, Lizzy. Agreed! Hey! It's too early to go home. Let's have a *deoch an doras*… a drink for the door. Why don't we go for one last pint to Ceoil agus Craic?'

Lizzy breaks into a wide smile. 'That surely means we are going to sing bro. Then we might be smothered by new fans… girls. Then we might never go home!'

'Ha! Ha! You are right, Lizzy. The city is packed with gorgeous athletic Welsh girls over for the hockey tournament this weekend.'

Lizzy comically raises his eyebrows. 'I can smell the wintergreen sports rub already. Jaysus, Rocky... a hockey tournament. You have me convinced.'

'Ha! Okay! Okay! Lizzy... we will have to be disciplined no matter what happens. Let's go and do a quick song. I want to be sure that your voice and our harmonies are as brilliant as ever.'

Chapter 8

Ceoil agus Craic

Ceoil agus Craic is a small pub where the customers are encouraged to sing and play musical instruments. It has always been one of the boys' favourite places, primarily because lots of awesome romantic opportunities have followed on from their singing performances there. It was where they experienced fan idolisation for the first time.

'Rocky, I need a new girlfriend.'

'Another one?! Calm down, Lizzy. What about Ping, the Chinese girl? Are you keeping in contact?'

'Yep, a phone call every night. I am meeting her tomorrow. But meeting new girls would be nice as well. Ha! Ha! We must experience everything. I want to meet loads of foreign girls while I am young. We must sow our wild oats! The world is our oyster.'

'Yeah, you just love tourists. But hold on, Lizzy. Today

we need to be disciplined. Please, try not to fall in love… just this once!'

'Oh God! As long as I do not get the whiff of wintergreen! All that adulation after we sing. I am not a man of steel, you know! Rocky, perhaps we should go straight home.'

"Listen, bro, for today, let's just make it a couple of songs and one last pint. We can then go home to Dad and say hello. I know he will not be pleased that I did not invite him along to the bus station to meet you. So, I don't want the two of us to arrive home totally *langered*…

'… and smelling of wintergreen. Oh, if only!'

Minutes later, they are entering the musical pub. As luck would have it, an old friend, Boxer Mullins from Smithfield, is performing, strumming his guitar badly and vocally annihilating an old Irish ballad. The bar is nicely packed with both local people and tourists, all taking a break from their Saturday afternoon shopping. Boxer suddenly stops playing and shouts out loudly, 'Jaysus, we are all in for a treat now. Hey, folks, it's the amazing Rockingham brothers. Hey, a round of applause for the Rock 'n' Roll Kids.'

A broadly grinning Lizzy embraces Boxer, who quietly mumbles into his ear, 'Hey, Lizzy, what the feck happened to your magnificent Afro hairstyle? And jaysus, you are after getting taller… and darker… and so bleedin' muscular. You must be training like crazy.'

'No need to whisper. It's okay. I joined the army since I saw you last. I had to cut off all my hair. You know, they want us to have a short back and sides haircut.'

'Ah Jaysus. No! No!' Boxer shakes his head. 'You! You! Lizzy in the army!' Boxer is clearly stunned, even somewhat distressed. 'What about the electric guitar and the music… and the band. You are an amazing lad, a brilliant talent. By now you should be a bleedin' millionaire like Phil Lynott or

Rory Gallagher. This is crazy news. Is this a joke? What the hell are you telling me?'

Rocky interjects, 'Good man, Boxer. That's what I have been saying to him as well.'

'Hey, Rocky, great to see ya. What are you up to?'

'Well… actually, I joined the army as well.'

Boxer covers his face and eyes with his hands, as if to cry. 'Oh, for feck's sake! I don't believe it. You, as well! Your beautiful mother Maria must be turning in her grave. The day the music died. I will never forget those lovely balmy summer nights on Ormond Square when you lads and Maria used to entertain the whole neighbourhood. Remember the crowd outside your house sipping flagons of cider. I was there so many times sitting on a timber box nicked from the fruit market across the road. We all loved you guys 'cause you were the only entertainment we could afford. Ah! So many wonderful, happy days. I thought I was looking at the birth of a superstar band. Oh, poor Maria. All her efforts gone to waste.'

Boxer is shaking his head and seems genuinely bitterly disappointed. The brothers know Boxer well enough to realise that he is a friend. A "salt of the earth" jackeen, always with their best interests at heart.

'Boxer, we are both just doing a short stint in the forces to keep our dad happy. But soon we will be back to the music, I promise. Okay, amigo! Don't worry!'

'Wow! I love to hear that word. Amigo! Amigo! Another flashback, Rocky. I remember you and Maria speaking Spanish together all the time. We were so impressed. When you used to call me "amigo", I felt like an actor in a Wild West film. You are the only person who has ever called me "amigo". I love it. Those were great times. The sun always seemed to be shining brightly on Ormond Square. We were poor, but we had community spirit, kindness and culture.'

Rocky and Lizzy head up to the bar and there is much laughter and embracing as they meet even more people who recognise them. Lizzy whispers into Rocky's ear, 'It's just great to be home, Rocky. I am only realising now how much I miss the incredible energy of this great city.'

The barman immediately knows the boys' drinks order and hands Rocky two freshly pulled creamy black pints. 'Hey, lads it's been far too long since we last saw you. You will do a song for us, I hope?'

Then Boxer shouts out, 'Yeah, lads, and I can give you a lend of my guitar.' Rocky gives Lizzy a revealing look and they both burst into laughter knowing that Boxer's guitar is usually totally out of tune. Boxer breaks into a grin as well. 'Ya cheeky brats. Here, take it. I tuned it less than an hour ago at the piano.'

Rocky gratefully accepts the guitar and pulls Lizzy aside. 'Are you sober enough for harmonies? Everly Brothers?'

'Yeah, I am as bleedin' sober as a judge. What about that "Dream, Dream, Dream" one? The pints have lubricated my vocal cords and I know I will sing even better than usual. I am sure we can manage it.'

'You mean "All I Have to Do Is Dream". Not an easy one, bro, but I'm with ya. Let's just slip out the back for a second to rehearse and check Boxer's guitar. I want to be sure we remember the words. I don't want to make a bleedin' bollix of it in front of our friends. Boxer will be very quick to tell us if our standards have fallen.'

They quickly rehearse the words in the back yard and return to the bar. Boxer's guitar is perfectly in tune and the boys speculate that he must have been taking lessons. The tiny pub is now jammed with customers. Seems people have heard that they are around. The venue by tradition is "unplugged" so they wait for the newly arrived customers to get served their drinks. A lot of the faces are local and familiar. They get many waves and thumbs-up signals. The barman then pauses his service and bangs a glass loudly on top of the bar counter. Then, as is customary, he calls, in the Irish language, for quietness in the house. '*Bi Ciuin! Bi Ciuin! Fan socair!*'

As the house rules dictate, the tiny bar falls totally silent. Rocky strums the opening chords. Then, with exquisite clarity, the professionally trained voices of the Rockingham brothers open up. The few pints they have consumed in no way diminishes their vocal capability. They stunningly handle the challenging vocal harmonies needed to do justice to one of the Everly Brothers' greatest hits. They know that their ability to perform this complex harmony is the result of endless weeks of Maria's demanding and inspirational coaching. They love the Everly Brothers because they are widely regarded as having a massive influence on the world music scene. Even the Beatles are believed to have gained inspiration from their work. Lizzy and Rocky know that their commanding performance of this song always impresses people, wherever they go. The pub customers seem awestruck as they stand on their tiptoes all around the bar, soaking in this marvellous musical experience. The intimate gathering of locals and visitors are astounded by their good luck to have stumbled upon such an impressive moment.

After rapturous applause, the boys are persuaded to do a second song. This time, they ask their fellow customers to join in the singing of another upbeat Everly Brothers harmony "Cathy's Clown". The little pub is filled with the sound of singing, as everybody seems to know the words. The brothers belt out their cultivated rendition and, with Rocky's skilful playing, even Boxer's guitar sounds perfect.

Then comes the inevitable call for more, but the boys

judge a pause to drink their pints and allow the barman, again, to make some money. They know the rules. The barman must have breaks in the music to serve drinks and make a living. Nevertheless, the atmosphere is immense with so many people coming up to shake their hands and wish them well. The chat includes requests for gigs, birthday entertainment and wedding performances.

Boxer quietly whispers into Rocky's ear, 'Are ya going to do another one?'

'The buzz is amazing, Boxer, but I want to get Lizzy home reasonably sober as he has not seen Dad in six weeks. He has been physically training so hard that he has lost weight and I am afraid the beer might go straight to his head.'

'Grand, if you guys want to quietly escape, I can start singing. It will get you off the hook.'

'Hey, Boxer, you are a real friend. You know, with the craic like this, both of us would stay here singing all night if we could.'

Boxer recommences his singing and the boys continue their many conversations out on the street, with both new fans and old friends. Then duty calls and it's time to go home to meet Piper Jim.

Chapter 9

Eclectic RRK

Rocky and Lizzy walk down Henry Street on route to Ormond Square. Their brief celebrity status vanishes as they melt into the hordes of Saturday shoppers in the city-centre, pedestrian-only streets. They are feeling pleased with the accolades and appreciation that they encountered. At the same time, Boxer's friendly critique left its wounds, impacting particularly on Lizzy. He starts mumbling in a quiet, slightly slurred voice, 'I think you are right, Rocky. You heard that slagging-off we got from Boxer. It brought some facts of life home to me.'

'What are you bleedin' mumbling on about now, bro? Right about what?'

'I think we should stick to the original plan.'

'Ha! Ha! Which original plan are we talking about now, Lizzy?'

'Why throw away our talent for music and all those years of hard work? We have come a long way and were amazingly lucky to have had a demanding professional coach in Mam. She devoted her life to making us unique. That's exactly what we are. Incomparable. There is nobody like us and that's really a good situation, Rocky. We have to respect Maria's memory.'

'You are right. Good! Good! Good! Thank God you have come to your senses, Lizzy! Thank you, Maria… in heaven! Thank you, my young bro! We are back on track. Now, I need you back in Dublin. Then we can resume our midweek gigs and rehearsals. Let's tell Dad nothing and just play along with him.'

Lizzy bursts into a slightly inebriated laugh and joins his hands in prayer. 'God, please send Piper Jim overseas and just let us do our own thing again. Ormond Square could be brilliant again if he were gone and there were just the two of us living there. Or maybe four of us. Ha! Ha! Rocky, you've got to date that other gorgeous Chinese girl.'

'Ha! You are a total rake, bro. Yeah, four would be perfect. I could get to love Chinese girls as well.'

They continue their journey home in silence and Lizzy looks at his watch. 'Okay, my time this weekend is so bleedin' short, Rocky, so here is my plan. Tonight, I will stay home with Dad. Tomorrow, I want to have time for a meal with Ping before I go back to Athlone. She is bringing me to her cousin's restaurant in Parnell Street, Chinatown. Then I will have to head directly for the bus.'

'Lizzy! You have everything under control. You are now more organised than I am. Fair play to you for keeping contact with that girl for all those months.'

'Well, you know her as well. You were really impressed. Remember, we met two girls, Ping and Lilly. They were the two who were jammin' with us at the student party at Dublin City University last year.'

'Yeah, yeah, wow! Now I remember. They were very talented, but I thought they had gone back to China. You kept in contact? Fantastic.'

'Look, they are great to hang out with. They are big into music. I must reintroduce you, Rocky. Both girls are, without doubt, up to our high musical standards. They are good enough to join us in the band. Ping is the drummer. Lilly has a voice like Stevie Nicks. Remember she sang some Fleetwood Mac numbers at the party.'

'Yeah! How could I forget? That was a superb night. Now you are talking, Lizzy. Let's get our focus back on the band. If these girls are up for it, and are as good as I remember, there just might be possibilities.'

'They often ask me if they could do some more gigs with us. They are keen and interested and they sort of look up to you as a leader.'

The influence of the pints has been to enhance Rocky's visualisation skills and enthusiasm.

'Hey, Lizzy, all the jigsaw pieces will come together if we quietly stay focused. We will be the most unique band in Ireland. We will have dark Irish, white Irish and two beautiful Chinese girls. We can sing in English, Irish, Spanish and Chinese. Totally different music.'

'Yeah, Rocky, we need to look at a new name as well. Did you hear Boxer calling us the "Rock 'n' Roll Kids"? I am more uncomfortable than ever with "kids" being in the name. We need a more mature name.'

'Yeah, something unique.'

'Rocky, you know… we are eclectic.'

'Wow, Lizzy. You were always so good at English. I love that word. Eclectic? It sounds like electric with a lisp. It's a groovy word. Ha! Ha! Now, what the hell does it mean?'

'It means that we are a totally unusual mix, pulling our influences and ideas from many different places and types of music. We can become Eclectic RRK.'

'Eclectic RRK... hmm! Lizzy, I think that name has a nice ring to it. You know, it could be a brilliant name. Our old fans will remember what RRK stands for. Then the new fans will see that we have a modern, cutting-edge identity.'

'Yeah, Rocky, I can see us on the front page of *New Musical Express*.' Lizzy holds apart his arms as if he were reading a broadsheet newspaper. '"Young, Irish-Chinese band, Eclectic RRK, launch their chart-topping album in China. Millions in sales predicted".'

'Lizzy, yeah! I can see it now. "First Irish band to sing in Chinese language. Concert in Peking sold out in three hours".' Rocky is enjoying the banter and playfully punches Lizzy in the shoulder. 'Hooray! Wow! Lizzy inspired as ever. We must have our dreams to make them happen. No dream, no route to success. We are going to be creative, brilliant and different. I am going to get you drinking creamy black pints much more often when you come back to Dublin. Now, tomorrow, be nice to Ping and get me a phone number for Lilly. I will invite them both to come busking with me next weekend in Grafton Street.'

The boys walk down Mary's Abbey Street to their home in Ormond Square. When their house comes into view, they can see that there are no lights shining through any of the windows.

Chapter 10

The Capel Street Fish and Chip Shop Agreement

Rocky opens the front door and immediately spots a note on the table beside the telephone. It's from Piper Jim and scribbled, typically, untidily on a scrap of old newspaper. It seems he has gone to a meeting and the note mentions that he will see Rocky later. No mention of a welcome for Lizzy and it seems that the homecoming of his stepson is either unimportant or has totally slipped his mind.

Rocky's cheeks turn red with a combination of rage and embarrassment. Lizzy is calm and seemingly unperturbed.

'Hey, Rocky, it's all right. Look, for me, this is an opportunity to spend more time with Ping. I can float the idea of her joining us in the new band. I know that she finishes serving in Dino's Bar and Grill at midnight. I will stay in her apartment tonight.'

Rocky attempts to deflect and regain self-control by making excuses for Piper Jim. This dreadful dereliction by his father must not be allowed result in the demoralisation of Lizzy. Rocky quickly concocts a plausible excuse. 'Okay, Lizzy. You know, I have noticed that Dad is becoming increasingly muddled. At times I am sorry for him. I hope he is not going downhill mentally.'

'Look! Dad just forgot I was coming. Like old men do. It's not a problem for me.'

But Lizzy is now hanging his head, sucking in a deep breath, and there is a slight shake in his voice. Rocky recognises the concealed deep hurt. He often wonders at how Lizzy tolerates Piper Jim's indifference while wearing a mask of false composure.

'Lizzy, I am so sorry. This is terrible. I feel ashamed of Dad's behaviour. He is an increasingly confused person. Maybe I am to blame. I should have brought him with me this morning.'

'Rocky, relax. Now look, I have two hours before I meet Ping. Why don't we head over to Capel Street and get some fish and chips? Anyway, there is something else I want to talk to you about. Now, this gives us some more time.'

'Great, let's do it.'

They lock up the house and briskly walk to the local "chipper" in silence. For now, Piper Jim is quickly forgotten, but Rocky remains a little tense wondering what Lizzy wants to discuss. Lizzy, in turn, is silent and seems to be rolling some profound thoughts through his head. Minutes later, they are in the vinegar-scented, local Capel Street chipper owned by the delightful Mary Byrne.

'*Howya*, Mary! Cod and chips for two. Two bottles of ice-cold Cidona as well, please.'

Mary has a loving, warm, almost maternal approach towards the boys and knows their family well.

'All right, luv. Hey! I haven't seen you two handsome young lads for ages. I hope you are not forgetting about Mary Byrne and my lovely fish and chips. Fresh cod caught this morning and landed in Howth Harbour. For young lads… remember, fish is great for your brains. Never forget. Take a seat and here is your Cidona, chilled of course. I will drop down the food to ya in about five minutes. Freshly cooked with TLC as always. Tell your friends about Mary Byrne, lads. I need the business. Times are tough.'

They take a table towards the back of the otherwise deserted chipper. Rocky wastes no time in opening the conversation. His curiosity has been whetted by the rather pensive face which Lizzy has suddenly adopted.

'Okay, Lizzy. Talk. You are worrying me. There is something on your mind.'

'Rocky, you and I both know something that we rarely ever dare discuss. I am not your stepbrother. We both know that.'

'Yeah, of course.'

'Rocky, I have been thinking a lot while down in Athlone. You know down there I have told everybody that I have a family. You will be meeting my new friends very soon at my Passing Out Parade in Custume Barracks. Rocky, we both know that my mother was not Jacinta, the local prostitute, and my dad was not a prostitute's customer. I loved Jacinta but she was my infant childminder not my mother. We need to finally sort this out because I cannot continue living the lie.'

'Hey, Lizzy, we have had this discussion before. We are both sons of Maria. You are my real brother… my best friend and I love you to bits!'

'Thanks, Rocky, you and Granny in Cadiz are all I have in terms of a real family. Piper Jim is your dad, but he is nothing to me. Nothing! I try to love him. At best, he tries to politely and coldly tolerate my existence.'

'Bro, Piper Jim has great respect for you. He is just a little emotionally brainless, that's all. He has a problem with empathy and love. Not just with you but also with our mother. With me, there is a problem too. I am used by him to achieve every dream in his life that he did not fulfil. Then there is envy about Maria's dominance of our upbringing. She dethroned him and his emotional state is often one of hostility for the things she achieved. Going back in time, I know Maria was ashamed of what happened. She tried to cover up her unfaithfulness because of the neighbours and the church. That's all it was. Just a convenient cover-up. Your coloured dad left Maria to cope with an unexpected baby. Nobody's fault. She did well, and we are both a big success now. We will soon be part of a world-class band. Now, Lizzy, in many ways, Mam even loved you more than me because she felt you needed her support more. Life was more challenging for you because you didn't look typically white Irish.'

'Rocky, everybody knows the truth. We look very alike, and the only difference is that we have different shades of skin. Of course, I am Irish. Like you, I was born in the Rotunda Hospital on Parnell Square. Mam's cover story fooled nobody, but it kept herself and Piper Jim on the respectable side of the community. Smiling and living the lie. Pretending that they were doing a great deed by adopting a poor coloured orphan. They felt that this story protected the family reputation.'

'This is a heavy conversation, Lizzy.'

For once, Lizzy is affirmative and strong in his argument. 'Rocky, we agreed to end the lie one year ago. Then what did we do? Nothing! I am still the prostitute's son. Rocky, you know that I am an easy-going person. But I want to have a life. I am worried sick that this falsehood is going to spread to Athlone where I am respected and even... kind of... well... I am actually... a popular person. Lots of the platoon members have introduced me to their sisters, some both gorgeous and smart. Quite a few of the girls seem to be attracted to me.'

'Lizzy, you are a great-looking guy, marvellous physique, kind, forever smiling and always behaving like a total gentleman. You deserve that attention from those Athlone girls.'

'Yeah, Rocky. But tell me, what will the situation become if the story gets down to Athlone that I am the accidental son of a prostitute. I now realise that I am carrying a terrible burden, bro... for a mistake that happened before I was born. Now, at last, life is getting good for me. Please, let's finally sort this mess out. Bro, it's time. Please help me.'

More than a year earlier, the brothers had agreed to end the untruthful situation. However, neither of them acted on that resolve. Partly this was because Maria, their mother, had not been dead for long. They did not want to dishonour her recent memory. They were also unsure about how difficult Piper Jim would find the change. They were both worried that he might become aggressive. But things have changed. They are now both independent adults and Rocky knows that there is only one correct course of action.

'Lizzy, yes, we have to take action. The silly cover story means nothing to me and never did. I was fooled for many years as a child, and I loved Mam. The cover-up is no longer necessary. Let's end it.'

The freshly cooked steaming cod and chips arrive, and Mary Byrne brazenly intrudes into the conversation in her heavily accented, loud voice.

'I could hear everything you two lads were saying. Now I will give you my pound of flesh. Every single person in this bleedin' neighbourhood knows you two are brothers. We always knew because you look so alike. We all just kept playing the game to keep your poor late mother, Maria, happy. She was a very religious woman who made a mistake lasting a few seconds. Look, lads, even in those horrible years, every woman deserved her occasional night of love and passion. Piper Jim was gone overseas all the time.'

She laughs and shakes her backside.

'Piper Jim... not much bleedin' passion there! Ha! Ha! That's for sure. Now, I hope that's a bit of help from Mary Byrne, your local fish woman, who has always loved you two lads and admired Maria.'

Mary Byrne heads back to her kitchen and, rather than being upset with the intrusion, the brothers burst into laughter and joviality. Lizzy leads the jocularity. 'In white, Catholic Ireland, it must have been a nightmare to have ended up with a dark son. Rocky, I can imagine that first day in the hospital...'

"Well, Maria, it's a boy... here he is... thanks, Doctor... ahhh! Oh, Jaysus, he is so feckin' dark... Jim will know it's not his! For feck's sake, what the hell will I do? I think I will escape down to Spain...

Lizzy gleefully snatches Rocky's upper arm. 'Mam says to Jim... let's tell the priest and the neighbours that he is the local whore's baby. Everybody will surely know the truth. But, Jim, living a life of lies is normal in Ireland and everybody will play the game.'

The bond between the brothers is so strong that they can laugh and tease with ease about such an incredibly sensitive matter.

'Hey, Lizzy, for our generation those days are nearly gone. Our poor parents lived in a fearful and pretend society. A bit of auld ridin' was something to be seriously ashamed of. Everybody doing it, living in fear, while at the same time standing in critical judgement of their neighbours who got caught.

Lizzy suddenly adopts a harsher tone. 'Rocky, it was sick. Even hiding and killing the babies.'

'You are probably lucky to be alive, Lizzy. Mam was strong and fought hard to keep you. She could have secretly sent you off for adoption. But, Lizzy, let's not get angry; let's move on tonight to final solution time. This time, we need to take strong action. From this moment onwards, I am never going to call you stepbrother again. The lie is over. You are my real brother, and I am going to tell Piper Jim that the cover story is being immediately ended. Terminated! *Terminado este minuto!* Rocky raises his hand and makes a sharp karate chop movement in the air in front of Lizzy. 'He will be furious and as thick as cow shite but is going to have to accept it. He can call you stepson if he wants, because that is the truth. For me, Lizzy, you are my blood brother and there must be no lies anymore. When we go to your graduation in Athlone, you can be proud of us, your real family.'

Mary Byrne has continued to monitor developments from in front of her deep fat fryer and shouts, 'Well done, lads. That's the way to go. Give some credit to Mary Byrne, your local fish woman. Come to me anytime if you want advice. Now, eat your meal before it goes cold.'

The boys both laugh again, and Lizzy gives Mary a thumbs-up signal while turning to face his brother.

'Rocky, that's great. I was a bit worried because you will be meeting all my new friends in Athlone soon. Having a family is really important to me, even if it's only a very small one.'

'Yeah, Lizzy, I totally understand. My family is very small as well… you, Granny and hairy arse.'

'I was just born. I did nothing wrong. I am working incredibly hard in Athlone to positively establish myself in my first real job. I am totally driven to succeed and create pride for you guys, my little family. Now, I really hope that Piper Jim accepts our decision. I am kind of scared that he might be very upset and throw me out of the house forever. I am the only jackeen doing recruit training in Athlone. I feel very worried about why that situation exists.'

'Well, Lizzy, if he is upset, that is his problem. If he throws you out, I am going with you. We are sticking together, and he can live alone. In fact, getting our own house is probably something we can soon afford. He, not us, will own any upset feelings. Let's meet at Bus Árus tomorrow a full hour before your bus departs for Athlone. We will tell him then what we have decided. I said "tell" because I am going to put it to him as our final decision. I will be on top of this conversation. Now, don't let me down by trying to be nice. Right?'

'Okay, Rocky. Have no fear. I will be strong as well. This means a lot to me.'

Chapter 11

Family Gathering in Bus Arus

Sunday morning, breakfast time, and Rocky is sitting in the kitchen tucking into a bowl of porridge. A bright sun is streaming through the window and Piper Jim joins him, striking a pose of a man full of the joys of life.

'Hey, good morning, son. It looks like it's going to be another beautiful day. Have you any plans for today?'

Rocky stays rigid and silent for a few moments and continues staring down at the table while eating his porridge.

'I have plans. Yes, plans for you, Dad.' There is a tense pause before Rocky confronts his father. 'Dad, did you forget that Lizzy is home from Athlone this weekend? I met him at the bus station, and he was full of enthusiasm for having pints and *sambos* with us in Molly's, your favourite pub. He picked the place especially for you, Dad. Anyway, we went ahead without you and then came back to the house around

8pm to see you. When you hadn't shown up by eleven, he headed off to his girlfriend's apartment. I am not sure if you met Ping, the nice Chinese girl. He is with her now and will be on the 3pm bus back to Athlone today. I think you and I should go down to Bus Árus around two and see him off.'

Piper Jim could sense the tone of admonishment in Rocky's voice, but his decision today is to deliberately act carefree and pleasant. 'Great, 1400 army time, good idea. Is he enjoying Athlone?'

'Yeah, he loves it. He is talking like he might be in the running for a prize at the Passing Out Parade on graduation day next month. He wants us to attend. He was really keen yesterday to tell you all about his experiences.' Rocky sees an opportunity to lay a false trail as to the brothers' future intentions. He uses a pitched, sarcastic tone. 'Athlone. You know, Dad, he is saying so many nice things about the freedom, independence and life that he has down the country that he has nearly convinced me to transfer down there as well. Sounds like a lovely barracks, great nightlife in the town, a beautiful river, great soccer team and marvellous people.'

'Relax, son, relax and enough of that talk. You have just landed the VIP bar job – that's the best position a young soldier can get in the entire Irish army, so be grateful.'

Rocky ignores his father and continues, 'And the house rents are great value down there as well. You can get a three-bedroom house for less than half the rent you would pay around here in Dublin. Lizzy and I could live like kings and even have enough money to buy a car.'

'Well, I'm delighted he's fully settled down in Athlone and he might even end up married down there.' Piper Jim is not to be drawn further on Rocky's pronouncements. He has more pressing issues on his mind. He continues, 'Just one thing, son, to briefly change the subject. I am kind of worried that they might work you to death in that VIP bar. So, let me regularly know everything that is happening. I can have a chat with the sergeant major if you need help. Will you do your old man that one favour? Tell me everything you see and hear. I will keep you well advised.'

'Huh! Dad, must I say it again? It's my life. I am never going to complain to the sergeant major or to you, Dad. That is not my way. What you genuinely might see as help, I might feel is unwelcome interference. Let's agree to give each other lots of personal space to do our own thing. For the moment, I want to stay living here with you in Ormond Square. But only if you treat me as an independent adult.'

'Okay, okay. But keep me informed. I am your dad and I do not want your eagerness exploited.'

'Dad, okay, where do you think I would really like your help?'

'Go on.'

'Can you please try to show some love towards Lizzy? Support him and encourage him. Be there for him. Most of all, give him your attention. Spend time talking and listening to the man. Behind his brave smile, he is actually a very sensitive person. He gets hurt easily but hides it well. He needs somebody who will give him some tough love. Remember, at school, he was often frightened because of his colour. I hope you will attend his Passing Out Parade in Athlone?'

'Of course.'

'Dad, from his description of life in the recruit platoon, he comes across as a driven man. He is desperate to impress us and is striving for just a little bit of recognition.'

Piper Jim raises his newspaper to hide his apathetic expression. He talks from behind the broadsheet. 'Rocky, look, I have heard all of this before. Just leave it now. That's enough.'

Precisely at 2pm, they arrive at Bus Arus. They spot Lizzy at the ticket desk. He looks around and seems very pleased that Piper Jim and Rocky have both come, as expected. Bus ticket in hand, he speeds over to greet them, gushing into immediate upbeat chatter.

'Hey, Dad, we had loads of ham *sambos* and pints in your favourite pub yesterday. Did Rocky tell you?'

Piper Jim stiffly embraces his stepson. 'Yeah, yeah, I heard you guys had a super day.'

'Then we sang in Ceoil agus Craic – awesome. We met loads of old friends. I got slagged off about my short hair. Hey, Dad! It's just great to see you again.'

The family now has a full hour together before the bus departs. They head to Bus Arus coffee shop.

'All is going well in Athlone, I hear. Will we have a Passing Out Parade soon? More important, young man, will you pass the course? I have heard that it's the most intensive and demanding recruit training in the entire Irish army. Custume Barracks always produces excellent soldiers and I worked with many of them overseas.'

'You bet I will pass, Dad. There will be a big buffet meal in the beautiful new barracks dining hall. A few pints and music will follow. There might even be free wine.'

'Sounds great.'

'We are starting intense practice for our drill display tomorrow. I think I am doing well. I am glad I took your advice. Joining the army... Dad, so far it's been the best experience I've ever had in my entire life.'

Piper Jim brightens up with this surprise endorsement. He is delighted. 'Well, that is amazing. Did you hear that, Rocky?'

Lizzy again hugs a now increasingly relaxed Piper Jim. Lizzy's warm, gentlemanly approach is in total contrast to Rocky's frequently belligerent attitude. Jim begins to feel that he might even be able to enjoy this meeting.

'Ha! Ha! That's great, son. I love your feeling of appreciation. Sometimes fathers do actually come up with brilliant ideas. I have never seen you so happy. Wonderful! Of course, we will take the train down to the Passing Out Parade. I haven't seen Athlone for years. I have loads of friends there so it should be a superb occasion. You will have a holiday then, I suppose? Will they give you some time off?'

'Yeah, we will have two full weeks off. We decided today that my girlfriend Ping and I will visit Granny in Cadiz and spend a full week there. I spoke to Granny on the phone last week and she is dying to see Ping. Sounds like she is healthy and in great form. It was lovely to talk in Spanish again. I was afraid that I was forgetting the lingo. Anyway, then we will come home. I will do a week of jammin' with Rocky. Should be a great two weeks of relaxation.'

Piper Jim is unable to control a grimace when he hears that the second week of Lizzy's holiday is going to be devoted to musical performances.

'Oh! Oh! Right, yeah, yeah. That flight must have been very expensive. Would you not make the best of it and stay in Spain for two weeks?'

'It's a cheap charter flight to Seville. Great value. We can then take the train down to the coast. I would love to stay for two weeks but Ping has an exam. Anyway, by then I will need to earn a few bob to pay for everything. I'm sure I will be flat broke. We can quickly make money with five or six nights of gigs. The two Chinese girls, Ping and Lilly, are starting to play with us in the band.'

Rocky interjects, 'Already booked, bro, are two student parties in Trinity College, and we have a licence for the Saturday afternoon busking at the bottom of Grafton Street. I have a promise of a gig till dawn on the Friday night. It's a prestige bash and will pay *mucho efectivo*. It's in a big house just off the Coliemore Road in Dalkey. There will be quite a few celebrities there from the UK film and music industry. Now, this could be a very special night. Fingers crossed we get that gig. If we are chosen, I expect to get the deposit tomorrow.'

Rocky throws in the Spanish phrase for "plenty of cash" as he knows that it bothers Jim when he cannot understand what they are talking about.

Lizzy rubs his two palms together with delight. '*Amo mucho effectivo.*' Lizzy's reply in Spanish, indicating that he loves plenty of cash, is joyful and instinctive but, unlike Rocky, is totally lacking any wicked intent. Piper Jim is immediately uneasy. The use of a language by the boys that he cannot understand is not the big problem. It is his detection that his battle to keep Rocky in the army is clearly not won yet. There are a lot of music gigs in the pipeline as well as two new band members. Rocky spots the reaction and bites his tongue. He realises that both he and Lizzy are revealing too much.

'Rocky, that's great news. You see, Dad? He is brilliant. A fantastic organiser and leader.'

'Yeah, I am really impressed. How do you guys get these gigs? Do you have an agent or someone like that?' Jim probes for valuable information that might help him understand the flow of work of a musical nature. He might be able to put a snag in the works.

'Dad, while I have been in Athlone, Rocky has been busking. Busking is brilliant for raising business. If people like what they hear, they take your card or buy a cassette. On our card it says that people must call us for bookings but only on a Saturday night at 10pm. Tell Dad about our Saturday night trick, Rocky.'

Rocky's cheeks turn a bright red, but the damage is now done. He might as well reveal all. 'The secret, Dad, is that we have picked a time when it's good for us to take a call on the hall phone. Our time is the half hour on Saturday night before *Match of the Day* begins on the TV. I am at home always at that time. The football begins at 10.30pm on BBC so we ask people to call us at 10pm. You have usually gone to the pub, but we get a lot of calls at that precise time.'

'That's smart. Well, your mother trained both of you well. I am proud of the two of you.'

Rocky now decides to unburden himself by informing his father of the decision he and Lizzy made the previous night.

'Dad, Lizzy and I want to tell you something. We made an important decision last night.'

Piper Jim visibly stiffens. 'Ouch... sounds serious, boys. Go on.'

'Lizzy and I have decided that we are no longer going to continue to pretend that we are stepbrothers.'

Lizzy interjects, 'We are not going to make any announcements or anything like that.'

Rocky continues, 'We just want to live our life with the truth that we both have the same mother. Also, we have decided that it's not fair on Lizzy that people should continue to think that he is the son of a prostitute. We really want all of this cleared up before the big occasion in Athlone. What do you think, Dad?'

Piper Jim raises his eyebrows. 'Eh... yeah... yeah. I don't think that I have really any issues with that at all. You are talking truthfully. Maria is dead eighteen months now and she loved you both very much. Jacinta is also dead. They both had to endure the neighbourhood gossips. I didn't because I was abroad, away from it all. You know Ireland has changed at last and these things are not life-shattering anymore. All I want is for both of you to be happy. Lads, I'm with you on this one.'

Rocky is dumbfounded by the reply. He is almost disappointed that the opportunity for the altercation, he had both expected and prepared for, will not take place.

Lizzy is exuberant. 'Wow, this is really good news, Dad. We expected you to be angry with us.'

'No. I am not at all angry. To be honest, I was always very uncomfortable with the idea of inventing such a story. But in those days, religious dogmatism and fear forced the decision upon your mother and I. Maria was highly spiritual and a devoted Catholic. She wanted peace of mind and good relationships with the local priests. Her calmness was vital for me also. Today, things are different, You lads are moving with the times. I am delighted with your idea of freeing all of us. We can finally bring an end to the burden of trying to hide in the shadows by inventing new lies to hide old ones. Lizzy, as far as I am concerned, you are totally free to tell the world that you and Rocky are real brothers. It does not make me look bad. That's for sure.'

Lizzy swallows so deeply that his Adam's apple visibly pops out from his neck. While a smile adorns his face, a small tear comes to his eye. Living the obnoxious lie that has haunted him at school for his entire youth is over. Rocky is also astounded that this change of long-term family policy has found such ready acceptance from their conservative, habitually obstinate head of household.

'You know, lads, Maria and I had a different type of marriage but, amazingly, it worked... eh... and it actually worked really well. Now, we had our difficulties, I am not denying that. For Maria, raising you two as children represented the total end goal of her entire life. She adored both of you. But she was also a woman who understood my need for travel and military adventure away from the marriage. We were both individuals and we respected each other's differences. For me, I did not ever want to feel trapped and limited. I never wanted to be suffocated by marriage.'

'Dad, I'm not sure either Lizzy or I know what you mean.'

'You know, lads, I did not want my desire for excitement taken away from me too young. Happiness for me was venturing forth into foreign lands, bringing the peace and being the solid family breadwinner. Happiness for Maria was nurturing you guys and making you into great little lads. When I was at home, I could see our total success as a family. What a noisy house. Laughter, music, wrestling, sport, loud Spanish chatter, great health and fantastic exam marks. Every time I came home from UN peacekeeping, I could see my household represented a place of total bliss for my wife and children. Maria loved her life.'

Lizzy moves to reassure his stepfather. 'Dad, when you arrived home, we were always delighted to see you. The blue beret with the white badge showing the globe really caught our imagination as kids. It's true that Mother always became tense and difficult around your arrival time. We did not understand it.'

Jim shrugs his shoulders while pursing his lips.

'Yeah, I did feel that every time I came home from overseas, I was an unwelcome, intruding stranger. Look, lads, both Maria and I enjoyed long periods of separation. I like to feel that this made our marriage rich in an unusual way. Neither of us had entered marriage, in the first place, because we feared loneliness. In fact, it was the very opposite. We were both people who relished and needed to do our own thing. We were happy to give ourselves lots of space. In funny ways, it was an incredibly successful marriage because we tolerated each other's individuality so well. But for certain, it is you two boys who acted as the glue that kept us all together.'

It is Rocky and Lizzy's turn to now shift uncomfortably in their seats. There is a momentary unsettling pause in the conversation. They have never heard this thoughtful, even intelligent, side of Piper Jim's personality before. It is the first serious adult conversation they have ever had about their uncommon family life. This is a fresh, eye-opening perspective.

Bus Arus public address system intervenes. 'Boarding call for the 3pm departure of the Bus Eireann Expressway serving Athlone and Galway.'

The conversation ends too soon. Lizzy checks his ticket and bag. He is clearly emotionally affected as he adopts a thankful silence. Everything has been agreed. Following handshakes and hugs, his lips move silently to form the word "bye". Rocky and Piper Jim wave as the bus leaves the station. They then walk in silence back towards their home. Rocky suddenly has a feeling that he needs some solitary time. He truthfully tells his dad that he will divert to hear a church choir performance in Marlborough Street. They part ways.

Minutes later, Rocky is sitting in a pew halfway up the middle isle of the historic Pro Cathedral. He knows that this pew is the optimum position from which to enjoy the acoustics of the old church and wonderful sound of the world-famous Palestrina Choir. The cathedral is filling with worshippers and Rocky has always found this place to be the perfect location for deep thinking. Rocky feels that he needs a brief retreat to sort out a growing sense of confusion. He is bothered with the sudden conversion of Piper Jim to the guise of easy-going and charming dad. Today's presentation of their family life, by his father, has a ring of truth. It was certainly a gloriously happy family whenever Piper Jim was away. The weather always seemed to be beautiful whenever Rocky recalls his youthful memories of Ormond Square. His thoughts of recent years always seem to be accompanied by dark clouds and rain. Rocky again turns his thoughts to his father. It continues to disturb him that if Piper Jim was still away travelling and Maria was still alive, Rocky and Lizzy would be pursuing their dream of rock-and-roll fame all over Europe. For better or for worse.

'Now, why is Dad suddenly turning on the charm? Is he trying to get us to buy into his desired world view? Jim the provider who put his family first. Maria, the mother who made the mistakes. Is this a kind of spin?'

Rocky is still very slow to trust a man who continues to obstruct and subtly discourage him from his dream of a musical career. But now perhaps the man deserves a chance. Today, Rocky has seen a side of Piper Jim's personality that is more complicated, less dogmatic and more liberated than he has ever allowed them a glimpse of before. Perhaps there are better times to look forward to as the old man mellows with advancing years.

Suddenly, the cathedral organ fires up and the Palestrina Choir burst into song from the balcony behind him. Rocky closes his eyes, empties his mind and becomes totally immersed in the performance.

'Wonderful.'

The last time he was here was with his late mother. This will always be a special place. This will always be an exceptional choir. The fragrance of burning candles and incense will always be a calming aroma. This religious musical performance brings back joyous memories of days with Maria.

After the thirty minutes of sublime choir and organ music, Rocky's personal vibration and disposition becomes calm. He feels spiritually encouraged to try to look at the bright side. 'Be grateful for what you have. Give thanks,' he tells himself.

Despite music now being his first love, he reminds himself that as a very young child, he always had dreams of himself wearing a United Nations blue peacekeeper's beret like his dad. Now, in a few more months, he has a good chance of realising that dream.

Now that will be some achievement. When I put that blue beret on my head for the first time, it will be the proudest moment of my life. I will be a young jackeen making my genuine contribution to harmony across the world. The Irish, a nation of peacekeepers. Dad deserves credit for my possibility of achieving membership of that elite group.

Then there is the emphatic transformation in his brother to be grateful for. Military service has done Lizzy a power of good. The meek, shy and untidy but gifted guitar player has become a beaming, tall, upright, increasingly self-confident and athletic soldier. *It's great. More marks for Dad. He certainly got that one right as well.*

Rocky tells himself that a change of approach is necessary. He and his brother must continue to positively enjoy the opportunities offered by their military service. Then, when they come to launch their band, they will be more experienced and mature. The self-discipline gained in the army and UN will be a massive asset. At the same time, they must both resolve to retain their keen musical skills through part-time gigs and rehearsal. Rocky persuades himself that a win-win situation is possible with the right attitude. He leaves the Pro Cathedral feeling calm and inspired.

Chapter 12

A Hectic Life in the Officers' Mess

With three weeks completed, work in the officers' mess has, in many ways, proven to be demanding and challenging for Rocky. His first week was tougher than he could ever have expected. He had to learn while performing many various tasks for the first time. It was a week when function followed function and there was non-stop pressure on the mess staff. At times, he was confused and frustrated, but the mess was so busy that there was nobody to sit down and teach him. Balancing his cash was a worrying new experience, when combined with the complexity of accounting for credit sales. He was expected by the customers to know what to do, but at times, he really had no idea. The young mess sergeant, Tom Gormley, summed it up on his first day.

'Gunner Rockingham, it will have to be on-the-job training for you, I am afraid. Just do your best and come to me if you have any questions. Try to figure it out. I will tell everybody on the staff to keep an eye on you, give you plenty of directions and help you if necessary. But we are going to be flat-out all this week. I have nobody to devote to training you.'

Now, after his initial baptism of fire, Rockingham has somehow reached a reasonable level of self-taught competence. He has already served at military top-brass functions as wine waiter and barman. Overall, he is just beginning to cope satisfactorily and gain poise in his job. The work atmosphere in the mess is more tense than he has experienced anywhere else in his entire life. Everything must be in the right place at the right time and his personal appearance must always be perfection. Many of the VIP meals are quite formal and ceremonial, with the requirement to serve specific drinks at appropriate times. Then he must ensure that his beverages are chilled to the right temperature. He must never run out of stock. At VIP meals, there is no tolerance of error. He has seen Captain Gilmore's embarrassed face when a slightly soiled tablecloth was pointed out to him by a VIP hosting a meal for foreign diplomats.

Behind the bar, Rocky has his own tiny barman's room. When not serving drinks, this is where he is required to hang out. The room is warm and cosy, but the decor is basic, and it does not seem to have been painted in decades. There is an exceptionally comfortable reclining armchair which he sometimes uses for short naps between functions. Also, the room benefits from a multichannel, modern colour television set and radio. During lull periods, Rocky enjoys the comfort, privacy and warmth of this tiny bolthole. He is delighted that the radio can clearly pick up the pirate pop station, Radio Caroline, from the *Mi Amigo* ship in the

North Sea. He usually fully closes the door to block the bar noises. When a customer requires a drink, they press a service button, causing a bell to summon him. Rocky likes the idea of hiding away when not needed for bar service, because it allows him full compliance with the rule of not listening to customers chat. With the door to the barman's bolthole tightly closed, all that can be heard is the background drone of multiple conversations. Rocky has discovered that it is only when the bar has very few customers that he, inadvertently and very occasionally, picks up titbits of information.

Rockingham always wants to do things well. He learns early on that many staff do not survive for more than a short period in the mess. They prove incapable of performing the job efficiently, are too slow to learn or just decide that the madness is not for them and leave. Gunner Rockingham is decisive in his determination that he is not going to fail. In fact, he begins to enjoy the turmoil as well as figuring out smart ways to cope when under pressure.

Despite the frequent work bedlam, the first three weeks' experience revealed that, depending on customer demand, the job can swing from massive pressure one day to total boredom the next. There are quiet days, and often the weekends are totally lifeless. This is a time for Gunner Rockingham to relax, wander around the kitchen and dining areas, have a laugh and hang out, making friends with work colleagues.

'Hey, Sergeant Gormley, what is that big building out behind the mess?' Rocky has come to know, trust and admire the mess sergeant. Gormley is a truly dynamic NCO from Duncannon, County Wexford. He shares much of the day-to-day operational management of the mess with Captain Gilmore. He has enjoyed fast promotion and always appears cool, smiling and under control, no matter how much work is piling in. He is a wizard at accountancy, stock control and, in general, is a rock of sense. He and Captain Gilmore make for a positively dependable management team.

'That's the old kitchen, Gunner Rockingham. Totally empty now. I think there are plans to make a gym out there sometime. But there is no money available now so it will stay unused for the foreseeable future... decades, probably. I know that was a loaded question, Rockingham. Why are you interested?'

'Well, it is a building made of solid concrete and only tiny windows. Sarge, you know how quiet it can be here some weekends for the barman. There is a lot of hanging around with little to do. I would love to use the old kitchen for song writing and music rehearsal during my breaks. Do you think anybody would object?'

'If you are not too loud and don't upset people, nobody will care. The first time you use it I will need to be here so I can be sure that the building retains the noise of any instruments you might be using. The keys are hanging in the little room behind the bar.'

'Sarge yeah, I spotted the keys and that is what gave me the idea. I was out there last night. The walls are an amazing two-feet thick. I am sure it will be fine for rehearsals. We can keep our volume down. Initially, it will be just me, but, perhaps occasionally, my brother and two girls will join me.'

'We have no issues at all. I remember you mentioned a lot about music in the interview. Do you still have a band?'

'At the moment I am a solo performer, but I am gradually pulling together a new band. My mother was a professional entertainer, so she taught me a lot.'

Sergeant Gormley scratches the bristles on his chin. 'Hmm... Rockingham, I have an idea myself which I will share with you. You know that Captain Gilmore's birthday is coming up. We are also going to close the mess bar for renovation for a week. However, the captain is going to use it privately for his friends one night while it is closed. You will be the barman and it would be great to surprise him with a little music.'

'Hey, Sarge, that's perfect. I can do a solo or we might be lucky. I can try to pull in a few talented friends to help.'

'This will be a nice surprise for the captain. I don't think he fully realises about the level of your music skills even though you did mention it in the interview. You can see the stress that he is under. Okay, keep things under your hat and tell nobody. I will get everything cleared with the mess president first.'

A week later, the renovation of the bar has commenced. Now it is close of business on Friday evening and, thankfully, the function season is stalled by the redecoration. Gilmore has strongly influenced the dates selected for closure. The staff were becoming cranky with exhaustion. He himself is feeling run-down and he is facing a big midterm exam as part of a master's in Dublin City University. As fate would have it, the exam is scheduled for his twenty-sixth birthday. He is now totally frustrated, finding it increasingly difficult to keep up with his course of studies by night while working incredibly demanding hours in the officers' mess. He unloads his feelings in the mess office to the empathic Sergeant Gormley.

'You know, Sarge, increasingly I feel that I have no life. All the staff are exhausted as well. As for me, those hectic three weddings in the mess in the past month have caused my studies to totally collapse. I am down in the dumps a little because it's so bloody hard to find free time. I am longing for just a little rest and even a tiny bit of social life. I need to escape this dreadful lifestyle but looks like it's not going to happen for a few months yet.'

'Sir, I have no idea how you do it. Six subjects, final exams, master's thesis and running this mad house as well. You are lucky that you are in such great health. You are lucky, as well, that you are still single. No woman would put up with her husband running himself into the ground like you do.'

'Well, I cannot give up the study in my final year. Just a few more months and I will have graduated. Then I will also be finished with my stint here in the officers' mess as well. I know that I am in line for a nice trip overseas, perhaps even for one year. I think it will see me back in the Middle East in the summer and it might be in a rather civilised office job in UN headquarters in Lebanon. That should help me get my bank account back in order.'

'More than well deserved, sir. I hope you are lucky enough to be selected.'

'I hope so too... as long as everything in this bloody officers' mess stays perfect. Really perfect. I pray all the time that nobody screws up. Sarge, I really appreciate your efforts. You are ensuring that we are actually thriving financially.'

'Thanks, sir, I love working here. It's a real high-performance team. Staff selection has been the key to our success.'

'Yeah, but I am now so glad that we are closed for a week so that all of us can get some time off.'

'Sir, are you going ahead on Monday after the exam with your birthday celebration? All the wallpaper has been stripped deliberately in case anybody dares to try to demand that we open. I left the bar looking like a total dog's dinner today with torn wallpaper all over the floor. I made sure to leave the customer door open to bring the message home that we are closed. Closed! Closed! I have signs up everywhere. Now Rockingham is going to tidy the place up again for your guests and he will be here to unlock the bar when you arrive. As Monday is an army holiday, I think the entire barracks will, pretty much, be deserted.'

'Great work, Sarge. Thanks for doing all that. The exam is over at eight. If Rockingham can be there to open at 2045, that would be perfect.'

'How many people are you bringing back after the exam, sir?'

'I am inviting around thirty of my fellow students back. We will just have a few pints and Rockingham can close at midnight. I am not doing any food. The cooks must get their break as well.'

'Sir, I should mention that the chief of staff will have guests in his own private suite down at the far end of the building. It's the naval flag officer, a group of French senior navy officers, their wives and a couple of civil servants. He wants no staff and we have set him up for self-service salads and finger food. The French are promoting the sale of some new naval hardware. A low-key affair. I have told him you are bringing a few guests into the main bar for a private function in case he hears any noise. I am going to drop-in myself just to keep an eye on the chief and to help Rockingham.'

'Hey, I really appreciate you doing that, Sarge.'

The weekend passes quickly, with Gilmore spending hour after hour attempting to catch up on his neglected studies. By Monday morning, he is beginning to feel confident. In the late afternoon, he is seen leaving the barracks in his bright, shiny, but ancient, silver Audi 80. His face is serious and there are dark rings under his eyes as he exits the barracks' gate. At the same time, Gunner Rockingham is walking up Blackhorse Avenue towards the barracks and spots Gilmore's familiar car. He waves and shouts as the vehicle slows down almost to a halt.

'Good luck in the exam, sir... and happy birthday.'

Gilmore's voice tone is solemn and without the usual cheer. The characteristic confident smile and dashing military enthusiasm are also absent.

'Thanks, Gunner Rockingham. I will see you tonight. I hope that I am in a celebratory mood when we next meet. I really do need a happy birthday after all we have gone through over the past month.'

'Ha! Ha! You will ace the exam, sir.'

Gilmore shrugs his shoulders, looks ahead without expression and then gives a feeble wave as he accelerates away.

Rocky is also looking physically drawn and feeling under pressure. What nobody yet knows is that tonight will be the first live performance of Rocky's newly constituted band. He and Lizzy have agreed on the new name Eclectic RRK and have prevailed upon Lilly and Ping to join them. He has been working feverishly all week pulling his personnel and rig together. As a newly formed band, things are not as tight musically as he would like but, with rehearsal, it has been improving. Then, all morning, he has been cleaning and tidying up the bar. Now he is to meet Sergeant Gormley, who he hopes will approve certain flagrantly cheeky liberties that he has taken.

Chapter 13

The Birthday Party

'Hi, Sergeant Gormley, I have the bar cleaned again and all of my stuff is ready for the musical performance tonight. Come on, I will show you. It's in the old kitchen.'

'Okay, Rockingham. So, is it to be you alone on guitar or piano or what? Your brother? Is he going to make it as well?'

'Okay, Sarge, come with me and I will explain everything.'

They enter the derelict old kitchen and, on opening the door, Sergeant Gormley is immediately startled. 'What! What in the name of God is all this, Rockingham? Where did you get this enormous gear? Is the birthday party going to be in Croke Park stadium or what?'

'Well, Sarge, I have pulled together a few musicians as well as a sound and lighting man. Now, we are going to set up everything for 6pm so we can do some soundchecks. I really would like you to be here so you can tell me how loud we can go.'

'Wow, you are talking like a man who is running a full-scale rock concert. This is incredible. Hold on! I am not at all sure about this, Rockingham. I was expecting just you and your brother gently strumming guitars or something.'

'My brother will be here. He is taking the train from Athlone specially for the occasion. He will be playing lead guitar. We have two Chinese girls in the band as well. One girl will be the main singer for our Fleetwood Mac set. The other girl will be our drummer, and we have a flute player borrowed for the night. My brother and I want to do a few Stevie Wonder and Thin Lizzy hits. We have a special song for the captain from the band Double. It's riding high in the charts now and called "The Captain of her Heart". It's going to be a tight sixty-minute gig, no longer.'

Sergeant Gormley's face is pensive. With untypical pursed lips, he seems bothered. He shakes his head. 'Oh my God. This is way bigger than I expected. You have totally exceeded what is acceptable in this mess. The music of Thin Lizzy… that means very loud electric guitar. The drum kit is huge. Rockingham, seriously, I am struggling with the wisdom of doing this. We are in the corridors of power and are surrounded by very stiff, conservative people. We might have to just tone it down a little. Do you have just ordinary guitars? These speakers seem far too big for the venue. Remember the bar ceiling is not very high.'

'Sarge, that is why I am doing soundchecks. Have no worries. It will be perfect. Big speakers mean clearer tone. Our soundman is really brilliant, and he will control the lighting as well.'

'Lighting as well. Whew! Look, it's a professional set-up,

Gunner Rockingham, but… you could land us in the shit. Do you get me?'

'You are in the hands of a perfectionist, Sergeant Gormley. As bandleader, I have it all fully worked out.'

He attempts to shake Sergeant Gormley's hand as if to introduce himself for the first time. 'Please, no panic, Sarge. Trust bandleader, Rocky.'

Sergeant Gormley responds with military authority. 'Okay, you are still Gunner Rockingham the barman for now. I am going to have to whisper into the chief of staff's ear. It is certain that he could be seriously disturbed by the loud music. I am not sure that this can go ahead.'

'But, Sarge—'

'Now, Gunner Rockingham, let's be very clear. I don't want you to set anything up until I get the approval of the chief of staff.'

Rocky shakes his head, facing the looming probability that all his preparation might be for nothing. Sergeant Gormley scurries away like a petrified chicken and heads directly for the chief of staff's private bar. He knows that career paths have been decimated for less significant trivia. He gently knocks on the door, feeling nervous and uptight.

'Come on in.'

Thankfully, it's a cheerful voice. Lieutenant General Johnny O'Dowd is alone, wearing an elegant civilian V-neck Curragh Golf Club jumper, cravat and creamy-white golf slacks. He is relaxing, sipping a Crested Ten Whiskey and reading *The Irish Times*.

'Hey, hello, Sergeant Gormley. How are you today? Listen, everything has been set up to perfection. Gunner Rockingham was here earlier and has been highly professional. Seems to be an excellent lad. The finger food looks delicious. This is a casual evening for my guests. We are all wearing relaxed civvies and bringing partners. These French people are always very light-hearted and sociable. I do not need any staff, as I mentioned on Friday.'

'Sir, that's great. Just to remind you again that we are having a surprise party for the mess captain. It's his birthday.'

'Oh! I see. Captain Paul Gilmore has transformed this establishment. Please send him my best wishes for a happy birthday.'

'I will, sir. But… well… I just want to give you a heads-up that we will have a… well… loud band for about one hour and you might hear the music. Is that a problem? We do not want to disturb your VIP guests.'

'Oh! Right! Okay! Hmm! Well, if it's music for Captain Gilmore's birthday party it will not disturb us. You two men are the miracle workers on my mess staff. I have noticed the light on in your office, often until very late in the night. I am fully aware that the standards Captain Gilmore and you, Sergeant Gormley, have achieved in this officers' mess comes at a massive price in terms of your own personal free time. Captain Gilmore deserves a bit of fun and so do you, Sergeant Gormley.'

'Oh! Thank you, sir.'

'You know, Sarge, I have an idea to put to you.' The chief of staff pauses, then continues, 'What if my group comes down to the main bar to hear the music as well? We might not stay long. Do you think that would be okay? I would not like to gatecrash. Just to show my appreciation and wish the captain well.'

'Sir, that will be a real surprise and honour for him. He might collapse with the shock when he sees you.'

'Great, then keep it as a surprise. It's agreed then. We will join you sometime after we hear the music commencing.'

'Well, that is great, sir.'

The chief of staff is not finished. 'In the army, far too often we "saddle the willing horse" and we run the enthusiastic young soldier into the ground. We then abandon the used, exhausted and broken person, never even bothering to say thank you. Tonight, I will enjoy the music. It's time to show my gratitude.'

Sergeant Gormley excuses himself and skips briskly back to the bar with the good news. He is smiling from ear-to-ear, uplifted by the praise received from the highest-ranking officer in the entire Irish military. He playfully growls at Rockingham, 'Okay, you are no longer Gunner Rockingham, barman.' He roughly grabs Rocky's top right shoulder.

'Sarge, what?'

'You are Rocky, bandleader. It's all systems go!'

Rocky punches the air above his head. 'Woah! Yes! Great!'

'I will serve the drinks while you, Rocky, bandleader, perform.'

Sergeant Gormley is now exuberant. It has been a long time since he received any form of recognition for his efforts.

'Rocky, the chief wants to join us for a while to hear your music. He is bringing his French visitors. Are you scared? Butterflies? Stage fright?'

Rocky, bandleader, momentarily stiffens up, wearing the strained look of a man about to face a firing squad. But he has confidence in what his band has to offer and seconds later is smiling. 'It's gonna be great. However, Sarge, I am glad now that I have put such a lot of work into this. We will start rehearsal as early as possible. I am going down to meet my band. They are waiting for me at the barracks' main gate already.' As he hurriedly leaves the room, he hollers back towards Sergeant Gormley, 'In fact, Sarge, I am actually getting really excited!'

* * *

At Dublin City University, the exam is nearly over. Gilmore is rereading his answer paper. Every question he prepared has thankfully come up. He feels sure of a top mark. The final bell rings and the students remain seated and silent until the exam papers are collected. Gilmore looks around and sees mostly smiling faces. It was a fair exam. Then, friends in his class gravitate towards him. The message is the same for all.

'The RV is Blackhorse Avenue outside the main gate of McKee Barracks in forty-five minutes. We must all go in through the gate together to keep the military police happy.

One girl smiles and teases, 'RV? Oh! Paul, how cute.'

* * *

Meanwhile, back in the officers' mess, Rocky, bandleader, has taken charge. Lighting and sound systems are carefully hauled into position and tested until everything is working perfectly. Band members check their instruments and perfect their memories of song lyrics. Soon, all is ready.

The bar door remains locked, and Sergeant Gormley waits in the hall to meet the guests.

The student group arrive, chattering happily, and assemble behind Gilmore.

'Hi, Captain Gilmore, how did the exam go?'

Gilmore's broad smile and bright eyes answers the question. 'Just great. We are dying for a few cool pints to celebrate.'

'We have the door of the bar locked so nobody can intrude on your group. Is everybody here yet, sir? When we have them all, we can open the bar.'

Gilmore does a quick count.

107

'Yeah, that's the lot.'

Gormley opens the door. The bar is in total pitch-black. Gilmore looks embarrassed. Suddenly, the hall light fails as well, leaving Gilmore's entire gathering standing in total darkness. One student friend of Gilmore gives a nervous screech. 'Sarge? Where are you? Have you a torch? What happened to the lights?'

Abruptly, out of the total darkness, the silence is broken by the crashing sound of cymbals. Gilmore's bewildered group begin to clutch each other in the dark for support and some nervous laughter emanates from the group. Then there is a dramatic drum roll. Suddenly, bright spotlights momentarily dazzle Gilmore and then swing towards a makeshift stage. There, Lizzy, wearing sunglasses, is disguised as Stevie Wonder. He bursts into song. It's the chorus of "Happy Birthday" of course, and he theatrically mimics the rocking head movements of the blind superstar. He pushes a serving trolley, containing an iced cake with a cluster of twenty-six lighted candles, towards the captain.

'What the f…' Gilmore gasps in total incredulity and then recovers his poise enough to blow out the candles.

Lizzy, in his Stevie Wonder role, gets everybody joining in the "Happy Birthday" song and immediately creates a rousing party atmosphere. Sergeant Gormley starts serving the drinks and the band launch straight into their Fleetwood Mac set. First is "The Chain" with Rocky and Lilly sharing lead vocals. They follow it with an extended version of "Go Your Own Way" in which Lizzy performs a short solo guitar piece. Then Lilly takes over centre stage for a set and if you closed your eyes, you would swear that Stevie Nicks was in the room. Her rendition of "Dreams" wins warm approval, particularly because she surprises everybody by singing the final verse in Chinese. Very quickly, everybody is relaxed, dancing and chatting. Rocky then sings the soft, chart song from the band Double, "The Captain of her Heart".

Then comes the serious musical business of the night as the band pauses to prepare for the Thin Lizzy set. The two brothers take centre stage wearing appropriate wigs and attire. To great cheering and laughter, Lizzy dons a fake Phil Lynott moustache. Just as they are ready to recommence playing, Rocky notices the arrival of the chief of staff and his French guests. There is much shaking of hands and hugs as the arrivals introduce themselves. Cautiously, Rocky starts the set with songs on the quieter side of the Thin Lizzy repertoire. "Still in Love with You", "Old Town" and "Sarah". They then ramp things up with "The Boys are Back in Town". Volume levels seem perfect, and as the night progresses, all the audience, including the VIPs, are clearly enjoying themselves. So, Rocky feels that it's time to let it rip a little to bring the night towards its climatic finish. No holds barred. He pauses the music to introduce each band member, deliberately leaving his brother until last.

'Well, thanks everybody for being such a great audience and congrats to Captain Gilmore. Tonight is our first ever performance. This is a new band called Eclectic RRK and I hope you have enjoyed everything. When we become famous, hopefully you will remember tonight and know that you were present the night it all began here in McKee Barracks!' Rocky pauses for audience cheering and applause.

'Autographs later and who knows, they might become valuable. For those of you who are curious, the man who looks like Phil Lynott is my brother. His nickname is Lizzy. I think you will shortly realise that he is one of the greatest emerging young lead guitarists in Europe. Brace yourselves for a treat. We will finish off tonight with our favourite Thin Lizzy piece of music and would like to dedicate it to our visitors from France. Ladies and gentlemen, "Parisian Walkways".'

Lizzy immediately rouses the crowd with his opening guitar chords, and Rocky acts as lead singer. The audience join in the words as a few air guitars emerge among Gilmore's friends.

When Rocky sings about the Champs Elysees, Mont-Saint-Michel and Old Beaujolais wine, there is loud approval from the French visitors.

While Lizzy is playing lead guitar, Rocky is watching for audience feedback from the stage. He notes the encouraging wide smile of approval from the chief of staff. Captain Gilmore is singing and dancing. Sergeant Gormley is contentedly pulling pints from behind the bar and chatting to everybody. Gilmore's guests are mostly dancing, singing and laughing. Rocky feels a sense of calm relief that everything has come together perfectly, just as he had planned. The "Parisian Walkways" performance is going well, and Lizzy skilfully raises the tempo by holding a screaming and shuddering electric guitar note for about twenty seconds, leading to loud acclaim from the gathering. Then comes the final three-minute guitar solo, expertly performed by the coloured guitarist ending in a definitive crashing of drums and cymbals by Ping.

The end of the music raises roars of approval and calls for more. But it's impossible to top that "Parisian Walkways" performance. It is fitting to end the night on this massive high. Rocky nods to his roadie to knock-on the house lights and, covered in perspiration, the band members leave the stage, circulate and delight in receiving many compliments, handshakes and cool drinks. Gilmore comes over to Rocky and is smiling profusely. 'Here, this will help you cool down.' He hands Rocky a pint of creamy black porter. 'Wow, your band is excellent. I loved every minute of your performance. I owe you one, Gunner Rockingham.'

Rocky grins and pleads, 'Sir, tonight, just tonight, please call me Rocky.'

'Ha! Ha! Yes, Rocky. You, the entire band and Sergeant Gormley were brilliant. Best birthday present... ever... in my entire life. I should have invited far more people. But I suppose it was the surprise element that made it so great.'

Rocky is chuffed with the feedback from his boss. Then the chief of staff comes over to him and shakes his hand.

'Gunner Rockingham, I did not know it was you. The wig is great. You do look like that blond American guitar player from Thin Lizzy. I am curious about one thing. How did you select the finale "Parisian Walkways"? Was I just lucky to have French guests? Or what? Perhaps you should be a diplomat.'

'Sir, to be honest I am not really a diplomat. We always planned to use "Parisian Walkways" as our high point at the end of the session. It's a superb guitar anthem and a difficult piece of music to play. I just dedicated it to your guests because it seemed like the right thing to do.'

'Yes, they were really impressed and appreciated it. Thank you. Your brother is a fantastic guitarist. The entire band are quality, and your own voice is immense. What a lucky surprise for me to stumble on such excellence.'

Rocky feels a sense of total elation. The band gelled together well, with Ping and Lilly making a massive contribution to its success. Lizzy was brilliant as always and must now take the first train back to Athlone in the morning. With his Passing Out Parade just a week away, it was exceptional luck that he managed to get permission to attend.

Sergeant Gormley gives Rocky some further good news. 'Listen, you can head away with your band. I am happy to stay on and pull pints for a couple more hours. It was a brilliant night. So, off you go. I will close the bar and lock up.'

'Gee, Sarge, that is absolutely fantastic. Are you sure? I really appreciate that.'

The band members say their farewells as they haul their gear out to the old kitchen for storage. Now, it's time to head to Lilly and Ping's apartment where there is loads of scrumptious Chinese food waiting to be enjoyed.

Eclectic RRK has been successfully launched but, that same night, there are strange events elsewhere.

Chapter 14

Sinister Happenings at Ormond Square

While Eclectic RRK are playing their debut gig at McKee Barracks, sinister events are simultaneously taking place at Ormond Square. Piper Jim is home, alone, relaxing, stretched out on the sofa, watching television. Suddenly his serenity is disturbed by loud banging on the front door of the house. He is momentarily startled as he is not expecting visitors and he hears deafening engine noise. He slowly and carefully creeps towards his front door. After a short pause he decides to cautiously open it, keeping the security chain in place. Jim is confronted by the sight of an unfamiliar masked motorcyclist. This dark rider is wearing a black helmet, all-leather, black jacket, black leather gloves and leather pants. He is sitting on a high-performance grey Kawasaki Sport motorcycle. He arrogantly has the front wheel perched right on the edge the house doorstep. In fact, he is so close to the house that Jim becomes immediately aware that he stinks of alcohol and cigarettes. The dark rider revs his engine impatiently. The backdrop of exhaust fumes and noise contributes an intimidating feel to the encounter.

Nothing is said but a right index finger beckons Piper Jim to lean forward. Nervously obeying, Jim opens the door fully because he feels that he probably knows the purpose of the visit. The dark rider's message consists of two words forcefully whispered mouth to ear. Jim can feel spittle spraying his earlobe.

'Paul Gilmore.' The dark rider stares directly into Jim's eyes awaiting an acknowledgement that the message is understood.

Jim nods his head immediately. This short message has been long expected. Within seconds, the dark rider is gone, accelerating into the darkness.

Piper Jim now, finally, knows that he has his first potential victim. Action to find negative information on the individual must be initiated without delay. But Jim is puzzled.

Why are they trying to eliminate a mere captain? Surely, he could not be that important. Why are they afraid of him? He must have information on them which is causing a level of trepidation in high places. Thank God it's not a colonel or general. That would be exceptionally risky for Rocky and I. We are already right on top of this first target. The job of uncovering shit might not be too difficult after all.

Piper Jim does not yet know that his son has established a massively enhanced friendship with the target that very night in McKee Barracks. If Jim had been coaching Rocky, as a spy, this is exactly what he would have encouraged him to do. Build the target's confidence. Do multiple small favours. Establish an optimum degree of open friendliness.

Jim would have told Rocky that friendship is the best fast-track route to unguarded talk. This is how a spy opens the door to privileged information, as well as to the disclosure of personal weaknesses and secrets.

Tonight, Rocky has enhanced his friendship with Gilmore for the very best of reasons. Rocky's youthful human kindness and work team spirit shone through with the band performing for free as a birthday gift. He still has no idea of his father's obnoxious task.

Piper Jim knows that Rocky will be difficult to tame. *Rocky can be independent, aggressive and as wild with me as he likes. But I know all the ways and means. I never fail. I know how to play the game. I can be cunning when it comes to gathering and twisting routine information into a scandal. That is why I am selected for jobs like this. I have my new elite warrior standing to preserve. Then I also have my retirement and civvy job in Switzerland to look forward to.*

Piper Jim grabs a beer from the fridge and turns up the TV volume. The Celtic rock band Horslips are performing their hit song "Dearg Doom".

'Yes! Brilliant!'

Piper Jim takes a long swig of his beer and leaps into the air, performing a celebratory Irish Jig.

'Yahoo! Switzerland here I come. Hurray!'

But his buoyant mood is to be fleeting in nature. As the song ends, he switches off the living room lights and television. Stretching out on the sofa in the dark, his mind begins to race with intense thought. Feelings of anxiety and foreboding plague him.

Is this the right way to live my life? What would Maria say if she was alive? She would go crazy. We are tasked with destroying a successful young officer's career and life. This could be a disaster waiting to happen.

Chapter 15

Lizzy's Big Day in Custume Barracks, Athlone

Lizzy's Passing Out Parade and big day is soon upon them. Rocky and Piper Jim both travel together down to Athlone in full uniform and by train. Piper Jim looks impressive. His chest is covered with numerous medals, and he is not wearing a kilt. Rocky is pleased that his dad seems to be enthusiastic about the ceremony ahead. They read the programme of events while eating their full Irish breakfast in the dining carriage of the train.

'Hey, Dad, this CIE breakfast is great. We will have to do trips like this more often. The carriage is so warm and comfortable. Okay, listen, it says here events begin at St Peters Church in the Market Square beside The Square House with Mass at 10am. The recruits will march from the barracks to the church and spectators are encouraged to line the route, applaud and cheer when they are passing. Sounds nice. I like that fun approach.'

'Yeah, we have a fifteen-minute walk from the train station to the church so we will be there in good time.'

Rocky reads on. 'After Mass, the recruits will march through the town behind the Band of the Western Command and on to the barracks square. Then there is the formal parade, national anthem, drill display and presentation of prizes.'

'Pass the jam, son. Well, does he know yet if he has a chance of a prize? Has he said anything?'

'Well, he feels that he did well, but everything is being kept very secret and the training staff are all tight-lipped. Okay, Dad, listen, here are the programme timings. 1pm Recruit Assignment Ceremony – Main Dining Hall. Then we have what is being described as the Count John McCormack Memorial – Army Prize. We then come to the best part.1.30pm food, drinks and speeches followed by some live music.'

'Wow, they have live music. That cost a few bob.'

'Actually, Dad, it's going to be just talented family members and friends who will sing while we are eating. Lizzy asked me to perform... just one song... of course, I have agreed.'

'He never asked me. The most talented piper in the Irish Army.'

'Nay, it's pop music they want during the meal, I think.'

'Perfect, that's very nice. I can relax more. When it's all over I would like to have a quick pint in the NCO's mess and then we have loads of time to make it for the 5.15pm train home.'

'I will help Lizzy pack for his Cadiz trip. He is travelling back to Dublin with us. Three of us in uniform together for the first time. Some of the neighbours want to see Lizzy so we will do a tour around the neighbours' houses on Ormond Square and Stoneybatter tonight.'

'Hey, Rocky, it's a real pity that Maria did not live for this great day. She would have been so proud. Ireland is just beginning to improve. I mean, it's fantastic that a young lad like Lizzy can afford to jet out to Spain tomorrow… at the drop of a hat.'

'It sure is, Dad. But he has worked hard. Remember, he made a lot of money busking last summer, so he has good savings. Granny in Cadiz will be amazed at how tall he has become!'

The train pulls into Athlone Station with a yank and screech. Jim and Rocky can immediately see that the town of Athlone, all along the Shannon riverbank, is decorated with festive bunting. In Athlone, a big occasion for the army is a big day for the entire town. Custume Barracks is a major source of employment in the entire midlands.

The father and son walk to the church. Many families are excitedly gathered outside on Market Square, beside the ancient castle. Piper Jim immediately spots several familiar faces, colleagues who worked with him on his many overseas missions. Hugs, handshakes, laughter and old war stories are the order of the day for Piper Jim. Rocky feels quite humbled by his own inexperience. There are spectacular uniforms, chains of honour and rows of medals to be seen adorning many chests.

'Hey, Dad, I feel naked without a medal. Hopefully I will have one soon.'

'Rocky, you will. Isn't the weather today just lovely? I am so glad for everybody. The forecast is good as well.'

'This looks like it's going to be a very big gathering, Dad.'

'Son, the Western Command is famous for hospitality. They go to town on these types of celebrations. I know their form. It will be an outstanding day.'

As the recruit platoon arrives, marching three abreast, the band strikes up and the crowd applauds and cheers. The recruits are dressed off by height and it is easy to spot Lizzy's dark, skinny features as he is one of the tallest.

'Okay, time to say our prayers, Rocky. Let's head into St Peter's for the church ceremony.'

The events of the day run totally to schedule and are timed to Western Command precision. Rocky is anxious. First, he has being praying that Lizzy will get a prize, and that will make their day. More importantly, he has his fingers crossed that Lizzy will be assigned to McKee Barracks in Dublin.

The assignment board results are always a closely guarded secret. Rocky knows that recruits' second uniform jackets have all been under lock and key in the barrack tailors shop so that their new rank markings and unit flashes can be sown on. Even the tailor does not know the identity of the owner of each jacket. The jackets are brought to the assignment ceremony where each recruit will come onto a stage and remove his old recruit jacket. He will then be handed a suit cover as he marches to a position behind a screen. When he opens the suit cover, he will find his second jacket adorned with his new unit flash, corps badges and lanyard. All will be revealed. For most recruits, it will be very straightforward as they will get to serve in their own local town. But many will not get their first-choice corps assignment. Lizzy wants the artillery. For all, it will be a tense ceremony with the possibility of both joy and tears.

The occasion moves back to the vast main square of Custume Barracks for the drill display and presentation of prizes. Then there is an incredibly exhilarating fly-past by Air Corps jets. Surprised family members scream, babies wail as the deafening noise takes all the visitors by surprise. For many of the families, it's their first ever time being exposed to the military, and everything around them is so incredibly exciting.

Disappointment as, contrary to best expectations, Lizzy does not feature at all in the prize-giving. In fact, the main parade ceremony sees all the prizes going to Athlone-based recruits.

'Nothing for Lizzy, Dad! I am gutted.'

'Look, Rocky, you should not be surprised. I call it home advantage. They must look after their own townies. None of the Mullingar, Donegal or Galway lads got a look-in for a prize either. The Athlone families are overjoyed, so let's be happy for them. There will be many other days for Lizzy. You know he might not be as good as he thinks he is.'

'Now, Dad, keep smiling and be sensitive to this big disappointment.'

One failure down and now for the assignment. Rocky tries to hide his tension from Piper Jim. He wants to give no indication that there might be a possibility of Lizzy returning to Dublin. This ceremony takes place in the large dining hall and commences with a public address announcement.

'Ladies and gentlemen, distinguished guests. Welcome to Custume Barracks Dining Hall where the best food in the entire army is prepared and served. The meal is almost ready and soon I will be asking you to find your family table, which will be marked with your name. As I know the food is smelling great, there will be no delays and we will get straight into the assignments. In order of the lots drawn by the recruits this morning, we will call each soldier onto the stage to receive his newly tailored jacket.

Rocky knows that the pain will be over quickly as Lizzy has drawn number seven. The ceremony begins. The first six recruits seem reasonably happy with their new assignments. There is plenty of cheering and applause. But now it's time for Lizzy.

'Number seven, Private Rockingham, come onto the stage please.'

Lizzy marches up, salutes and is handed a suit cover with his military destiny inside. He disappears behind a screen, unzips the cover and pulls out his jacket. He immediately sees that his command flash is different to everybody who has preceded him. His is the yellow and red of Eastern Command in Dublin. His uniform is decorated with a white lanyard, unit flash and the collar badges of the Artillery Corps. Lizzy immediately realises that this is good news. He emerges from behind the screen, maintaining his stiff military decorum but smiling from ear-to-ear.

Piper Jim looks startled.

'Congratulations on your assignment to the Second Field Artillery Regiment in McKee Barracks, Dublin. From this moment, you will be called Gunner Rockingham.'

There is a loud round of applause and cheering from the platoon members. Lizzy marches smartly from the stage, proudly wearing his new identity. Rocky is unable to contain himself and he immediately pounces on his brother while jumping up and down with delight. But Piper Jim does not join in the celebration and seems frozen in shock, not even offering Lizzy a handshake. He hurriedly disappears from the ceremony and into the men's toilet.

The ceremony continues with some surprise assignments, but most of the platoon members are happy with their new units.

'Ladies and gentlemen, I would like, on your behalf, to thank the assignment board for their wisdom in sending every platoon member back, as close as possible, to his hometown.'

There is a loud cheer. Now the hall is buzzing with commotion and excitement as the families discuss the appointments. The master of ceremonies determinedly moves to complete the event. 'Okay, I know there is a lot of excitement in the hall, but I will ask your attention for one more moment while we move on to the Count John McCormack Memorial – Army Prize. This is a totally new prize and is sponsored by the town of Athlone in celebration of Ireland's greatest tenor who was born here in 1884. This prize will be presented by His Excellency the Mayor and will be awarded to the person who has been voted by the soldiers in the platoon as the colleague who they think is the "Person Most Likely to Succeed". Hand me the envelope, please.' The master of ceremonies cuts open the envelope and pulls out a white card. 'Well, we have a very interesting winner. Like Count John McCormack, this man has amazing musical talent. The platoon member who has been voted as "Person Most Likely to Succeed" is Gunner Philip Rockingham, stage name Lizzy.'

Applause and cheering fill the room. The dark-skinned kid has captured the only prize that will leave Athlone. He is presented with a magnificent miniature copper bust of Count John McCormack, as well as an envelope and scroll stating, "Philip Rockingham, Person Most Likely to Succeed".

The ceremony is over and there follows a half hour of unmitigated bedlam with an eruption of hugs, handshakes and mutual introductions. At last, everybody present gets to enjoy total relaxed informality. Lizzy is at the heart of the action, moving around from friend to friend. Rocky knows very few attendees but gets dragged into the crowd by Lizzy to be introduced to numerous people. The platoon soldiers are clearly a tight-knit, cohesive group with a strong spirit of solidarity. This military bonding seems to have decisively influenced his brother to confidently succeed like he never, ever, did before. Rocky walks to the side of the room to observe everything. He suddenly realises that he is standing beside the lieutenant platoon commander and decides to thank and congratulate the officer.

'Wow, sir, this was the best military occasion I have ever attended. I am not sure how you did it, but my brother tells me that, here in Athlone, he experienced an amazing level of camaraderie.'

As they warmly shake hands, Rocky yaps on enthusiastically without giving the officer a chance to talk. 'My brother Lizzy was extremely shy and timid when he left Dublin. We were really worried about him because of his dark skin. He seems to have thrived here in Custume Barracks. I have to say that the training he has told me about seems to have been incredibly intense, almost like a Ranger course. He tells me that only the best and totally committed soldiers survived the pressure.'

'Hey, I see a white lanyard and Artillery badges. You must be the famous Rocky who is Lizzy's brother. He told me so much about you. All good, let me add. You two will be together now in McKee Barracks. I do wish that Lizzy was staying here with us in Athlone. What a worker. What a performer. You know it was a hard fight to get him back to Dublin, and there were strange barriers put in our way. It was weird, but we prevailed. Lizzy got what he deserves. He also got the Count John McCormack Trophy. I will let you into a secret. Lizzy won that vote by a mile. A very popular lad, your brother. Dedicated, helpful, humble and always quietly smiling. He seemed to love the training, probably because he is incredibly athletic and fit. The training staff are all delighted by the result of that vote.'

They both look towards Lizzy in the crowd. He is surrounded by fellow platoon members, lots of soldier's sisters and even a few admiring mothers. The lieutenant excuses himself and continues to circulate to shake more hands. Rocky looks to find Piper Jim so that they can head for a celebratory drink. However, he is nowhere to be seen. Finally, Rocky captures Lizzy's attention.

'Lizzy, what's in the envelope? Open it so we see what else you won.'

'Okay, here, hold Count John's head.' He hands Rocky the bust of the famous tenor and tears open the brown envelope.

'Hey, wow, Rocky, it's a cheque for a hundred quid. Feckin' great. Just in time for my trip to Cadiz.'

'A ton. Wow!'

Piper Jim suddenly reappears. 'Hey, did I miss something? What in the name of God is that silly ornament you are carrying?'

Lizzy's smile fades. He did not realise that Piper Jim had missed his awesome, hard-earned, first ever, adult moment of glory. Rocky quickly intervenes to prevent Piper Jim making an even bigger buffoon of himself.

'Hey, Dad, you missed it. You were a little dizzy there for a while. But you look okay now. Just look at the scroll that comes with this trophy. Lizzy was voted "The Person Most Likely to Succeed" by his mates in the platoon. He won the first ever Count John McCormack memorial trophy.'

But Piper Jim does not appear to be listening and is distracted by someone at the far end of the room.

'Fine… fine. Now, lads, I am going to circulate as I have seen a lot of old friends.'

Lizzy makes an anxious plea, 'Dad. Please… let's go to the bar and have a celebratory toast. Please stay with us for the food and first drink. All the families are staying together. We have our own family table… and, Dad… I have my photo album of the training to show you while we eat.'

Piper Jim was just not getting the significance of the message. 'Yeah! Yeah! Look, there is one man I must talk to over there. I will be back to you guys shortly.'

Rocky leans over towards his father, placing his pursed lips right up beside Piper Jim's ear to emphatically, but quietly, renew Lizzy's plea. He whispers, 'Dad, this is Lizzy's day. Stay with us. Don't ruin it for him. The family tables are all arranged. This whole family thing is very important to him. Dad, you also need to congratulate him on winning the top prize. You need to be here for him… with us. What the hell is wrong with you?'

Piper Jim turns around to face Rocky and rolls back his shoulders. He snarls, 'I will be back shortly, I told you. You never listen. That civvy is an important contact.'

Rocky continues in a low but increasingly irate whisper, 'Look, Dad, don't bother coming back. We can celebrate without you.'

Piper Jim walks away, only to be followed by Rocky, still tugging and pinching the back of his arm, while whispering aggressively in his ear. Piper Jim lunges his elbow backwards and firmly into Rocky's stomach. Rocky is not hurt, but Lizzy sees what is happening and is afraid there is going to be a scene and even punches thrown. Rocky spits his words into Piper Jim's ear, 'You are one selfish pig. I am totally sick of you.'

With the remainder of the room oblivious to the exchanges, Rocky quickly regains his composure and walks back to Lizzy. The roller coaster emotions of the day are now beginning to tell on Lizzy. He has overheard the aggressive exchanges between Rocky and Piper Jim and his smile fades. For Lizzy, that long-held suspicion of being unloved and unwanted, shockingly, has come to prominence on this crucial day of his life. All the other family tables are full of people and now he and Rocky will eat their meal without the head of the household joining them. There has been no handshake and his enormous achievement has gone unrecognised by a vital person in his life, his stepfather. He experiences a sinking feeling.

Rocky regains his joviality and instantly comprehends his brother's adversely changing emotional well-being. He realises that he needs to rescue this happy occasion from the intransigence of Piper Jim. He knows exactly how to grab this predicament by the scruff of the neck. Many times, when Lizzy was bullied at school, he intervened effectively to avoid an emotional meltdown. He looks Lizzy straight between the eyes.

'Lizzy, *cut*. You hear me, *cut*.' Rocky makes a sideways hand-chopping movement through the air with his fingers outstretched.

Lizzy immediately looks up, startled, remembering that *cut* was Rocky's long-time signal that there was an immediate requirement to pull his emotions together. It worked.

Rocky smiles broadly. It has been a couple of years since he last had to use that *cut* signal. Now it's time to immediately change the subject to re-establish the upbeat mood. 'Hey, Lizzy, it has been an absolutely super day. You know that trophy is significant. You are the most admired person in this room. It's a huge achievement. The platoon saw you under the savage physical and mental torture of recruit training. Remember, Athlone run the toughest course in the entire army.'

'Ha! My platoon knows me even better than you do, Rocky. The training exposes everything about your character. Every little flaw or weakness emerges. But also, your dependability, honesty and loyalty to your comrades is revealed.'

'That is what makes your achievement so massive. What a brother I have. Now, let's bring the food to our family table and polish off the free bottle of wine before that fat arsehole returns.'

Lizzy immediately laughs. Rocky is so hard on his father. 'Ha! Ha! Rocky, I have to keep saying it… some things never change'

'Okay, Lizzy, down the hatch. Let's get a glass of wine into us fast.'

Moments later, they are joined at their family table by three popular young corporals from the training staff.

'Hey, Lizzy, can we join you guys? We are supposed to join different family tables but the three of us want to stick together and have a laugh with you guys. Hey, you are Lizzy's brother. I am sure you know that Lizzy is one amazing guitarist. You are called Rocky, right? I hear you are quite a decent singer and performer as well. You are doing a song for us today. Is that true?'

Lizzy intervenes, 'Oh! Rocky, it's not a problem if you have nothing prepared.'

'Huh, that's not the way I operate. Little bro, for your special day I have spent a long time fully preparing and rehearsing one great song. Can I sing it now and then I will be more relaxed to enjoy my food and wine afterwards? I perform best on an empty stomach.'

One of the corporals stands up. 'Right, let's do it, Rocky. I am going to introduce you. We will organise your meal while you are singing. What's it going to be?'

'I picked a song of thanks, and I can see from the whole atmosphere here today that it is the right choice. Let's go!'

The corporal assumes the job as master of ceremonies and grabs a mike. 'Ladies and gentlemen, while you enjoy your meal, we have persuaded the brother of one of the platoon members to sing the first song of the evening for us. A round of applause for Gunner Rockingham from McKee Barracks in Dublin, please.'

Rocky is already sitting on the performer's stool. He checks the tuning of the guitar and, by ear, makes some small adjustments. He carefully selects the volume of the speaker and, without further delay, introduces his performance.

'Ladies and gentlemen, today I will perform a very special ballad which, I expect, you have all heard many times on the radio. It has been made into a massive hit by Bette Midler. I have selected this song as a tribute to the people behind the scenes who supported all the platoon members and helped you all get through this incredibly tough course. It is often unnoticed supporters who champion people's efforts. Ladies and gentlemen, "The Wind Beneath my Wings".'

Rocky sings the song with intense emotion. He is deep in concentration as he succeeds in vocalising and bringing out his understanding of the lyrics for the audience. There is a second of stunned silence as he completes his performance. Then there is a rapturous ovation. Rocky returns to his seat to enjoy his meal, together with Lizzy and the training corporals. Eventually, Piper Jim joins them, and the occasion becomes light-hearted and relaxed. As people finish their meal, they begin to circulate again. The Rockingham family table is surrounded by talkative friends, and a festive spirit prevails. Lizzy is again bubbling with joyful chat, and Piper Jim now pretends to celebrate and appreciate the moment. Rocky keeps his distance from his father and just observes. The false, exaggerated mannerism of Piper Jim now includes him stiffly draping his arm across Lizzy's shoulders and posing for photos. Rocky throws his eyes to heaven. He is still furious that Piper Jim has undermined the vital element of family recognition on the biggest day of Lizzy's life. He crunches his teeth in disapproval while watching and thinking about Piper Jim's sham, unnaturally stiff demeanour. He is somewhat bewildered.

No wonder Mother wanted him out of our life most of the time. He just cannot grasp the importance of genuine fatherly love. I am certain that he disappeared today when he heard that Lizzy was assigned back to Dublin. Someday, I am going to understand this man's real agenda. What is his problem with my brother? What is he trying to do to me? He shakes his head and purses his lips. *Something is just not right.*

Chapter 16

Rugby International Weekend

The week after Lizzy departs for Cadiz is one which Rocky will remember as one of the most turbulent of his entire life. The Ireland versus England rugby international is being played in Lansdowne Road on Saturday and the mess is inundated with requests for accommodation, meals and parking. On Saturday night, after the international match, the bar will stay open until late. Rocky has been told to call last drinks at 1am.

Sergeant Tom Gormley sums up Rocky's tasks. 'Okay, this will be the biggest bar sales of the year. Get your cash into the orderly officer's safe once you have more than a grand in the till. I am giving you two extra barmen from 5pm until midnight and then for the last hour, things should fizzle out and you should be able to manage by yourself. Okay. Now, I want you to check your stock and be sure that we have enough glasses. I have a cleaner also with you as well but try to let him go home around 1am. Gunner Rockingham, I expect the usual high standards. No evening food is being served so neither Captain Gilmore or myself are around on Saturday night, but we both can be contacted by phone.'

'Great, I love to be busy and then time flies. Thanks for getting me all the helpers. Looks like I will need them.'

'I am not fully finished yet, Gunner Rockingham. There is more.'

'More? Wow!'

'On Sunday morning, the head chaplain is hosting a coffee morning in the lounge area of the bar. It will commence after 8am Mass in the garrison church. It's for his congregation who are mostly elderly folks living around Blackhorse Avenue. There will be a few young families as well. The two civilian waiters on duty will expect the bar to be spotless and clean so they can commence their set-up early. The waiters are not responsible for the cleanliness of the lounge area. You are. The bar itself will not be open for alcohol service for the chaplain's group. So, good news is that you need not be there and can have Sunday off. However, I want no smell of alcohol anywhere and you are the one who must have the place spotless… all before the waiters arrive. The bar must look like no rugby function took place the night before.'

'Okay, Sarge. I should be able to start cleaning the carpet and scrubbing out stains by about 2am. Right?'

'I wouldn't bet on that, Rockingham. Look, you will get some customers, who have booked bedrooms in the mess, lingering on in the lounge till all hours. You cannot start deep cleaning until everybody is gone. But pull down the shutter at 1am, then serve last drinks and head off to get some rest. If there are still people finishing drinks, just leave them alone in the lounge and they will depart in their own good time. Do not try to clear the lounge area because this might cause unnecessary friction. You can come back around 6am when everybody is gone and complete the cleaning at that time.'

'Okay, Sarge. I got it. I am going to earn my week off for sure.'

'Well, actually, I have bad news. There is more.'

'More again?!' Rocky laughs and throws his arms up in the air.

'You will not be getting all of next week off as usual. The sergeant major of the regiment wants to see you on Monday.'

'What the f… ah, Sarge, I have gigs planned… Sarge, you know I work hard. I do not want to be dragged over to the regiment for even more duties on my week off. I know they are short of gunners for geli patrols… you know… explosives escorts, I mean. But after this tough weekend in the mess, that would not be fair.'

Sergeant Gormley hands Rocky an envelope. 'It's not my decision. The sergeant major was quite emphatic with me. There is no messing with that man. It's bad news for me as well. He left this instruction for you.'

Rocky is now becoming quite alarmed. He quickly tears open the small envelope and unfolds the typewritten sheet contained within. On the front page are the words: *WARNING ORDER.* 'Oh shit, I'm on a warning from the sergeant major.' His cheeks turn bright red as he looks up at Sergeant Gormley. 'What the hell? But, Sarge… I did nothing wrong. Did I?' He immediately suspects that somebody might have reported the clash between himself and Piper Jim at the Passing Out Parade in Athlone. He gingerly opens the second page and reads on.

Gunner Rockingham. The officer commanding 2 Field Artillery Regiment wishes to inform you that you have been selected for United Nations peacekeeping service with the Heavy Mortar Troop of the Irish Battalion in Lebanon for a six-month tour of duty commencing in mid-May. United Nations battalion concentration area will be the Curragh, County Kildare area, and you will be located there from the second week of March until departure. Congratulations. Full briefing in Regimental Headquarters on Monday from 0900–1000 hrs. You are directed to attend. Dress is number one uniform. You will be meeting your new Mortar Troop commander.

Sergeant Gormley is now grinning from ear-to-ear as he had already been briefed on the contents of the envelope. 'Well done, Rocky. Looks like we will only have you here in the officers' mess for just one more month. Then you will be leaving us for Lebanon training. You will be sadly missed. How do you feel?'

Rocky waives the letter over his head. 'Wow! Fantastic. Great news... Sarge... my lifelong ambition to become an Irish peacekeeper. I will be so happy to work on Monday and in full uniform.'

'Great. I am delighted for you. Well deserved. Now, get back to me in less than one hour if you need any stock ordered for the bar. You need to keep impressing me, Rocky. Remember, you are not overseas until the plane touches down in Beirut. So many guys... dozens, in fact... screw up and miss their peacekeeping trip for a variety of silly reasons. Rocky, let me remind you of an old soldiers' proverb: "there's many a slip twixt cup and lip". Understood?'

'You know me. I will run the bar brilliantly this weekend. You can go home to beautiful *Playa del* Duncannon knowing that everything will be under my control.'

'Thanks, Rocky. I already know that.'

Saturday afternoon comes and Rocky is well prepared. The bar will stay closed until 6pm as most of the prospective customers are expected to be at the game in Lansdowne Road rugby stadium. Rocky is not a rugby follower so decides to relax in his little room behind the bar and take a nap. On a freezing-cold day, it's a cosy place to hang out while he is waiting for people to arrive.

By 10pm, the bar is crammed with customers wearing green Ireland rugby shirts. There follows four hours of intense pressure, leading Rocky to retain his helpers beyond their scheduled finishing time. He promises them extra money and is sure that Sergeant Gormley will agree and pay up on Monday.

Then Rocky finds it impossible to close the bar as arranged as people are still arriving and piled up three deep at the counter ordering drinks. However, by 2am, he feels confident enough to rattle the shutter and even pulls it down over the bar to the half-mast position. His call for last drinks leads to a further, frantic, surge in demand. However, he manages to have the bar totally closed by 2.45am, with the lights behind the counter turned off. He is tired, but the time has flown, and he has enjoyed the energy of it all.

Now the head chaplain's coffee reception, later in the morning, becomes foremost in his mind. He is worried that his cleaning task will be a nightmare job. His assistant barmen finally depart, but he persuades his cleaner to stay around for another hour removing empty glasses and wiping tables. He does not want to reappear in the bar or lounge area himself as he knows that some customers will pressurise him to resume bar service. The lounge area is still packed but Rocky's job is completed, so he decides to head across the barracks to F Block to catch a few hours' rest. He heads out through the deliveries back door to the rear of the kitchen. As he opens the back door, he is blasted by an ice-cold breeze.

Wow, it has snowed. It is freezing hard. That wind would cut you in two. I don't think I can cope with the cold in F Block billet tonight. I will just be awake all night, shivering in my bed.

Rocky realises also that he will have to return to the bar to complete the cleaning at 6.30am. It is certain that there will have been some spillages on the carpet, and these will need to be washed. There is no way he is going to let the head chaplain and guests arrive to a lounge stinking of alcohol. He decides that the barman's cosy, warm bolthole is probably the best place to catch a few winks of sleep. *I have my sleeping bag there and that reclining armchair is almost like a bed.*

Rocky returns to the bar, being careful not to be seen. He discretely shuts himself into the little bolthole without turning on the lights or television. He removes his sweaty clothes and crawls into his sleeping bag. Then he fully reclines the armchair. Within minutes, he is totally asleep, despite the persistent drone of customer conversation coming from the lounge.

Sometime later, a startled Rocky sits up suddenly. Loud, inebriated voices, almost shouting in the bar, have succeeded in waking him. He holds his breath and listens.

'I am telling you now, he is going to destroy it for everybody. The lads in the cabal have plans to sort him out, you know.'

Rocky looks at his watch and the glowing hands indicate that it is 4.10am. There are still people in the bar and now they have become louder and more verbally outspoken. The usual background drone of multiple conversations is absent, so Rocky figures that it must be just one small group who are now alone but noisily dominating the bar.

'Look, shut up! Listen, ya-boy-ya Look! Close that feckin' door so we can talk.'

Rocky hears the bar door slamming shut and now speculates that it is just two people that are still in the bar. He picks up snippets of conversation.

'The bastard has found out how we control things. Our entire secret chain of influence is in danger. He found out about our network. He knows how we do the seeding. Some guys are worried that they will be exposed. He is a clever and dangerous bastard. He is going to ruin us. I am sure of it.'

'You know he is due another top job abroad again shortly. I heard that he has nearly finished a master's degree. That will enhance his CV and make him unstoppable in the promotion race. If he gets into a position of power, he will do damage, for sure.'

'So… what the hell are we doing about it? What about the usual hate campaigns?'

'Yeah, we have about four of those making slow but significant progress now.'

Rocky is then shocked to overhear a name that he knows well.

'That bastard Gilmore has left us very little to go on. He is a workaholic. Some juicy sexual gossip is beginning to gain a little bit of traction, but there are no hard facts. A few of his closest friends are beginning to shun him.'

'Hmm! We also are soon to have a plant here on the mess staff spying on him. He is sure to make some financial blunder or balls up a big function… or something… nick a few bottles of whiskey, maybe. We will know about it straight away and spread the shit all over the place. We can package it as theft or corruption. His denials will be useless because we will have the muck spread to every corner of Ireland. Even if he is innocent, nobody will hear his side of the story.'

'Go to hell! Mistake in the mess, my arse. Again, that's not going to be enough. What about roofies?'

'I know nothing about them. It's a date rape drug or something. He is not the type that would use them to *flah* some unwilling bird. Not his style.'

'Yerra, you are talkin' shite now. Our contacts can get us Devil's Breath. They use it for interrogation. You know who I am talking about. The lads from Virginia.'

'I never knew there were date rape drugs in Cavan.'

'Ya feckin' *ejit* ya. Listen, once a victim even smells Devil's Breath or consumes it in their drink, they will do anything you tell them to do. It's amazing. Once you spike a drink with even a gram of it, it takes away a person's free will. They become totally obedient. You tell them what to do and they do it. Then, the next day, they remember hardly anything.'

Rocky is hardly breathing, still in the dark, stretched out on his reclining chair. Now, he can clearly hear every word of the conversation and is immobilised by fear. He cannot believe what he is hearing. He is afraid to stir, even slightly, lest his presence be detected. He realises that he might have stumbled upon a bizarre conspiracy.

'Then we should be setting him up. Protecting the secret existence our cabal is priority. With drugs, we can obliterate him forever in ten seconds. Even if he does nothing weird, we can still have him screwed by setting him up for the new random army drugs test. When he tests positive, he will be unable to explain it and be forced to resign.'

'You are right ya-boy-ya. Listen, are you comin' up in the autumn for the marathon? They asked me to come up for a flag event or something. Not sure what's happening. Might be a flag day fundraiser or something. It's all hush-hush for some reason. Sure, I'll help out anyway.'

'I heard it might be a false flag, but I really have no idea what that is all about.'

The drunken voices seem to move location and appear to be drifting into the distance. Rocky hears the lounge entrance door opening and again banging shut. There is silence. He is relieved and takes a deep breath. But seconds later, the voices become louder and look to be approaching his bar back entrance door.

Bang! Bang! Bang!

A fist is hammering on the wooden door of his tiny bolthole. Suddenly, the loud voices seem to be just inches away from him. He is momentarily unsure if he locked the door. He prays that he did. Then he hears shouting.

'Hello! Hello!'

'Barman! Barman! Open up! Is there anybody there?'

The door handle moves and springs squeal. Rocky becomes increasingly scared as he knows that somebody is now trying to force open his bolthole door.

Crash! Crack!

A boot has been applied to kick open the door. Now there is anger in the voice.

'Barman! I know you are in there. Open this door. That's an order. Do you hear me?'

Rocky holds his breath in the hope that his hiding place has not really been compromised. He is not sure how much punishment the flimsy timber door can withstand.

'Barman!'

The door is pounded again violently, and inches from his nose, he sees the handle shaking vigorously up and down.

'Barman, just two Redbreast whiskeys, please. Then you will not be in trouble.'

'Leave the door alone ya langer ya. Hey, listen to me. You are wasting your time ya feckin' *ejit!* He closed hours ago. Let's try to break into the kitchen fridge for some food. There might be cooking sherry there as well.'

The voices drift away from the door and Rocky can hear the distant clanging of kitchen steel presses, pots and utensils. He is still somewhat anxious but begins to feel more physically secure. The door has not been damaged badly and he now must stay quiet and not sleep in case he snores. He lies fully back on his reclining armchair thinking about what he has just heard. Captain Gilmore did warn him never to listen to customer conversations. In this instance, Rocky feels that he is not at fault. But it is the content of the conversation that worries him the most. He is vaguely aware that Gilmore is a rising star in the officer ranks. He has heard that Gilmore is not universally popular. Nevertheless, this plot against him is unbelievable. Rocky's mind starts racing.

What's a roofie? What in the name of God is Devil's Breath? Sounds disgusting. If I report this, I might be in serious trouble for eavesdropping on officers' conversations. I wonder, were those people officers or civilians? They seem to have a secret network. If they are officers, then, should I report it? But this is so bizarre, nobody will ever believe me. They will just laugh. Perhaps these were just drunks playing around with idle threats.

For the rest of the night, Rocky's mind is in turmoil. The good news about his trip to Lebanon is now eclipsed totally by this outrageous event. Perhaps worst of all is the revelation that somebody on the mess staff is spying on Captain Gilmore. For Rocky, that means he cannot trust anybody on the officers' mess staff.

Should I warn Captain Gilmore? What the hell am I going to do? If they spike his drinks with date rape drugs here in the officers' mess, as barman, I might be implicated. If I don't tell him and his life is destroyed, I will never forgive myself.

At 5.45am, Rocky emerges from the barman's bolthole having tidied up the room to give no indication that he has stayed there overnight. He commences cleaning the lounge bar area. He is jumpy and full of fear, worried that last night's final customers might return looking for more booze and asking demanding questions. He works with nervous intensity so that he can escape home quickly to safety. Suddenly, Rocky hears two sets of footsteps in the corridor, and they are getting louder. It's 6am. *Who the hell could it be, at this unearthly hour?* He suddenly feels somewhat light-headed. Then, armed and in full uniform, the orderly officer and barrack orderly sergeant enter the bar. Rocky springs to attention, though it is not customary for staff in an officers' mess to do so. The orderly officer has his left hand on his leather holster which contains a 9mm Browning automatic pistol. He addresses Rocky. 'Gunner Rockingham? What are you doing here?'

'I am cleaning the bar for the coffee reception, sir.'

'Have you been here in the bar all night?'

Rocky becomes momentarily incoherent with stress and exhaustion. 'No, it wasn't me sir... I didn't do anything wrong... I mean... I mean... I am just back. I just started cleaning a short time ago.'

'Okay, there is a serious problem.'

'What is it, sir?'

'Did you notice anything strange?'

'I don't know, sir. Am I in trouble? I think there was two very late rowdy customers, but I didn't notice anything else strange at all.'

'Well, Rockingham, open the shutter. I want to see behind the bar.'

The barrack orderly sergeant and orderly officer follow Rocky into the barman's bolthole.

'Rockingham, what happened to this door? There are boot marks and cracks in the timber.'

'I have no idea. They are new but not mine. Look, sir, I have my keys. I have never needed to kick doors.'

'Okay, how much did you hand me to lock in the safe around 3am?'

'Exactly £2,300 in cash, sir. See, it's written here.'

'Where is the receipt I gave you? Show it to me. Read what it says.'

'You signed on this receipt for… hey, wait a minute… for £3,200, sir. You entered the wrong amount. The smaller amount is the correct figure. It's my error as well, sir. Please, can we correct it now? Sir… eh… sir, I didn't mean to cause trouble for you.' Rockingham is standing to attention.

'Everything was so rushed; the bar was packed… but I am certain that £2,300 is the correct amount because I kept a careful tally all during the night.'

The relieved orderly officer immediately seeks to defuse the situation and becomes supportive of this clearly distressed and overworked soldier.

'Phew! Gunner Rockingham, relax. No need to stand to attention. I nearly collapsed when I did the final cash count in my safe a few minutes ago when I noticed that I was down a pile of money.'

'Sir, I presume there will be no trouble about this now that it's sorted.'

'Everything is a hundred per cent, Rockingham. You are an honest guy. Hey, this bar and lounge looks great. Well done on the cleaning job. The head chaplain is sure to be very pleased.'

By 8.30am, Rocky is walking towards the city centre down Aughrim Street. Today, he decides to walk all the way home despite the cold weather, icy paths and sprinkle of snow. The Sunday bus schedule is irregular, and he cannot be seen hanging around at a bus stop. Escape to home and total safety is his objective. He pulls a hood around his ears to defend against the cold but also to hide his identity. He has no idea who his final customers last night were, but he is sure that they will remember what he looks like, being the highly visible barman. He is apprehensive in case he unexpectedly meets anybody who might start asking him difficult questions. Rocky is unnerved and worried that he also might become a target of these undoubtedly evil people.

As he strolls through Stoneybatter, he wonders who he can trust and confide in. Lizzy is in Cadiz but even if he was in Dublin, Rocky feels that this issue is way beyond his young brother's capacity to advise. Sergeant Gormley is a great guy, but can he totally trust him? He might be the person who is spying on Gilmore.

Rocky is now uncertain about everybody. He concludes that the presence of a spy means that he now dares not trust a single person on the mess staff. But for Rocky, this is too big an issue for him to handle alone, and he has no idea what to do. He has a brainwave. It might be time to make friends with his dad again. They have not spoken since Rocky dished out the insults in Athlone. Perhaps there are uses for his dad's military experience after all. He is family and, in this crisis, he is the only person Rocky can trust.

Chapter 17

An Enigmatic Father

Rocky enters home through the front door. From the wonderful smell of cooking rashers, he immediately knows that his dad is preparing a traditional Irish breakfast. The sizzle from the frying pan and the sound of Piper Jim humming in the kitchen fills the entrance hall.

'Hi, Dad, I'm home.'

'Well, that's good news. Do you want me to top up my frying pan with some breakfast for you? Rashers, sausages, eggs and a bit of black pudding? I have a few mushrooms and onions as well.'

'Wow, that would be super, Dad. It's freezing outside and I'm starving. I need ten minutes to have a quick wash. I have been working nearly all night because of the rugby international function. Then I had to clean the bar this morning because there is yet another reception. Just give me a few minutes and I will be back down for breakfast.'

'Okay, fine, I will wait for you. Hot grub to warm you up after your hard night's work.'

Rocky is somewhat relieved that he and his father still seem to be on friendly talking terms. The aggressive exchanges at the Passing Out Parade are being conveniently, mutually, ignored and seem to have left no permanent scars.

Piper Jim has had time to absorb the Athlone confrontation. He now fully realises that he stumbled unwittingly into moronic thoughtless blunders. He was not sufficiently guarded and stupidly exposed the actuality of his lack of any feeling of love towards Lizzy. He knows that he is getting ever closer to a permanent end of his relationships with his boys. Nothing ever seems to go smoothly. He worries that the next confrontation will see Rocky drift away to find a new home. For the past few days, Piper Jim has been trying to come to terms with how he can revive some sense of unity. He has also continued to be gripped by mental turmoil. How will he cope with the demands of the sickening mission which involves having Rocky destroy Paul Gilmore?

Rocky quickly rushes upstairs to his bedroom, washes himself and pulls on his fresh army-issued cotton pyjamas. After having a hearty breakfast with his father, he will have no difficulty in getting some sleep. He returns to the kitchen where Piper Jim is serving their fry onto piping hot plates.

'Well, son. There was a massive crowd around the city yesterday for the rugby. What a fantastic buzz. I had a pint with some well-travelled English fans, and they told me that Dublin is the greatest city on earth to watch a rugby international. A lot of them come with no match tickets and are delighted to just soak up the electric atmosphere in the pubs. A few of the lads from the pipe band and myself did a pub crawl and, in a few places, the craic was probably even better in the pubs than at the stadium. So, how was your day? The mess bar was packed, I suspect.'

'Yeah, Dad, it was bedlam… pressure, pressure, pressure. People just kept arriving in droves and, even as late as 1.30am, it was just impossible to close. I worked flat out all night, but I enjoyed it. I got quite a few tips and made a nice few bob.'

'Great, now get stuck into your breakfast while it's hot. Let me know what you think of the home-made brown bread. I bought it from an old lady in Moore Street Market yesterday and it was so fresh, it was still warm. Straight from her own oven in Dominic Street flats.'

'Okay, I have some big news, Dad. The names for the Lebanon trip have been released. I will be heading out in May.'

For once, Piper Jim has had no advance notice of Rocky's big news. 'Oh! Jaysus, that is just great.' Piper Jim hops up from the breakfast table and shakes Rocky's hand. 'Fantastic, I'm gonna miss you.'

'Dad, I have just one more month in the officers' mess and then it's off to the Curragh of Kildare. We will go directly from there to the mission area. It will be my first time ever on an Aer Lingus jumbo jet. I'm really excited.'

They sit silently, enjoying their breakfast, but then, strangely, Rocky notices frowns beginning to appear on Piper Jim's forehead as his eyebrows twitch up and down. Piper Jim seems to be momentarily lost in a conversation inside his own head and seems suddenly worried. Finally, he breaks the silence. 'And, of course, you are sure you really want to go to Lebanon? I can talk to the sergeant major and have the trip put back until the autumn if you wish. It might be a better option.'

Rocky feels like screaming. 'Good God, are you crazy? Dad, please don't start this again. Don't get involved.'

'No, I mean—'

Rocky raises his voice. 'Dad, that would be a terrible thing to do to me. I am so happy about this overseas trip. If I lose it, I will be devastated. In fact, Dad, if I am taken off the list, I will never... *ever*... forgive you. Now, I mean that. This conversation is over.'

'No, no, sorry! Relax, son! I am just thinking about how well you are impressing everybody in the officers' mess VIP bar. Are you sure you are not needed there? Then your brother is coming back to Dublin. I just thought that you two boys might like to be together for the next six months. That's all I am saying. Don't jump on me, son.'

Rocky continues talking in determined, strong terms. 'Dad, this is the biggest thing that has ever happened in my life. It somehow makes up for me losing out on my musical career. I *am going* overseas in May! I have no worries about Lizzy. He is an adult now and has managed very well without me down in Athlone. I have no interest either, in further impressing people in the officers' mess. I have done my bit there and have made great friends.'

'That's fine with me, son.'

'Dad, thanks. I am excited and now the only thing I want is my peacekeeping trip to the Middle East. Nothing else! I am highly focused on getting on that beautiful green jumbo jet.'

'Okay! Okay! Of course, son, you are dead right. I am delighted for you. Don't get me wrong. You are a man who is growing in experience and it's time for me to take a back seat.' Piper Jim immediately changes the subject to avert, yet another, altercation. 'It will be great here in Dublin as well. Lizzy will be back to Ormond Square to keep me company for the summer. We will get on superbly together. I hope he will join me in the Phoenix Park every evening for some serious exercise – I must shed a lot of weight, or I will never again see an overseas trip myself. I would not pass the medical or fitness tests in my current state. The doctor warned me that I am bordering on being obese, possibly even unfit for promotion. Blood sugar is up. Most certainly, I would not pass an overseas medical test. The weight just piled on after Maria's death.'

Rocky is feeling relieved and the positive remark about Lizzy's return is good news. He becomes more relaxed. 'Yeah, it will be great for both you and Lizzy, Dad. If you change, it will work, for sure. But you must change, Dad. I really mean it. You have seen that Lizzy is a real calm, easy-going person. The man most respected by his fellow recruits. Some achievement. You will come to love him. Please try. He is very athletic and will encourage you to shed the pounds.'

'Rocky, look, I know that I have not been a great stepfather. I am going to organise events for the two of us to attend and try to improve our relationship. You are hard on me, son… but I know that this time you are right.'

'Dad, that is perfect. It will help me to enjoy my time overseas as well. I want to know that you two are supporting each other while I'm away.'

'Have no worries. I can organise some good times with Lizzy… you know… a few nice events we can go to together. I am thinking of the two of us dressing up and taking the train down to the Irish Derby festival at the Curragh Racecourse. Bubbly, smoked salmon, a few flutters on the tote… the lot. We can take in a few Dublin matches at Croke Park. Then we might even head over to London in August to see a Chelsea game.'

'Dad, that would be great for the two of you. I will be jealous. Great idea. Lizzy loves Chelsea and still has that old poster from *Shoot Magazine* of John Dempsey, Peter Bonetti and Ian Hutchinson. He has never been to Stamford Bridge.'

'Look, son, we will both do fine while you are away. It's very important that you mentally carry no family worries or baggage with you to Lebanon. It's tough enough out there without having stress from home to cope with as well.'

The conversation pauses for a few minutes and Rocky debates in his mind if it is advisable, and a good time, to discuss the dramatic overheard conversation from the early hours of the morning in the officers' mess. He decides to trust his father and get it off his mind. 'Dad, I need your help. I want your advice on something.'

Piper Jim looks up, surprised by this rare deferential request for help from Rocky. 'Oh! Yeah? Okay. Anytime.'

'I overheard a conversation in the early hours of this morning which relates to my boss, Captain Paul Gilmore.'

Piper Jim sits up attentively. Perhaps the task of tarnishing Gilmore is about to nicely fall into his lap with no effort at all needed.

'Tell me more, Rocky.'

Rocky reveals everything about the bizarre events and conversation he heard during the night. Piper Jim immediately strongly advises that his son should stay away from controversy. He counts out his arguments on his fingers.

'First, son, the reason you were warned to avoid overhearing conversations in the mess is because officers talk terrible shit when they have beer on board. Secondly, you have no idea who these customers are except you believe them to have culchie accents. Thirdly, it's highly inadvisable, as a young barman, to make allegations against your superiors or mess guests. It's not your place.'

'I know that, Dad but…'

'I am not finished. Fourthly, you have just told me that the peacekeeping trip is now the most important thing in your life. Be careful, because I am sure that you do not want to end up being kept in Ireland to give evidence to an investigation.'

'Wow, Dad. I want to avoid that kind of disaster. I am absolutely sure that I do not want to ruin my United Nations opportunity.'

'Exactly. Now, son, you said that these two culchies mentioned that Gilmore is also going overseas. You should have no worries about the captain. He can cope without your help. He is a rising star and you even told me that the chief of staff described him as a miracle worker. What about you... a gunner, private three star, a jackeen from a tough part of town, fresh face, zero medals, one trip to the Border but otherwise absolutely no experience. Who is going to listen to you? Does the rising star need help from a young twerp like you?'

'Yeah, I get you, Dad. It all was probably just rubbish talk after booze. It's just that I was shocked and actually scared when I heard about the drugs.'

'Now, son, overall, I would strongly advise totally forgetting that this happened at all. It's none of your business. It's not your fight.'

'Okay, I agree. But, Dad, what if somebody uses a drug like Devil's Breath on Captain Gilmore? I will feel very guilty to see his life destroyed by these dirty bleedin' culchies, whoever they are.'

'Ahah! Yes... whoever they are... exactly! You have no idea who it is you might be making allegations against. They could be civvies. Most likely this was pure drunken, exaggerated bravado. It is you who could get in trouble for wrongfully eavesdropping while improperly sleeping behind the bar. That is conduct to the prejudice of good order and discipline and could be considered an offence under military law. Officers in secret illegal cabals have a habit of closing ranks when one of them is exposed.'

'Yeah? You seriously think they might try to destroy me as well?'

'Absolutely, son, I am sure they would and your father. Your brother, as well. They would not think twice about eliminating any threat you might represent. But… son… are you fully sure you were not having a nightmare? You were always big into mystery and conspiracy since you were a child. This Devil's Breath? Are you still reading those Enid Blyton *Famous Five* children's books?'

'I read one last month… in Spanish… just to keep up my language skills. Now, I am reading Tom Clancy a lot.'

'Ha! Ha! Devil's Breath. Even Tom Clancy would be proud of a fictitious name like that. Rocky, really, it sounds like something out of a spy novel.'

'Dad, I know what I heard. But you are right about one thing. The last thing I want is my peacekeeping trip ruined.'

'Not just your trip, Rocky. A silly allegation like this could destroy your entire life. Officers have power and some have rotten politics advancing their careers. You have nothing. Now, don't mess with dangerous bastards. Heed Gilmore's instructions. He clearly told you that the VIP barman must not be compromised.'

There is a pregnant pause as Rocky, hand on chin, stares down at the dining table, absorbing the message. 'Okay, Dad. You don't need to convince me anymore. There is going to be no "slip between cup and lip". Never a word again about Devil's Breath. You know, Dad, I now realise that, at times, I am totally out of my depth. Thank you for keeping me on the right track. I am now going up to bed and will happily crash out for the rest of the day.' Rocky lands a rare kiss on his father's cheek.

'Ha! Ha! You are a "gas man", Rocky. At times, you are only a little kid. Other times, you are such a strong personality that I must remind myself how young you are. Okay, son, I am heading for a walk and I'll probably say a few prayers for us all in the Adam and Eve Church on Merchants Quay. We want to keep Devil's Breath away from our house and out of our pints. I will get some holy water. Ha! You head up to bed and relax now. Forget about everything. Start thinking about your overseas trip and the fitness tests which must be passed. If what you overheard is correct, Captain Gilmore will be there in Lebanon earning double your pay. You can treat him to a bottle of Almaza beer in the UN bar in Lebanon.'

'Thanks, Dad.'

Piper Jim pulls on a heavy coat and hat and strolls along the north bank of the River Liffey. He walks over O'Donovan Rossa Bridge to the south side of the river and the church on Merchants Quay. Never one for religion he, nevertheless, always enjoys admiring the beautiful interior of this exquisite building. When Maria was alive, he would come over for an hour of peace and quiet. He would enjoy a welcome solitude, away from the effervescent babbling of the children, as his wife taught them singing, dancing and the Spanish language.

Piper Jim sits in a pew facing St Anthony's side alter in the almost deserted church. He looks at the magnificent liturgical art while momentarily deep breathing. He feels a new sense of tension induced by the eye-opening information he has just heard from Rocky. He will appropriately circulate the news about Gilmore's likely selection for duty overseas to those that need to know. His influential friend will not be happy that the target is soon to leave the country. Equally, the loss of Rocky as a potential informant in the VIP bar is guaranteed to be treated with the utmost of hostility.

Hmm, it looks like Gilmore will soon be out of harm's way. Unless they scandalise him in the mission abroad. However, it is most unlikely that a tactic like that would pay dividends in the UN multinational community. Not as easy as in Ireland's "squinting windows".

Piper Jim feels that he can view these new developments somewhat positively. His repulsive mission might be moving outside of his sphere of influence. The natural flow of events could be said to be unburdening him of a heinous task.

Thankfully, Rocky will be back with his young soldier pals, peacekeeping in the mountains of South Lebanon. Pure soldiering with devoted friends and safely away from involvement in sickening intrigue. It's probably for the best.

Jim takes in a deep breath and concludes to himself that he should not be faulted by his influential friend for not accomplishing the mission. He wonders if Rocky is the spy that the two drunks were referring to. Perhaps there are multiple spies stalking Gilmore. He takes in a deep breath and shakes his head while thinking, *wow, Devil's Breath drug. Oh my God! That's scopolamine.*

A year earlier, Jim had completed a one-day community course on parental drug awareness which included a frightening lecture on Devil's Breath from a visiting South American doctor. Jim learned that the drug is commonly blown through the air towards the victim. It can also be sprinkled into a drink. Within two minutes, it causes the person to become highly suggestable with no sense of right and wrong. They do exactly what the perpetrator tells them, including, for example, disgraceful acts in public.

As Jim mentally digests Rocky's revelation, he becomes

increasingly disturbed. *My God, it would be the perfect drug to use for ending a person's career through total humiliation. The most easily administered, dangerous drug in the world. I remember we were told that one ounce is enough to kill up to fifteen people. Where the hell did they find that in Ireland? These are sick bastards, and currently I am one of them.*

Since his meeting with his influential friend, Piper Jim is being tortured by guilt and is suffering from massive feelings of regret about his past. He kneels in front of Saint Anthony's Alter and places his two hands over his entire face.

'Thank God that Rocky never came to realise the shit that I was up to. I feel terrible about my own outspoken silly gossip down through the years. I was just trying to impress those who I regarded as superior to me. I never knew I was doing real damage. I will take my regrets to my grave with me because I can never forgive myself. My stories ruined the lives of at least two decent men. Dozens more lost out as well.'

He remembers the sudden resignation of one lieutenant colonel he was told to smear and, apparently sadly, there was no farewell lunch or presentation to him. Then there was that poor sergeant who he spread rumours about. They magnified a silly incident into a highly circulated scandal. Then his wife attempted suicide and finally left him.

Piper Jim knows that there could be serious recriminations over his unwillingness to stop Rocky's overseas trip. *Maybe they will try to use Devil's Breath on me. Hopefully they will leave me alone. I am facing a lose-lose situation. They have waited six months for this infiltration of the VIP bar. I could easily, but will not, stop Rocky's overseas trip. He would be certain to blame me if he was removed from the UN list. Things are bad already. Rocky is no fool. I don't want a total family break-up.*

Piper Jim's mind continues in turmoil as he now also admits to himself that he has been an angry man for eighteen years, ever since Lizzy's conception which occurred while he was overseas. He knows that Maria never told the boys about a proposed visit to an illegal backstreet clinic which he had demanded. His arrogant coercion of his pregnant wife was a disastrous misjudgement. Maria never forgave him and, de facto, she ended the marriage. For far too long, he has allowed anger about his late wife's infidelity to drive his actions. He has lived a life ceaselessly seeking flight and escape from this entire horrific family predicament. Piper Jim knows that he foolishly confided in his dangerous influential friend at that time, telling him his marital secrets. What a mistake. Now they have him in a corner if they want to destroy him. For the moment, he still seems to have Rocky's trust, even though it is heavily overshadowed by suspicion. For Piper Jim, life has been a series of traumatic lessons and many colossal blunders. He realises that he should no longer continue to ostracise Lizzy. He will also have to come to terms with the likely eventual re-emergence of music as the chosen career path for both boys.

'Even though my motives were not right, God, I have provided them with their military opportunity. They are now more disciplined and organised due to the intensive training. But from now, they can take the army or leave it. I am stepping back.' He takes in a deep breath and whispers another prayer, 'Listen to me, God... or Saint Anthony... whoever is listening. I know I need to change, but I hope that I am not a total psychopath. I accept that Rocky's needs are not best served by him becoming an officer through a political back door. He is strongly spiritual and there is no way that he would accept an order from anybody to betray his closest military comrades. God, I pray that my son's fantastic musical talent gives him financial and career independence. I have my piping talent but, unlike Rocky, I do not have youthful energy. I am totally dependent on the army and my influential friend. Alone, I am nothing. Life makes no sense... no sense at all. I am all mixed up.'

Piper Jim breaks down with tears flowing in profusion from the brutish man's eyes. Since the debacle in Athlone, he has had a lot of time to examine his future. He realises that the two boys, in his senior years, will become increasingly important. Now that he is advancing towards retirement, the escape and comradeship offered by United Nations duty will soon be a distant memory. Then, Ireland has changed as well, with many children being conceived unashamedly out of wedlock. Looking at the positive side, becoming a loved grandfather might not be too far down the road. He must try to rebuild the boys' confidence in him because he would love to be at the centre of their future family lives. He can no longer continue to conspire to separate them. He can no longer stymie their natural career paths. He can only pray that his influential friend does not now decide to destroy him and everything he holds dear.

'God, please don't let them smear me with the backstreet clinic story. If they do, it's all over and I have nothing to live for. I am finished. I need the boys. Don't let them frighten my friends and army comrades away using gossip and character assassination.'

For Jim, life is becoming seriously complicated, and he is tired. He decides to immediately withdraw his participation from the entire Paul Gilmore elimination attempt. He knows that this is a very dangerous decision. He will announce nothing but just avoid contact with his influential friend.

'No retirement job in Switzerland... c'est la vie. I can still advance in life by putting myself in line for a promotion vacancy in the pipe band. That vacancy, for Company Sergeant, is coming up soon. It will be hard for them to politically block me thanks to the strict seniority system.'

He rubs the tears from his face, blows his nose, stands up and heads for the church exit door onto Merchants Quay. As he steps down onto the street, he hears a familiar voice behind him.

'Hey, is that Jim Rockingham?'

'Ah, hello Father Broderick. I heard that the church had been newly decorated, so I just dropped in for a quick look around… and a prayer of course. Sorry about my eyes. I have a bit of a cold.'

'Jim, we always love to see you. How are Rocky and Lizzy?'

'Well, Father, it looks like Rocky is heading for Lebanon. He just got the word on Friday.'

'Ha! Ha! Wow! A chip off the old block. You are overdue a trip yourself. You seem to love it over there. Or is it that Ireland is just too boring for a man of adventure like yourself?'

'Ah, you are right, Father, I always miss the United Nations every time I come home. Soldiers often feel down in the dumps for a while after returning from a trip. It can be really tough to adjust.'

'Wow! That's not the first time I have heard military men say that. Very interesting. What do you put it down to?'

'It's lots of things, Father. I miss the teamwork. The UN job is clear… authentic. I feel fantastic about being part of something important. Something bigger than myself. The Irish peacekeepers make a massive difference by creating safety for frightened, poor villagers.'

'Jim, everybody in Ireland is so proud of our peacekeepers. Nothing on this earth is of greater importance than your task abroad with the UN.'

'Yeah. Thanks, Father. Most of all what I miss is the strong bond of friendship among the troops. On a UN mission, because of the danger, almost every task is done as a team. This creates high levels of what we military men call "esprit de corps". What that means, Father, is that we have tremendous loyalty to each other, pride in our identity and devotion to our job.'

'That is very interesting. At home in Ireland, it's different? Right?'

'Yeah, you face peacetime soldiering which is often a mind-numbing daily grind. I always have a feeling of apathy. There is an environment in the home army where people are anonymous "ships in the night". There is a lack of that sense of belonging and identity.'

'Jim, that indicates very poor leadership from the top.'

'Absolutely, Father. In Ireland, the army lacks a dynamic task to bond the troops together. I always struggle with a feeling of purposelessness. Then, for me, things were particularly tough because my marriage was not strong. So, down through the years, I always have had the urge to escape from Ireland. Despite the danger abroad, I am much calmer and happier there. ' Jim finds himself talking from the heart. He is, now, not sure if he will ever be picked for overseas service again.

'Jim, so the UN gives you a sense of community whereas in the home army you face a sense of anomie.'

'Anomie? What does that word mean, Father?'

'Jim, it's a sense of futility. Anomie is also a breakdown of social bonds due to lack of a properly defined purpose.'

'Wow, Father, thanks. Lack of clear mission at home? Absolutely correct. This causes the feeling of emptiness and despair.'

Chapter 18

From Mingie Street, Naqoura
to the Blue Note in Beirut

By the end of May, Paul Gilmore is fully settled into his staff appointment in Naqoura, South Lebanon. He is working under an excellent and highly operationally experienced French colonel in the prestigious operations cell. The UN in Lebanon is comprised of over six thousand troops from many nationalities, and his job is to write detailed assessments of the ongoing military conflict and political situation. His reports are signed by the force commander and are used as decision-making material at the United Nations headquarters in New York.

Gilmore now loves his life and relishes the prospect of spending a full year enjoying fascinating office work as well as a coastal Mediterranean climate. He feels that this new, perfect situation is well deserved. His final four months in

Ireland were torturous with the requirement to finish his master's thesis, pass the university exams, pass overseas fitness tests, medical tests, inoculations as well as keep the VIP clients in the officers' mess happy. On arrival in Lebanon, Gilmore is both physically and mentally drained. He is satisfied that no matter how tough his new job turns out to be, it will be easy, compared to his experiences of the past year.

Meanwhile, Rockingham manages to avoid the proverbial "slip twix cup and lip" and successfully travels to the tiny mountaintop Lebanese village of Ayta Zutt in the Irish peacekeeping area. He becomes a surveyor of heavy mortars, a technical, indirect fire task which he had to learn in just three weeks. However, news of his musical skill does not take long to circulate, and he quickly ends up spending a lot of his time doing gigs all over the Irish peacekeeping battalion area. In the desolate and dangerous mountains of South Lebanon, the importance of providing the troops with some form of social life, music and relaxation is a very big challenge. There is competition from the various commanders to have entertainers visit each remote outpost to help keep the troops smiling and maintain their mental well-being. Rocky knows that this was a role Piper Jim had perfected for many years as a top-class bagpipe player and Celtic traditional storyteller. Rocky immediately becomes known as the legendary Piper Jim's son, a label that he is not overjoyed with. He relies solely on his vocal skill and a guitar. His repertoire is pop and charts which is perfect for the youthful demographic make-up of the UN mission. On an ad hoc basis, he regularly teams up with other soldiers who also have musical skills. Occasionally, he can pull together a full band for a night of superior entertainment.

As a much sought-after performer, Rocky finds himself increasingly being dragged away from his primary military task. He not only covers the entertainment needs of the Irish troops but also travels around entertaining many other UN peacekeeping nationalities. When the security situation deteriorates, he gets a break from the music as it can be too dangerous to travel. His priority then becomes his conventional military peacekeeping role with the Heavy Mortars.

In early June, Rocky gets his first chance to visit the south Lebanese town of Naqoura, with its huge, sprawling, United Nations headquarters located close to the Israeli border. He performs on an open-air stage for a multinational audience comprising of UN bureaucratic staff, Italian helicopter crews, French armoured mobile reserve, Polish UN hospital staff and Swedish logisticians. This becomes his biggest gig with over 250 in attendance. The audience includes some Irish personnel, including Gilmore, who he has not seen since he left McKee officers' mess almost four months earlier. After the gig, Rocky and the other entertainers are rewarded with a guided pub crawl of Mingie Street. This is the only commercially vibrant street in the area and is lined with souvenir shops, restaurants and bars. *Mingie* is a term used by UN soldiers for souvenir.

During the pub crawl, Rocky spots Gilmore and immediately scrambles through a crowded bar to shake his hand. 'Sir, you made it to Lebanon, and I made it as well.'

Gilmore does not realise the profound significance of that statement. But for Rocky, there is a massive sense of relief and delight that his former boss is unharmed. Rocky has been plagued with worry for being so self-serving in not telling Gilmore of the existence of a potential plot to destroy him. This was particularly the case after he found a frightening reference to the Devil's Breath drug in the local ILAC Centre Library in Dublin. Rocky read that, in many countries, political cabals use Devil's Breath to have drugged opponents engage in compromising behaviour which then provides blackmail opportunities. Few people in Ireland seem to be even aware of its existence. Yet, Rocky is certain that one of the voices in the bar that night had spoken about it coming from Virginia, a tiny town in County Cavan near the Border with Northern Ireland. Rocky remembers being frightened as he left the library that evening.

Enid Blyton my arse. Jaysus, what kind of insane psychopaths did I overhear that night? This is big. Very big. I am so glad that they did not know where I was hiding. At least I hope that is the case… or they might pursue and harass me in the future as well.

Now, in Mingie Street, Rocky is certain that everything has turned out well as Gilmore is on his feet, suntanned, socialising and laughing. He looks calm and content.

'Gunner Rockingham, it's great to see you and that was just another great show tonight. Reminded me of my birthday. You did a full twenty minutes and were the most impressive of the performers.'

Rocky is suddenly overcome with emotion. The terrible guilt he has been harbouring can now be put to rest. He awkwardly and firmly hugs his former boss, nearly knocking the beer from his hand. 'Jaysus, sir, I am so glad to see you.'

Gilmore is taken aback by this stirring reunion as his overall relationship with this gunner has mostly been friendly but, also, normally quite formal. He admires Rockingham and considers him to be a brilliant soldier but never thought of him as a close friend. He is surprised, therefore, at Rockingham's apparent euphoria in meeting him.

Rocky exhales strongly before releasing his potentially embarrassing embrace of the officer. 'Whewwww.'

'Hey, Gunner Rockingham, are you okay? Ha! Ha! I am delighted to see you as well. Is everything going okay for you up in the battalion? Nothing going wrong on your tour of duty, I hope. Are you a bit tense after the gig, perhaps?' Gilmore pauses and stares into Rockingham's face, searching for some hint as to this unusual emotional behaviour. There is silence and, not waiting for an answer, Gilmore glances sideways and spots that the barman is free and can immediately serve him a round of drinks. 'Hold on, wait there a minute and I will get both of us a fresh, ice-cold beer.'

Rocky quickly regains his formal military composure while Gilmore is at the bar buying tall cans of Almaza. Gilmore returns with a beaming smile on his face.

'Sir, apologies. Yes, you are right. I am a bit emotional after the pressure of the gig. It gets to me like that sometimes. Big crowd tonight. Overall, the mission is going well for me. I am having an amazing time travelling all around the UN villages and performing for so many different nationalities.'

'That's brilliant. The UN is a massive education. You get to talk to so many different nationalities. You see so many different places and hear different points of view.'

'I never did so many gigs in all of my life. Enjoying every minute of it. I think I know now why my dad, Piper Jim, wanted to be on UN missions abroad all the time. So, how is your job, sir?'

'Interesting and far nicer than running the officers' mess in McKee Barracks. Life is good and I am no longer a captain. I was promoted to Commandant so it's a bit of status and reward from the top brass.'

'Wow, I noticed the new rank markings, but I was afraid to ask. So, it's true that you are a rising star. Fly me to the moon with you, sir.'

'Hey, Rocky, who said that I was a rising star? Ha! Ha! I hope you were not listening to silly gossip back in McKee. I am just a simple, ordinary, small-town guy, loving my new job, working long hours and now doing my best for the UN peace process.'

They sip their beers and enjoy some casual small talk. Gilmore has been building up expertise on political developments in Lebanon's capital Beirut.

'Hey, sir, I have a question for you. How dangerous is Beirut? It looks like they are sending me up there next month to perform at the request of the Irish embassy. I will be there for a week of rehearsals and then we play for a big group of local and international dignitaries.'

'Beirut is okay towards the northern end. But the route there is not so safe, nor are the southern suburbs of the city. You are okay if you are travelling up in a large convoy which is well armed. Get into an armoured car if you can. I go there for meetings regularly. You need to be streetwise and I now am. But, if it's your first time, you should ideally travel in a convoy and I recommend staying in secure, protected accommodation in the UN military police compound. When are you going?'

'Next month, sir, but things are still vague. I have no date yet.'

'Okay, Rockingham, let me know, particularly if there are a few spare tickets. I could arrange my schedule to be there and might try to take in the gig.'

'Wow, for sure. I will call you and let you know, sir. I think I am back here again in Naqoura two weeks from now for another performance and I will know everything by then. I will try to get you either a ticket or a backstage pass. The gig will be in a famous old venue called The Blue Note, right in the city centre.'

'If I can make it, I certainly will. Entertainment is something that is in short supply everywhere, so any excuse to schedule my work in Beirut and take in a little bit of music will be most welcome.'

They part company as Rocky continues with his pub crawl group to a nearby restaurant.

* * *

A full six weeks passes before Gilmore hears from Rockingham again. The security situation has been intermittently tense, with a reduction in both ease of movement and UN social event opportunities. Then, contact from Gunner Rockingham comes in an indirect manner. A stylish envelope arrives on Gilmore's desk, embossed with the logo of the Irish embassy, Beirut. It's an invitation.

International Musical Celebration, The Blue Note, Beirut.
Dress Formal, UN Personnel – White Uniform, Blue Cravat, Medals.

Gilmore is delighted and immediately revises his travel schedule to ensure that a working research assignment in Beirut coincides with the gig.

Two weeks later, as planned, Gilmore is in Beirut, travelling in a large Cherokee Jeep, accompanied by his French boss. His boss is not staying in Beirut, so he drops off Gilmore close to The Blue Note. Gilmore is way too early for the gig but wants to meet Rocky for a quick chat before the venue fills up. Gilmore now knows that what is planned is a Latino night with the Spanish, Argentinian and Mexican embassies sponsoring the food and drinks.

Rocky has apparently been almost a week rehearsing with a local Lebanese band and backing group. He has been told that he represents the entertainment contribution of both the United Nations and Irish embassy to this special event for diplomats. On entering The Blue Note, Gilmore is immediately taken aback by how professional the entire set-up at the club is, considering they are in the middle of a war zone. The stage props are of theatrical quality and many of the performers are already scurrying around wearing traditional Latino costumes. He spots Rocky among the entertainers, wearing a full-length, all-white stage suit. Rocky immediately breaks away from his group and heads towards Gilmore.

'Welcome, sir, glad you could make it.'

'Wow! Jaysus, Rocky, that is some costume. You look like Elvis Presley or even... let me think... yeah... John Travolta in *Saturday Night Fever*!' They laugh loudly and shake hands. 'Hey, it was just great to get the ticket. Thank you.'

'It's going to be a super show tonight, and all of the costumes are stunning. There has been some impressive sponsorship as far as I know. The quality of performers here in Beirut is very good. I have a brilliant backing group, including dancers. We have had to work really hard on the dance routine, so let me know what you think of it.'

'So, what is your role in the show?'

'Well, the various Spanish-speaking ambassadors are, not surprisingly, fanatics for Latino music, and we are onstage after the interval. We plan to do five numbers in Spanish and one in English. I am lead singer with my Lebanese backing band.'

'Wow, did you have to learn all of the songs from scratch?'

'My Spanish mother actually specifically trained my voice using Latino music. Then, I also had a month to prepare. I performed some of the songs during gigs in various United Nations mission areas. I could also quietly rehearse by myself in the "glen". It's a beautiful, lonely valley near our platoon mortar position in the mountains near Ayta Zutt.'

'Then it should be a really enjoyable night. I am glad you are so well prepared. A good report from the Irish ambassador will be a great feather in your cap. The Irish battalion commander will be very pleased. Now, Rocky, good luck tonight. I am going to my hotel to check-in and have a shower. I need to get out of this dusty, green uniform. I will be back in good time for the show. No more talking. Save your voice. Let's meet for a beer after the show. I am sure you will be brilliant. Just to remind you that you are picking up a Land Rover for me tomorrow morning at the military police compound. I am obliged to always have a second person in the vehicle and tomorrow you will be my signaller on the radio as we travel back south to the UN area. Unfortunately, there is no UN armed convoy tomorrow, so we will be on the road alone. It's a little bit risky but my French boss and I have done it many times before.'

'Yes, sir, the military police have that vehicle ready. In fact, I saw it in the compound this morning. I am up to speed on the various net disciplines and radio voice procedure. I am staying, as you suggested, in the MP compound so it's all very convenient.'

Two hours later, Gilmore arrives back to The Blue Note on foot. Already, the venue is beginning to fill up. Security in the surrounding streets is intense. There are numerous Lebanese army heavily fortified checkpoints backed up by armoured cars. Snipers dominate every rooftop. The arriving diplomatic cars are luxury, armour-plated models, and many are adorned with national flags. There are many different uniforms with top army ranks, chiefs of police, fire chiefs and politicians attending. Gilmore spots the UN force commander's spectacular white limousine coming to a halt at the entrance door.

Jeez, this looks like a who's who of Lebanese society and the international community. It's staggering how glittering occasions like this can take place while there is savage fighting and killing going on just a few miles down the road.

Gilmore is frisked by security but quickly gains entrance and immediately finds a seat midway back from the stage. He is lucky because it's a packed full house, with many people having to stand at the back of the hall near the bar. The Latino theme fully extends to the food and beverages. Waiters circulate with trays of finger food and bottles of Spanish Rioja. One busy corner is the location of the self-service bowls of sangria. Gilmore spots a tray marked "From Mendoza, Argentinian Catena Malbec" and he gravitates towards his favourite sumptuous, silky, dry vino tinto. As the temperature rises and the cigar smoke becomes thicker, Gilmore wonders how the performers will cope with the sweltering heat when the show begins. He calculates that there could be almost three hundred people crammed into the venue.

Finally, the show begins. The curtain opens to reveal a lady in a bright red dress standing under the spotlight. The opening performance of the night gets underway. It's an energetic, dynamic flamenco dancing show which is welcomed with much cheering. The Latino members of the audience are quick to lead the rhythmic clapping at appropriate times during the dance. Gilmore has never seen flamenco before and is fascinated by its energy. The fervent dancing sets the tone by instantly creating an uninhibited atmosphere which goes on to last for the entire night.

The show quickly moves on with a Mexican Carlos Santana tribute band. Now The Blue Note pulsates with Latin-infused salsa, rock, jazz, blues and African rhythms. Performances of "Samba Pa Ti" and "Black Magic Woman" spellbind the audience, bringing everybody to their feet singing and dancing. Gilmore wonders if the young Irish UN representative will be able to cope. The standard is high, and it must be tough on Rocky and his group waiting backstage to perform. The incredible din of audience appreciation for the early acts must be adding to the tension.

During the interval, Gilmore opts to stand for the rest of the show at the back of the hall, strategically positioning himself close to a large air conditioner and near the tray of Catena Malbec. The lights flash once, and people jostle their way back to their places. Silence descends again for a split second. The show recommences, and Gilmore recognises a voice emerging from behind the stage curtain, calling for the audience to dance and have fun.

'*Esta noche vamos a bailar. Vamos a divertirnos.*'

The curtain slowly opens to reveal the new stage set. Rocky is at the centre surrounded on both sides by dancers, support singers and musicians, all wearing traditional Latino costumes. He belts out his first number in perfect Spanish. Then, more Spanish songs follow which fire up the Latino members of the audience. The VIPs are getting increasingly pissed and are gradually losing the run of themselves. Rocky seems to be absorbing the positive feedback on the stage and is smiling broadly. He confidently dances in synchronised, split-second precision with his backing singers. Despite the cigar smoke, his voice is crystal clear.

The time comes for the last number and Rocky is joined on centre stage by a tanned Lebanese girl from his backing group whom he introduces as Adeline, a student at the American University of Beirut. She and Rocky look into each other's eyes while performing a magical old number. It's a Julio Iglesias and Dolly Parton song "When You Tell Me That You Love Me". They complete the song, and the entire night's entertainment, with an inordinately extended kiss and embrace as the curtain closes.

It's over and Gilmore decides to escape to cool down and enjoy his final glass of Malbec in the fresh air. The limousines are already lined up outside the door under the direction of the Lebanese police. He sits down in the fresh air, judging a long pause to allow the hall to empty. The bar will stay open for another hour and, as Gilmore re-enters the half-empty venue, he spots the photographer from the *Litani*, a United Nations magazine. Posed photos of the various bands are being taken, and everybody seems to want to be included in a group picture. Minutes later, Rocky and his beautiful stage partner are standing at his shoulder.

'Adeline, this is my boss back in Ireland, Commandant Paul Gilmore. Sir, can you join us for a photo for the *Litani* magazine? We can do it on the stage with all the props behind us.'

Gilmore is impressed. Despite all the fan adulation, Rocky retains his humility and finds time to seek out his ex-boss. Photos ensue and Rocky circulates among the VIPs, chatting with ease in either English or Spanish while enjoying a beer. Adeline becomes separated and Gilmore seizes the opportunity to chat to her about the performance. She is wearing a knee-length red dress, and Gilmore immediately is impressed by her warm, broad smile.

'Commandant Gilmore! You are the boss that Rocky speaks so highly of. I am delighted to have this chance to meet you. First, thank you for doing such a superb job in the south of my country. My granny and grandpa live in the

169

Irish area. We worry about them all the time. But they are happy because you are bringing the peace and security they so badly need. The UN has saved so many innocent lives.'

'Wow, thanks for the nice comments. I am delighted to meet you. We just do our best. You can call me Paul, by the way.'

'Paul, I hope the show was enjoyable. The audience feedback for us on stage was immense. I am just an amateur and have never experienced anything like this before. You know that Rocky set up most of the stage arrangements and the dance routine. He is a professional. Then we had the soundchecks.' She laughs. 'They went on and on. Nothing was left to chance. When we got tired, Rocky demanded more. He told us that Freddy Mercury and Queen did four hours of soundchecks before every gig… and we were going to do the same. It was hard, but we solved so many little problems on the last day. So much knowledge and experience. A perfectionist.'

'I never knew that he organised the choreography. You were brilliant yourself and your duet with Rocky was, for me, the highlight of the night. I loved that long final kiss. Ha! Ha! How often did you rehearse… the kiss, I mean? Not as long as the soundcheck, I hope?'

Adeline flushes red as she giggles. 'Actually, Paul, Rocky stole that kiss! I was overwhelmed. There was no kissing rehearsal… totally impromptu. That awesome kiss was a special stage moment. Wonderful! Seems the audience loved it and I was, truthfully, a little surprised but… I admit… enchanted. We both got carried away by the cheering from the crowd.'

Adeline looks around as she hears her name being called by the photographer. 'Well, Paul, it has been great to meet you. I am doing my studies in the American University of

Beirut. I am hoping to do some courses in London next semester. I am very interested in visiting Dublin as well. In the meantime, I am in the AUB Business School. Rocky has my number.'

Adeline is gone and Gilmore is suddenly alone. He is disappointed that she left so suddenly. He momentarily feels a little down and slightly envious. He is a senior army officer but, unlike Rocky, he is not the superstar of the night.

The time comes to seek out Rocky to brief him for the hazardous journey back to the United Nations zone the next day. He discretely calls the superstar aside for a moment away from his adoring VIP fans.

'Hey, Rocky, it doesn't have to be a crazy early start, but we do need to get over the Litani River before dusk. It's potentially volatile all the way south on the coast road until we get into the UN area. We will travel back in a fitted-for-radio, FFR Land Rover. We should have good communications most of the way to the UN controlled zone. We have a Motorola as well for communication in the Beirut area. The reports I have is that the radio relay stations are working well. That is vital for our safety considering the kidnap and hijacking risk. The military police will bring the Land Rover to my hotel at 7.30am so you should arrive with them. You are secure and sleeping in the military police compound – right?'

'That's right, sir.'

'Great, okay, Rocky, I will treat you to a good hotel breakfast before we depart. Dress will be bush greens, boots, blue helmet and flak jacket. Remind me not to forget to take the radio charts from the MPs.'

'Sir, I will see you tomorrow then at 0730 hours sharp.'

Suddenly, it is all back to the business of living in a war zone. Gilmore correctly takes the reigns and becomes the commander with military responsibility. Deep in thought, he sips his final glass of wine, alone outside the venue. Feeling a slight sense of anti-climactic emptiness, he finds himself shaking his head.

Life is so funny sometimes. What an amazing night. Rocky, aka Gunner Rockingham, has been the undisputed master of ceremonies. The audience hung on his every musical note. Ambassadors, chiefs of police and generals were grovelling for his attention at the end of the show. Invites to visit embassies proliferated. Glamorous daughters of VIPs surrounded him.

Gilmore sees the night's events as confirming his long-held conviction that talent or expert knowledge of a task naturally generates leadership. During the performance, Rocky, entertainer and superstar, was the complete commander of the entire room. While entertainment was the task, Gilmore saw himself as, quite rightly, unimportant and passive. The end of the entertainment signalled a return to a realisation of their presence in a war zone. Gilmore finds himself using his military expertise to take the lead in organising that potentially dangerous journey back to the UN zone. He recalls the old military college adage about how the task should naturally be permitted to strongly influence the selection of an appropriate leader – "authority flows to the man who knows".

Tomorrow, roles will be transformed by the nature of the changing task. The superstar becomes the senior officer's humble radio operator. Commandant Gilmore again calls the shots and takes over military responsibility for their safety, security and navigation.

Chapter 19

Breakfast in Beirut

Next morning, Gilmore is awake early and immediately tunes his transistor to Radio Kol Israel. 'This is the voice of Israel broadcasting from Jerusalem.'

Gilmore knows that, after the Hebrew programmes, there will be news in English at 7am. All significant overnight developments in the security situation in both Lebanon and Israel will be covered. Gilmore resets his watch using the five-second Kol Israel countdown bleep. After the fifth long bleep, he pushes the winder to restart the second hand on his beloved Seiko Sports 100 watch. He has been doing this every day since arriving in Lebanon. The watch never leaves his wrist, twenty-four hours. A belief in the need for military timing precision has evolved in armies around the world from the crucial operational importance of H-hour. Gilmore's enthusiasm for his military life means that he considers it vital for an officer to possess a tough, dependable watch which keeps the exact time, to the second.

The news bulletin is reasonably comforting. Beirut and the Lebanese coastal highway are not mentioned. The news reports overnight artillery shelling in Qana in the UN Fijian peacekeeping area with three civilians injured. A roadside bomb, which was discovered in the Israeli-controlled southern Christian enclave, was defused by the Israeli Defence Forces with no casualties. Neither incident is anywhere near the route south, which Gilmore and Rockingham will be taking. The level of violence seems lower than usual. The Kol Israel weather forecast mentions a risk of rain for the afternoon. Gilmore knows, from experience, that tarred, wet roads combined with typically bald Lebanese vehicle tyres usually results in total traffic chaos. This is a good reason to get moving down south no later than the early afternoon. He knows that the military police will have a more detailed weather briefing for him when they come with the vehicle at 7.30am.

Gilmore rarely suffers from hangovers. Despite him imbibing on delicious Argentinian Malbec wine at the gig, after his shower this morning, he feels nothing more than slightly dehydrated. He heads down to the hotel dining room to wait for the MPs and his vehicle. As he has promised Gunner Rockingham a top-class hotel breakfast, he decides not to eat until he gets the vehicle hand-over formalities completed. He can then relax over the breakfast meal. He sits in the dining room sipping chai – Lebanese tea with mountains of sugar in the glass. It is his normal practice to order *chai bidun sucre*, tea without sugar. This morning, he decides to combat dehydration, and his experience is that sugar provides him with a desirable immediate energy boost.

The military police arrive precisely on time at 7.30am but immediately, Gilmore senses a slightly anguished look on the corporal's face.

'Sir, I'm Corporal Kirwan from Mike Papa Beirut.' They exchange salutes in the hotel car park followed by a handshake. 'I am here to brief you. Let me say straight away that the Land Rover is okay but not perfect. The gear change is a bit tricky. Other than that, it's fine. I am happy it will get you back down south; just go straight from second to fourth gear. We should do a run around the block. I can show you how I bypass the third gear problem. Here are your radio charts, and the good news is that the forty-six set is a good one, new, I think. All radio relay stations are working fine. You will be able to pick us up here in Beirut, using the Motorola Radio, for the first half hour of your journey. The Lebanese army reported about one hour ago that all roads as far as the Litani River are open. There are currently zero security issues. Weather is different, unfortunately.'

Corporal Kirwan has the latest updated report. 'It's raining in the south on the mountains so the many local "bangers" of cars, and trucks with bald tires, will be skidding all over the road once that wet-weather front reaches you. So, be careful. Gunner Rockingham is waiting for you in the back of the vehicle and the fuel tank is full. I have drilled Rockingham on authentication procedures and radio net discipline so he should be good at that. Also, sir, there is a jerrycan full of additional fuel should the need arise. Finally, Rockingham has been provided with four large bottles of water and some sandwiches.'

Gilmore is highly impressed by the completeness of the military police briefing. 'Hey, that's great, Corporal Kirwan. Well done, very comprehensive. So, the only real snag is the sticky gear change.' Gilmore examines the vehicle with Corporal Kirwan and is satisfied that it is overall in good condition. The gear change problem turns out to be a minor issue and something that can easily be overcome.

'Okay, Corporal, let's park the car here. Back it right up to the window of the dining room. I have booked that dining room seat just inside the window. We can strap down the canvas back as well until I am ready to go. Thanks for your assistance. I will do a radio check with you in about an hour when we are leaving this location. I would appreciate you closely monitoring our progress until we go out of signal range. I have a small bit of business to do near Jounieh before I leave your area of operations, so you will get us on the Motorola until about noon.'

'Absolutely, sir, drive carefully.'

Rockingham has been uncharacteristically quiet, letting the corporal do all the talking. 'Sir, if you don't mind, I would like to go for a short walk to buy a *mingie*. I spotted it in a local shop just two hundred yards away.'

Gilmore agrees but suspects this request is for the benefit of the corporal's ears. He can see that there is tension between them.

Rocky carefully plays the game. He knows that the MP corporal might be a little resentful if he finds out that Commandant Gilmore is allowing a humble three-star soldier to dine with him in the posh hotel. So, the cover visit to the souvenir shop is necessary to bide time until the corporal is gone. Gilmore plays along with the appropriate military formality and gives no indication of his intending preferential treatment for last night's superstar. He takes his seat in the hotel dining room, which is now packed with local Lebanese and Syrian customers. Not sure if Rockingham will have the confidence to join him, he makes his first visit to the running buffet. He half fills his plate and takes a tall glass of fresh, locally produced, orange juice. As he is sitting back down with his plate of food, a smiling Rockingham returns.

'Jeez, sir, that MP corporal has had a saddle on my back all morning! He had me up at 5am washing the car, painting the tyres and sorting all the MP communications data. He knows I am doing a lot of entertaining and thinks that I am on a bleedin' holiday out here. He made some remark about me being on a "jolly". He is right, of course. Ha! Ha! Long may it last, sir. He kept telling me that you were a strict, professional officer and that I would want to watch my manners... yeah... my bleedin' manners. Jeez! I will grab some food, sir, if that's okay.'

On Rocky's return to the table, Gilmore is grinning. 'I am sure you are well able to cope with a little bit of envy, because that's all it is. He is a newly "minted" corporal who is trying hard to do well and advance his career. Now, forget about that MP because now you must cope with me. The strict one.' Gilmore chuckles. 'Yeah! Let's talk about jealousy. Even I was envious last night. Tell me all about the gorgeous Adeline.'

'Ha! Ha! Sir, yes, she is stunning. Educated and sophisticated, and you heard her remarkable singing voice. Her gorgeous, permanently tanned skin is so... well, let's say, inviting... you remember that kiss. Yeah, well, the truth is that it was not in the script. It was my instinctive reaction to the words of the song and the audience cheering. I was overjoyed with the reception we were getting, lost the plot and my instincts took over. You know, sir, every day, as we rehearsed, I became more and more attracted to her laughter and fun. Then I was so happy to have come to the highlight of a super gig. Then, it just happened.'

Gilmore sees a golden opportunity to tease. 'She told me to tell you, Gunner Rockingham, that she was totally shocked by that kiss.'

Rocky immediately becomes flushed with embarrassment and is a little worried by the sudden formal use of his rank.

'Oh, no, sir. I didn't... look... sir, I didn't mean to upset anybody.'

'Calm down, I am only joking. What she really said was that she was floored and delighted. She told me that the entire show was just a superb experience.'

Rocky's face immediately brightens up. The beads of sweat which had suddenly appeared on his forehead are brushed away with the back of his hand.

'Wow, sir, you had me scared there for a minute. That's good news. I will drop in a gift to her on my next visit to Beirut. That's if I am ever here again.'

Gilmore now notices a further opportunity to slag Rocky. 'Rocky, you seem to have bruises on your neck. Are they mosquito bites or were there some lengthy soundchecks with Adeline?'

'Oh Jaysus, no! Have I hickeys? That old flamenco dancer ate me alive backstage. I gave her a polite hug and suddenly she was nearly on top of me... eating my neck. And she told me she was fifty-eight years of age. Yuck! Oh God. Sorry, sir... I will have to put a plaster on my neck so that the lads back in the mission area do not notice. No, it wasn't Adeline... unfortunately.'

'Yeah! Yeah! Yeah! Old flamenco dancer... hmmm. Ha! Ha!'

Gilmore loves the banter. They continue eating but something comes to mind, causing Gilmore to adopt a more serious tone.

'Rocky, this has been a great visit but, to put a slight damper on things, just be careful if you are up here again. You have heard of Brian Keenan and Terry Waite?'

'Yeah, sir, of course, they were kidnap victims.'

'Now, Gunner, friend and colleague, I am this minute wearing my official UN HQ hat. Let me advise you that having a relationship up here could be more than a small bit risky. We all know that interpersonal relationships with locals is forbidden by the UN. The UN rule is in force all around the world because in the past, there have been, not only kidnapping incidents, but also murders of peacekeepers. It's far too easy to target a soldier by luring him into a secret romantic rendezvous. Proceed with extreme caution. This is a wild and violent city.'

Seeing Rocky's disappointed face, Gilmore then changes to a more upbeat tone. 'Of course, now wearing my friendly mentor and coaching hat, I realise that there are ways around the rule which are totally legitimate. You could end up bumping into a Lebanese girl on Nissi Beach while on UN leave in Cyprus. That's not in the mission area, so it's okay. But be careful not to end up in Beirut alone with a local girl. Your Mike Papa Beirut friend might be glad to find fault with a soldier on a romantic jolly.'

Rocky is momentarily silent, thinking over the probabilities. 'Yeah, you are right, sir; I know that regulation. Everything seems so normal here today that it's easy to forget how dangerous a city this is.' He pauses, then suddenly becomes upbeat. 'You know, if I date Adeline in Cyprus, that would be an incredible coincidence. It would be astonishing for one reason. You know my dad met my mother, Maria, in Cyprus a couple of decades ago. She was a professional singer in a nightclub in Aya Napa, and when he saw her on the stage, he was immediately smitten. You know, I often suspect that I was conceived in Cyprus. They never told me, but I have done the maths. I might have been the reason my parents got married... a shotgun wedding perhaps. Ha!' Rocky smiles widely but then suddenly retreats to a more contemplative tone. 'Anyway, meeting Adeline again would be a real long shot. I would not bet on it happening. I have her contact details anyway so we can stay in touch by post. I know she visits her uncle in London occasionally. But last night will live in my memory. It was just a great gig. A super moment in my life. Now, I suppose, I simply move on. Plenty more adventures in many different places to come.'

Rocky quickly again becomes optimistic as he arrives back from the buffet with more lush Lebanese fruit, fresh from the trees. 'Hey, sir, after you left last night, I had a great chat with the editor of UN *Litani* magazine. They took a picture of Adeline, me, the dance troupe and the Spanish ambassador. The Carlos Santana lookalike guitar player was in the photo as well. If the photo comes out bright enough, they hope to use it as a front cover picture on next month's *Litani* magazine. Now that will be special if it happens. What an honour. Even my famous dad never got his picture on the front cover of the UN *Litani* magazine.'

'Perfect. Like father... like mother... like son! Rocky, even as a soldier you are being constantly lured back into music.

For sure, last night will have done your musical career no harm. I expect some of those embassies will want you back. You are being put on the stage more and more often. You are spending less and less time with your military troop of Heavy Mortars in Ayta Zutt village.'

Rockingham has always felt guilty about not doing his share of real "soldiering" with his comrades back in Ayta Zutt. He wonders if Gilmore is trying to tell him something indirectly. Perhaps he really agrees with the MP corporal's "jolly" remark.

Gilmore notices an emerging glum expression and immediately reassures Rocky. 'That's not something to worry about or be ashamed of. It's too dangerous now for any band to come out from Ireland so what you are doing is important. The mental health of the peacekeeping troops is vital. On that subject, Rocky, I have a question.'

'Yes, sir.'

'You were a bit emotional when I met you a few weeks ago in Mingie Street, Naqoura. In fact, you were trembling a little. You gave me a long hug. Is there anything wrong that you want to discuss?'

Rocky looks down, embarrassed, and the conversation falters. Then he takes in a deep breath and looks directly at the officer. 'It was relief, sir. Relief that you were safe and well.'

'What? That I was safe and well. Me? Good Lord, what do you mean?'

Rocky initially hesitates, but then continues. 'Sir, I will keep it brief. I broke one of your golden rules and, unfortunately, I overheard a conversation in the McKee bar one night. There were two very drunk customers talking about you in threatening terms. They were worried, even angry, about your potential for success. They said that you knew too much about, what they called, their cabal system. They planned to block you. What they said frightened me and made me feel that they might be part of some secret illegal organisation or conspiracy.'

Gilmore's face flushes a bright red. He shakes his head and purses his lips. 'Oh, no! Not more of this.' Gilmore clenches his teeth, his eyes burning with sudden anguish and anger. 'So, now they are even getting at my young staff. It's disgusting. Very worrying. I hope that they have not turned you against me, Rocky.'

'Of course not, sir. I really enjoy working in a highly disciplined, busy environment where the orders are always clear. I hate wasters no matter what their rank is.'

Gilmore abruptly stands, leaves the table and heads in the direction of the toilets. He needs a few minutes alone lest he betrays his agitation to the young soldier. To Rocky, he appears calm but is joyless on his return.

'Well, Gunner Rockingham, I am sad. You have told me the truth so let me explain. In recent years, among officers, sadly, there has been a diminished respect for hard work. Personal interests have taken over. For many, the best interests of the service are no longer important.'

'Oh!'

'We now have a secret, treacherous political backchannel which is populated by the lethargic. This backchannel has resulted in the lines of authority becoming blurred. Do you understand?'

'Just a little, sir.'

'The environment I work in is one that is both a friend of mediocrity and is highly threatened by talent. This backchannel is a politicised domain of influence. It is constantly expanding through vilification, smear and attempts at humiliation. One dares not stand out through excellent work performance.'

'Wow, I get the message. That's why I was so worried.'

'Yeah, the entire politicisation increasingly deprives talent of the influence in the army that it deserves. Talent is cynically portrayed as the stain of dangerous individualism. Then there is our oath. Officers swear not to become involved in politics. Young Rocky, in our democracy the swearing of an oath is vitally important. Oaths of office are sworn by the president, judges, policemen, trial witnesses, doctors. Oaths are, in many cases, fundamental to the workings of the entire democracy. A collapse of our society's respect for the integrity of oath-taking is worrying. It brings with it the potential for a catastrophic democratic failure in the future. The creation of secret chains of influence inside the security services has the potential to bring down the entire country. Our loyalty as soldiers must be to the Constitution and to whatever government the people select. The people vote. We respect. We must be above any political power games. I am sad that you heard certain things, Gunner Rockingham. These stupid people are playing with fire. Their involvement in politics is potentially treasonous and a national betrayal of the most serious nature.'

'Sir, I felt very guilty for not telling you about this sooner, but I was really afraid.'

'You are right to be afraid. I am afraid too and often deeply depressed. Yeah, depressed far too often for a successful person who loves the army.'

Rocky does not totally understand everything Gilmore has said. But he listens attentively as his mentor and hero unexpectedly divulges a massive burden of emotional pain.

'Other times I feel sad, lonely... isolated. I feel that there are powerful elements in Irish society which are driving us towards kakistocracy.'

'Jaysus, sir, I have no idea what that means.'

'Kakistocracy. Yeah, Rocky, a big word but a simple meaning. It comes from two Greek words with a literal meaning "government by the worst people". It is a system of government which is run by the most unscrupulous citizens. In Ireland, there is a lot of regard for native cunning. The con man is always smiling and seems popular as he slyly wins your friendship and confidence. There is this sick jocular approval for the brutal, calculated sting that follows unexpectedly. I am tired of people cheating and smearing. I am tired of wasters winning. Instead of impressing, and offering devoted public service, they attack and hurt those public servants who outperform. They attack your family. They hurt your parents, wife and kids. They work to alienate you and destroy your friendships. They can only thrive if they devalue you in the eyes of your significant colleagues and friends. But, Rocky, if there is a national crisis with corrupt simpletons in charge, the results will be totally calamitous.'

Rocky is silent but is not as stunned by Gilmore's emotional revelations as might be expected. This is because he had begun listening deliberately to customer banter while preparing drinks back in McKee. The negativity in overheard conversations was far too frequent for his liking.

'Now, Rocky, keep quiet about anything you heard behind the bar, or you will become a target. They will not allow you to expose them and will try to drive you out of the country. Forcing emigration upon their opponents is a far-too-frequent tactic.'

'Emigration?'

'I hope you have told nobody about your knowledge of the plot against me.'

'Oh! I only told my dad. He gave me the exact same advice as you.'

'Oh n... I see... hmm. Piper Jim. You told him... okay... right.'

The tone of Gilmore's voice is not encouraging. Rocky studies the officer's face for a clear signal and he probes gently but interrogatively.

'Could my dad... I mean, sir... do you mind me asking, could my dad be involved in this?'

They fall silent and no answer to that question seems forthcoming. Gilmore adopts a faraway look with a facial expression that seems tinged with indignation. As a lengthy silence takes possession of their breakfast table, Rocky realises that the officer may have suffered deep mental wounds.

'Sir, one conversation all the staff talked about in the officers' mess bar was a remark by the chief of staff that you are a "miracle worker".'

Gilmore manages a smile, welcoming the change of subject.

'Yeah, the chief is a great guy and straight down the middle. A man of very rare integrity. No toleration of idiots. He really enjoyed the Eclectic RRK performance at my birthday. He was so impressed with the band. He could not understand why you were in the army. He said that he was afraid that your roots in a central Dublin working community might lead you to having ambitions which were far lower than was justified by your talent.'

'Wow! No, I am very ambitious.'

'He asked me to keep an eye on your progress and not allow you to set your sights too low. The words he used were, "they are very special... we will never hang onto these two brothers as soldiers... nor should we try to do so".'

'Phew, sir, from the chief of staff that is really encouraging.'

'It's sad, but Lieutenant General Johnny O'Dowd has suffered disloyalty as well. They leaked confidential information to the media to get him in trouble. It's a sick, well-known, political tactic called "poisoning the well".'

'Wow!'

'"Poisoning the well" is entirely premeditated, planned and executed by highly organised political cabals. It is done in the same way as criminals put into motion their performance of a crime. They have secret planning meetings... the whole works.'

'Jaysus, sir, this job in the officers' mess has exposed me to a horrible new reality. I am never going back there.'

'Ha! Me neither. Just in case you become a target, Rocky, watch for sudden new friends who want to socialise with you. Watch for smiling con men who flatter you with admiration and want to get into your inner circle of buddies. Watch out for that loaded question, late at night after a few pints, at a social occasion. These people are clearly definable in literature as psychopaths. They will simultaneously show you surprisingly warm friendship to win your confidence. At the same time, they will be quietly destroying you with any innuendo they can get a hold of. Be careful of these people because, Rocky, you already know far too much. The personal destruction can be extensive, and it can unfold at many different levels and places. Political psychopaths are slowing growing their numbers in the army and police as religion and morality collapses.' Gilmore suddenly taps the table gently three times. He manages a grin provoked by Rocky's startled expression. 'Going! Going! Gone! That's religion, Rocky. Let me emphasise, amigo, that a sudden new admirer, who clearly targets you for friendship, is often the one you can trust least. Army political cabals use friendship like the proverbial Trojan Horse. They get close to you. Then they twist the things you say and do to try to ruin your life.'

'Oh my God, friendship is so valuable to me. I met the best friends of my entire life in the army. But we are just privates and not under the same pressure for power and promotion as officers. Among us gunners, there is no interference that I know of from outside. Soldiers are not really competing for promotion or power, so we are not politicised. Most lads just do three great years in the army and leave.'

'Yes, you are right. Officers are different. First realise that the lifetime value of a job in Ireland's public service, including pension, can be worth a small fortune. Putting that in context, bank robbers often murder people for as little as twenty grand. So, for a job and pension for life, worth millions… what kind of shit will people do for that?'

'How do you cope, sir?'

'I focus on what I can control and that is mostly my own present moment performance. I take massive pride in what I do. I focus my efforts each day on the job and simply do my best to achieve as close to excellence as possible. I devote time to making good choices. To focus on things I cannot control, like criticism for example, is to allow anxiety to take over my life. I just work hard, do the right things and then let destiny take its course. I am a self-starter. It tends to work, like now for example, finding myself in this excellent appointment in UN headquarters. I am truly living the best, most interesting, days of my life. I regularly endorse myself.'

'Endorse?'

'Yeah, I tell myself many times every day that I am a super person and better than all the rest.'

'Ha! Sir, that sounds like a Tina Turner song.'

187

'Yeah, exactly. "Simply the Best". I sing it in my head or whistle the chorus quietly. That helps me persist. Currently, I think about how I love my job and my delight to be wearing this blue UN peacekeeping beret. By being simply the best, my work can save many lives here in Lebanon. That's my focus.' Gilmore places his blue beret on his head with the white UN badge carefully positioned above his left eye. He glances at the empty plates, then at Rocky, then points to his Seiko sports watch. 'Time to make a move.'

.

Chapter 20

Notre Dame du Liban

A few minutes later, Gilmore and Rockingham are driving northwards, in their Land Rover, on the picturesque Beirut-Jounieh highway. Gilmore explains, 'Rocky, before we leave Beirut, I have to do a quick visit to the suburbs of Jounieh and Harissa in the north of the city. My French boss was up there last week visiting a place he described as Notre-Dame du Liban. At UN headquarters, part of my job is to assess religious tension all over the country. The Maronite Christians have a large community in Jounieh and are protected by an ardent, determined group called the Lebanese Forces. My boss says that it's a beautiful part of the city suburbs but not always completely safe. We must do a quick drive around and keep our eyes open. If time allows, we can have a glass of chai with the locals. I want to get a feel for the security environment. I want us to observe if people can practise their various religious faiths without intimidation.'

'Wow, great. This is really interesting, sir.'

'Yes, so now, young Rockingham, you get to experience being an assistant UN information officer. We gather intelligence so that the UN in New York can make reliable decisions to maximise the calm in the region.'

'Okay, sir, so we are visiting the famous statue of Our Lady of Lebanon. I have seen pictures of it.'

As they drive northwards, the war damage and number of destroyed buildings decreases. Very quickly, they find themselves in a neighbourhood that appears to be affluent and thriving. Rocky notices the increasingly impressive stone-faced apartments and houses. 'Jeez, sir, this is the bleedin' Killiney of Beirut. Nothing like the dilapidation we have in Dublin's inner city, that's for sure. I cannot believe I am in Lebanon. This is more like the south of France. Look, sir, a lot of the local signs are actually in French.'

'Yeah, this is Zouk Mikael. Looks beautiful and tranquil. But they have had their own tragedies here as well. See that church coming up. It was bombed. Two large explosive devices were placed under the alter and were triggered by a timing device set for when people were receiving Holy Communion. Ten people waiting at the alter rails were blown to pieces and the entire congregation was injured, many severely. Sixty taken to hospital, many with limbs missing. Totally innocent lives destroyed.'

'Oh my God. It's so beautiful and calm here today. It's hard to realise. What an outrage. Terrible. I can now understand how vitally important your job is.'

They continue driving until Gilmore decides to park the Land Rover in a heavily policed car park near the coast.

'Okay, Rocky, time for some information gathering. We are heading now to the shrine. It's up in the mountains in Harissa. From here at the coast, we face a climb of nearly two thousand feet, but the good news is that there is a cable car with gondolas so we will not have to work up a sweat. I will talk to the Lebanese police to ensure our vehicle is not interfered with.'

Minutes later, they are in a smoothly ascending gondola, skimming through trees and past the top of high-rise buildings. The sound of the Mediterranean Sea and din of the coastal highway traffic quickly fades to an emerging total stillness. A white blur in the distance becomes more prominent until they gradually realise that they are approaching the famous statue. The sea behind them is a spectacular azure blue, and the sun is now radiating agreeable morning heat. In less than ten minutes, they reach the summit. The distant seascape, with Beirut and Jounieh in the foreground, is awe-inspiring. In front of them is the fifteen-ton bronze statue of Our Lady of Lebanon perched on top of a stone, spiral-shaped house of worship. There is just a sprinkling of pilgrims to be seen at the shrine. The plateau is so serene that it is the heartening sound of chirping birds and the fragrance of wildflowers that captures their attention. They both fall silent, enjoying the view and the contemplative solace inspired by the magnificence of the entire setting.

Gilmore immediately becomes totally absorbed in taking notes. Rocky seizes the opportunity to independently explore alone. He is immediately moved by the unique peacefulness, finding it hard to perceive that they are still in a tragic war zone. His thoughtful wandering eventually takes him into the small stone church beneath the massive statue. Rocky enters the beautiful building and finds himself alone. Spiritually inspired, he decides to make a wish and takes the opportunity to pray.

'Notre-Dame du Liban, while I am young, I want to give music a go. Please do not allow my father or the army to interfere in any way. Also, I want my brother Lizzy and our Chinese friends, Ping and Lilly, to be part of the band. One last thing is that I want to meet Adeline again somehow. That's my wish at this beautiful shrine. I promise that I will come back here as a rock superstar. I will do another gig in Beirut and raise money for the war-injured people of Lebanon. I know my desire might come about in a roundabout, even strange way.' Mother Mary, "Let it Be".' Rocky sits back while he quietly, in his mind, sings the John Lennon and Paul McCartney song.

He is about to stand up to leave the church when a tall, grey-bearded man, dressed in priestly vestments, greets him with a warm handshake and whispers in his ear, 'Welcome, young UN peacekeeper.' He glances down at Rocky's shoulder flash. 'Ah! From Ireland… a superb peacekeeping nation. Are you a pilgrim?'

Rocky is slightly unnerved by this unexpected question and shies away from a direct answer. 'Well, Father, yes, it's such an inspirational place that I feel… well, I hope and pray for some big changes in my life.'

They both continue to whisper in deference to the sanctity of the shrine.

'Well, change frightens everybody. Are you a little bit worried?'

'I suppose sometimes I am, Father.'

'Well, just remember, young soldier, that change is all about belief in yourself. Plant, within yourself, beautiful, inspirational success feelings to be enjoyed immediately and every day. Flood your mind with happy thoughts of your dream fulfilled. Create a success chant or song inside your head and repeat it often. Power up that song with a colourful mental film of your achievement. Watch as your self-belief massively grows. Ask, believe, receive. Things begin to happen. This is a form of prayer which is beyond any limit known to man. You, soldier… yes, you, my humble young Irish peacekeeper, now have massive spiritual power inside your own head.'

With his right hand, he performs a "sign of the crucifix blessing" over Rocky's head.

'Wow! Thank you, Father.'

'God bless you and thank you for visiting Notre-Dame du Liban.'

The priest is suddenly gone, leaving an elevated Rocky with gems of wisdom to digest. He grabs a pen to immediately write down the profound, life-changing advice provided by this elderly venerable priest. He reads and rereads his notes before leaving the little stone church with an excited smile on his face.

'What has just happened?' he asks himself.

Gilmore is sitting close by, now enjoying the morning sunshine. 'Hey, Rocky, I hope you said a prayer for me. This is one marvellous place. It's also my first time here.'

'Yeah, I'm really glad you included me. What an experience. You have done a lot for me today. Together with The Blue Note gig, I think that these have been the best few days of my entire tour of duty.'

'Perfect, Rocky. You are suddenly very upbeat.'

'Okay, I will tell you. Something amazing happened a few minutes ago. I was about to leave the church and then, out of the blue, this very old, tall priest comes up to me and whispers a welcome into my ear. We spoke for just about a minute, but he left me with some fantastic advice.'

'Yeah? This is beginning to sound like serendipity.

'Serendipity?'

'It's the art of finding nice things or experiences that you have not been looking for. It tends to flow to people who feel supported, loved and happy with their mission in life. Suddenly a flow of meaningful lucky coincidences occurs. Rocky, you seem to have had that experience this week in Beirut. Tell me more about the priest.'

'You are right sir. The priest advised me to constantly flood my mind with intense thoughts and feelings of success. In my head, I must include a success song, like what you spoke about, and a victory film. I must keep repeating them constantly.'

'Yep, I hope your first single is called "Serendipity". You know everything in life depends on a man's attitude towards himself. Sow the seeds of success through your own decisive inner talk and imagination. Then watch for serendipity.'

Rocky falls silent for a few seconds. 'Because I am constantly thinking about music, I keep being attracted towards the career I love.'

'Yep, no doubt. Don't be scared. Your uniqueness puts you in a different boat to most other people. In a crisis, countries can train thousands of people to become soldiers and officers in a matter of weeks. But to train just one person to be "Rocky the entertainer" you would need to have a professional coach every day for a dozen years. You had the devoted attention of your Spanish mother. Pure talent will allow you to move ahead on your own merit. In the business world, they would describe you as "highly differentiated". You are authentic, original and as scarce as gold. Show business is risky, but there is nobody I know who is more capable of beating the odds. Being a soldier is about sameness, marching in step, wearing identical uniforms, not standing out. In fact, it is about *not* being unique. We do not want independent-thinking private soldiers or eccentric, oddball officers. Show business is the very opposite because creativity is vital to success as a band.'

'No wonder I'm so confused and torn apart. My mam and dad had totally opposite views of life. I had an exciting, highly creative mother and a dad who is a rigid military system man.'

'Yeah, you are right. I bet it was not your father who showed you how to dance.'

'Haaaaa! Are you out of your mind? Dad, dance?'

'Rocky, I should mention that the dancing was exceptional during the show last night. Adeline hinted that it was you who arranged all the choreography.'

'Yes, it's true, sir. We spent hours getting the rhythm and foot co-ordination right.'

'I think you have been keeping your dancing skill a secret.'

'I will dance up here in Beirut where I feel uninhibited. Last night, there was nobody from the battalion present to hate me or resent my dancing. I want to be accepted as a macho professional soldier by the lads. Survival means that it's important that I hide my creativity. If I dance back in the Irish battalion, I will be ripped apart.'

'Ha! Yeah, in Ireland, you dare not be flamboyant. The sad thing, of course, is that we never get to see people's full, uninhibited depth of talent. They are afraid.'

'Well, sir, the best has yet to come once I get my band back on the road. We will probably travel a lot around Europe and China where we will feel free to be different.'

'Yeah, emigrate for creative freedom. Anyway, China. That's exciting. Very few Irish bands have done that. But then you are an eclectic Irish-Chinese band. Just one hit record in China and you will be millionaires overnight. I love the band name, Eclectic RRK. With the Chinese girls playing such an important role, that name sums it up.'

'My brother Lizzy is already able to sing quite a few songs in Chinese with the two girls. He is a sponge for knowledge.'

Gilmore glances at his wrist. 'Oh, Seiko says time to move.'

Minutes later, as they descend in a gondola, Rocky breaks into a broad grin. 'Sir, look who is coming up. It's the United Nations *Litani* magazine photographer and his reporter. Do you mind if I have some fun? I want to flood the atmosphere with some positive thoughts.'

Gilmore grins and shrugs his shoulders. With a beaming smile, Rocky screams comically at the group in the ascending gondola, 'The cover of the *Litani* magazine. *Yeeees! I wanna do more!* Dr. Hook, rock 'n' roll! I want to be on the cover of the *Rolling Stone.*'

They shout back, 'You will be, Rocky! Yeah, for sure. Fantastic performance last night. I want your autograph for my kids before you become famous.'

Gilmore takes in a deep breath, feeling almost that he is privileged to be in the company of such an unstoppable force. *I'm the senior officer, but this lad has the greatness. Seems that he has already begun to take the priest's advice, instinctively flooding his mind with thoughts and images of success.*

Minutes later, they dismount from the gondola right beside the car park. Rocky takes his position in the signaller's seat, in the back of the FFR Land Rover. Gilmore jumps into the driver's cabin. Flak jackets and blue helmets are immediately adopted as the appropriate safety attire. It's time to get moving in the direction of South Lebanon. Rocky, as signaller, professionally establishes communications on the two nets with radio checks on the forty-six set and Motorola.

As they leave the car park of Notre-Dame du Liban, neither Gilmore nor Rockingham have any idea as to how close they are to massive, life-changing events, for both of them.

Chapter 21

An Rod seo Reoibh
The Road Ahead of Us

Traffic on the Beirut coastal highway is unusually light, and Gilmore is delighted to be able to rapidly move through the, often volatile, southern suburbs.

'Hello, Mike Papa Beirut, this is UNIFIL 3892, we are making steady progress south. Send SITREP, over.'

'UNIFIL 3892, this is Mike Papa Beirut. Leb army report steadily moving traffic on the coastal highway. No security threats to report. Weather conditions still good as far south as Sidon. Mike Papa Tyre reports arrival of weather front and you should expect tricky road conditions once you come close to the Litani River crossing.'

'UNIFIL 3892, thank you. Out.'

Rocky, competing with the radio traffic and engine noise, shouts forward to Gilmore in the driver's seat, 'Hey, you heard that, sir. We should have good weather until we get close to the Litani River crossing.'

There is no reply from Gilmore. Rocky stares through the holes in the steel radio mounting and notes that the officer appears to be deep in thought. He relaxes in the back of the jeep, stretching his right leg out over the open vehicle tailboard. On dangerous journeys, Land Rover tailboards are always kept open to prevent vehicle occupants from being trapped if they come under fire. Rocky tries to ignore the pounding headache he is experiencing which he blames on the exhaust fumes. He closes his eyes and imagines himself with Adeline, lying on the white sands of Nissi Beach in Cyprus. *Hmm, yeah… I've got to flood my mind with positive thoughts!*

He will be going home to Ireland, for good, soon, so he must quickly find an excuse to meet her again. She was the highlight of the entire tour of duty. He wonders how he always seems to be attracted to foreign girls. The dark, tanned skin is certainly a plus as well as those big, brown eyes.

What a girl. I will dream about her every night until I see her again. I know we will both find a way to get back together. Nothing can stop us. I wonder if the lads back in the battalion will notice the love bite on my neck. The feckin' commandant noticed it, and I am sure he didn't believe my little white lie. His thoughts recede into those beautiful moments with Adeline backstage at The Blue Note.

Suddenly, there is a problem. He sits up in alarm as the vehicle brakes are being slammed on. He is thrown forward, impacting the forty-six-set radio with his right shoulder. Gilmore roars with ferocious anger… the maddening scream of a frightened man. '*Get out, Rockingham!* Debus! The bastards!'

Rocky understands the "debus" order. He must jump out of the back of the moving Land Rover and take cover in the nearest ditch. Suddenly, the vehicle is accelerating and swerving violently. Rocky has one foot on the tailboard, but it is not enough to steady him. A sudden violent acceleration forces him uncontrollably out of the back of the vehicle. His head and shoulder simultaneously hit the road. As he skids along the road surface he feels the skin on his knees and hands becoming severely torn. Then he violently rolls into a grass roadside margin before losing consciousness.

As Rocky comes to, he has no knowledge as to how long he has spent on the grass roadside margin. He is dizzy, wet and relying on blurred vision. He spots his blue helmet in the middle of the road a few metres away from him. His shoulder and head are painful but not bad enough to prevent him from climbing to his feet. His olive-green UN slacks are soaked in blood and shredded. He feels liquid on his face and realises it is his own blood. He begins to walk and notices an eerie silence. He is puzzled as to why there is no traffic moving on this normally busy road. He wonders where Commandant Gilmore has gone, seemingly abandoning him. He cannot see the Land Rover. He stumbles forward, despite the bleeding and pain, hoping to find it around the next bend. After fifteen minutes of agonising progress, he sees a cluster of people in the distance and there is a blue emergency light. *Could be an ambulance, and it seems like it might be just a few hundred meters away. Jeeeez, that must be the jeep. I hope the commandant is okay.*

Soon, he is close enough to pick up a conversation that seems to be coming from the direction of the blue flashing light. Sounds like a Lebanese army ambulance crew talking in Arabic and then in broken English. He catches a snippet of their radio conversation.

'The leg is definitely broken. Ribcage crushed. Possibly bleeding into his lungs.'

Rocky feels a gentle, warm rain on his forehead. As he limps towards the blue light, he can gradually see the number plate of UNIFIL 3892. The Lebanese medics do not notice him approaching, so involved are they in attending to their patient. As Rocky gets closer, he can see that the Land Rover door is both badly buckled and crushed into the driver's cabin.

'We need to get this door open. It's impossible to attend to the patient. We need a crowbar or wedge.'

The ambulance crew start shouting at the onlookers in Arabic, appealing for help. Rocky is still dazed with limited vision. But at least he is on his feet. He rubs more fresh blood from his forehead to stop it running into his eyes. He looks at the indent on the front top side of his blue helmet. *Wow, it definitely saved me.*

With his vision gradually improving, he can see that the Land Rover is damaged all along the driver's side. Gilmore is still sitting in the driver's seat, possibly trapped. He slowly walks up to the vehicle and stares through the driver's side window. A semi-conscious Gilmore still has his hands in the ten-to-two position rigidly clutching the steering wheel. Fortunately, he is breathing and seems to be muttering something. Rocky realises that the driver's cabin has partly collapsed. He can see a broken bone protruding through the skin below Gilmore's left knee. He begins to realise the gravity of what has occurred. He manages to drag the driver's window open and tries to speak to Gilmore.

'Okay, sir, you will be okay. It's me, Gunner Rockingham. They've gone to get a crowbar to prise open the door. Try talking… just whisper if you can. We will have you free in a jiffy.'

Gilmore, hearing Rocky's voice, momentarily moves and mumbles something incomprehensible. He takes his hand off the steering wheel and beckons towards Rocky to come closer. Then Rocky picks up a whispered sentence. 'They zapped me… zapped my eyes. I'm sorry, Rocky. Are you okay?'

'I'm okay, sir, you will be fine too. Somebody used a laser to attack us… is it?'

Gilmore momentarily manages a weak nod before drifting into unconsciousness again. A Lebanese paramedic now climbs through the rear Land Rover cabin and over the radio mountings. He starts attending to Gilmore from inside the front of the vehicle. Then there is the sound of the bark of the forty-six set in the back of the vehicle. Rocky is suddenly energised by the sound of the radio. He knows he can contribute to their rescue. He stumbles to the back of the vehicle and grabs the handset to find that it is totally undamaged. He presses the transmit switch and it is working perfectly. He has been drilled hundreds of times on UN road traffic accident – RTA – voice procedure. He instinctively presses the handset switch and opens a transmission.

'Hello, Zero, this is UNIFIL 3892. Medevac, medevac, medevac. I need a medevac. Romeo Tango Alpha – two UN personnel injured. Urgently need Rainbow with full medical team to come to my location. Over.'

'UNIFIL 3892, this is Zero. Wilco. Send immediately your present location. Over.'

In the total confusion, Rocky has lost the map. He has no idea where he is. Suddenly, he remembers that just before the accident, he had sent a grid reference location to call sign Zero.

'Zero, this is UNIFIL 3892. Map missing due to accident. We are approx. 1km south of last location sent. Over.'

'Roger, this is Zero. I have that. Out to you.'

UN operations control room immediately contacts call sign Rainbow One, the UN Italian medical evacuation helicopter flight crew on duty.

'Hello, Rainbow One, did you pick up that last communication? Over.'

'Zero, this is Rainbow One. We got it. Leb army medical team have also been onto us with exact co-ordinates. We are already in the air and departing zero location now.'

However, UN operations control, nickname Seagull, immediately intervenes on the net and issues a warning. 'Rainbow One, this is Zero. Seagull speaking. From SUNRAY UNIFIL. I Repeat, SUNRAY UNIFIL. Warning! I say again. Warning! 155mm artillery shelling of a wide area to the north of Tyre city imminent. Coastal area unsafe and already in groundhog. Danger area extends to the Litani River Bridge. Rainbow One – this is a direction, I repeat, a direction. Fly at least 4km offshore over the Mediterranean until you are north of the Litani River estuary. Confirm, over.'

'Rainbow One. Roger, 4km offshore confirmed. Wilco, out.'

This is not good news. The term "groundhog" means that the situation is so dangerous that all UN personnel have been evacuated into underground shelters. Villagers have been warned to stay indoors. However, the Lebanese army have confirmed that the accident happened 6km north of the groundhog zone, so the rescue can continue.

Meanwhile, the Lebanese army medical team, with the help of some hefty Arab truck drivers, manage to force open the driver's door of the Land Rover and they remove the still semi-conscious Gilmore from the wreckage. The medical team surround him and prepare him for medevac. Rocky remains sore, bloodied but surprisingly very alert. Now the rain and dark clouds are leading to reduced visibility. Rocky is worried about the whereabouts of the helicopter.

'UNIFIL 3892, this is Rainbow One, now ten minutes from your location. Ask Leb army medical team if they have a flare. Urgent, please reconnoitre for a safe landing site.'

Rocky responds, 'Wilco, will get back to you in figures three.' Rocky immediately recognises that the road offers the best landing site. He calls on an Arab driver who he hears speaking English and asks him if he can get some of the vehicles to back up. He needs to create plenty of room for the helicopter landing. The accident has blocked all the traffic so the area of road past the accident is almost totally clear. He looks for overhead cables which might destroy the helicopter blades, but there are none. He then approaches the Lebanese army paramedics and asks if they have a flare to signal the chopper. A red flare is produced from the back of the Lebanese ambulance.

Rocky rushes back to the forty-six set radio. 'Rainbow One, this is UNIFIL 3892. Land on road south of the accident site. Zero overhead cables. Watch for red flare and blue flashing ambulance beacon.'

'Roger, we are approaching from the sea. Echo Tango Alpha two minutes. Out.'

A few seconds later, Rocky hears the welcome flapping sound of distant helicopter rotary blades. He leaves the radio and goes to the landing site, immediately igniting the bright red emergency flare. Contact. The helicopter hovers over the accident site. The side door is opened. A crewman leans out, conducting his own visual examination to verify the safety of the landing site. The helicopter touches down and two UN paramedics immediately run to the stricken Land Rover. Notes are quickly exchanged, and within seconds, Gilmore is being transferred on a stretcher to the helicopter. An Italian paramedical sergeant approaches Rocky. He shouts because of the noise of the helicopter. 'Soldier, you are covered in blood. You are hurt. You are our second patient, right?'

'Sergeant, I am fine. I was thrown clear from the back of the Land Rover and my UN helmet saved me. I am just a bit groggy.'

'Right, come with me. You probably have concussion and could have some fractures or dislocations. You are wet from the rain and blood. Get into the helicopter immediately. Are you fit to walk?'

'Sergeant, I am fine. I must stay here to look after the vehicle and forty-six set. I cannot just abandon the military equipment.'

The Italian medical sergeant is having none of it and loudly bawls out a determined response. 'Now, I am the medical sergeant.' He aggressively points at his rank markings. 'I am in charge. You are my patient. I am not interested in heroics. Let's go. You are holding up the medevac. Just get into the helicopter immediately. Understood? That's an order.'

'Yes, Sergeant.'

Rocky knows when not to argue with a superior. Besides, he is already losing the accident adrenaline rush and is beginning to feel severe head pain and drowsiness. A minute later, the helicopter is in the air and heading out to sea. The two casualties immediately receive attention as the dusk descends. Rocky barely knows what is going on and begins to fade in and out of consciousness. It's twenty minutes back to the UN hospital. At a point midway through the journey, Rocky opens his eyes. He can see the flash of artillery rounds exploding on the distant hills. He can see multiple streams of heavy machine gun tracer. *The fighting must be really bad, but we are safe out here over the sea.*

Rocky feels no fear until the chopper banks suddenly and steeply. There is a massive flash of sheet lightening in front of them. Despite his condition, he knows that they are now in immediate danger. He prays that these are not the last moments of his life. The storm intensifies. The pilot for some reason takes the helicopter further out to sea. Finally, the unmistakable white huts of UN headquarters in Naqoura become visible along the coast in the far distance.

The helicopter then hovers, but the pilot makes no move towards the UN hospital helipad. Rocky is disoriented but is sure he sees smoke and some flames near the hospital huts. It seems that there are more exchanges on the radio. The pilot and medical team engage in constant chatter using their speakers and headphones. Rocky has no headset, so he has no idea what is going on. He closes his eyes, resigning himself to the fact that things are totally outside of his control. He slowly drifts again into unconsciousness.

A sudden thud startles Rocky. *Oh, no! What has happened?*

The helicopter has landed, and the doors slide open. He immediately feels himself being lifted. The hospital medical teams swarm around the two patients. Rocky is placed in a wheelchair. He can see Gilmore ahead of him on a wheeled stretcher. Despite his barely conscious state, Rocky knows that they have not landed in Lebanon. As he is being wheeled into the accident and emergency room, he sees an overhead sign in Hebrew script and then its translation into roman script "Ram Bam". Rocky immediately surmises that the intensity of the artillery and heavy machine gun exchanges forced them to overfly the UN headquarters. It looks like they have travelled 20km further south into Israel. Rocky knows straight away that this is the famous Ram Bam hospital in Haifa. Despite his injuries, his spirits are raised as he knows that they are now in the most advanced war casualty hospital in the world. The primitive, backwards world of South Lebanon seems light years away. He begins to feel that his face and head are very swollen as his pain intensifies.

As he enters A&E, Rocky finds himself surrounded by a medical team. 'Risk of fractured skull. Possible brain injury,' he hears an elderly nurse say. 'Don't worry, soldier, it sounds worse than it is. We are going to test you for everything. It's routine. Your head has a few nasty bumps. Your vital signs are good.'

That is all Rocky remembers as he fades into a coma. Time passes, and when he regains his senses, his body is clean. He is wearing a white hospital gown and is surrounded by complex dials and machines. He realises that he must now be in intensive care. There is a nurse sitting on a stool directly in front of his face, monitoring his every essential life sign on an array of complex machines. She smiles as she adjusts a life support machine setting.

'You have been out of it for a few days. The team of consultants will be here soon. You are doing very well, and I think we will be able to move you out of intensive care. You are heavily bruised, a few dislocations, concussion, but all your organs are functioning. You had a little brain swelling but we controlled it and there is no permanent damage. You are a lucky man. You will make a one hundred per cent recovery.'

'Can I see myself in a mirror?'

'Yeah, here, look.'

Rocky is shocked by the amount of purple bruising as well as swelling all over his head and face. He closes his eyes and thinks about how he had no pain after the accident at all. He remembers guiding in the helicopter and wanting to continue working. He did not realise the extent of his injuries.

'Okay, Rockingham, I am going to give you a little pad which you can squeeze if you need to control any pain. You should never be in pain because we believe in managing it.'

Rocky is moved out of intensive care a short time later but continues to be wired up to a variety of tubes and machines. The team of consultants visit him, and they are encouraging and upbeat.

'In the next few hours, you will see us gradually removing machines as we see more positive test results. I hope to release you, all going well, in about a week.'

Rocky continues to drift in and out of sleep. Suddenly, he hears a ringing sound coming from the side of his bed. *Oh wow. I even have a phone. This is an amazing hospital.*

He looks at it for a minute. How can he get to it without his tubes and wires becoming tangled or disconnected? He extends his left arm and manages to stretch his fingers to pick up the receiver.

'Hello. This is Gunner Rockingham of Irishbatt UNIFIL here.'

'Hi, Rocky, guess who this is.'

'Oh my God, Lizzy. It's just great to hear from you. You might have heard that I was in a little bust-up. But all is well. I am pulling through and getting out of hospital in about a week.'

'We know, we heard about the accident. We were really worried about you, so I took a few days off the Ranger course to be with Dad. He is out of his mind with worry. They would not allow calls through to you up to this minute.'

'Yeah, that is understandable. I was wired up to machines in intensive care. I was just totally zonked… you know… out of it a lot of the time. It's great to get your call. How did you hear about the accident? I am surprised the news travelled all the way to Dublin so fast. You know, the truth is that I was not going to tell you about it until I was released from hospital.'

'Rocky, the accident was five days ago. Dad rang five times yesterday and twice this morning, but we were told you were getting treatment. He has gone to the pub now for a pint. He is very upset that he could not talk to you. You know, it's all over the newspapers here. I am proud of you to have pulled through. He lost it totally when he heard about Paul Gilmore being in the accident as well. I never saw him so upset in my entire life.'

'Yeah, the commandant got a worse hammering than me. I was thrown clear out of the back of the vehicle.'

'Rocky, you probably heard that they brought Gilmore home yesterday on the government jet.'

'Wow, that's great.'

'The funeral is in Arbour Hill Church here on Friday.'

'Oh! Wha…'

'Rocky, it's sad that Commandant Gilmore didn't make it.'

'Make what?'

'He passed away shortly after arriving in the hospital in Israel. Surely you must know. I am so sorry, bro. I thought… did they not tell you?'

'Ahhh! No! Lizzy, I never knew… this is terrible! I cannot believe it. Jeez, I am totally devastated. I must hang up. I am not feeling well. Ahhh!'

A nurse comes running into the ward. She has heard Rocky's screech and immediately realises what has happened. 'Oh no! You were not supposed to get any phone calls until tomorrow.' Rocky is uncontrollable with grief. The nurse holds his hand and hugs him. 'I am so sorry. The Irish priest has been trying to get here to break the news to you. But the border is still closed due to the intense shelling. Nobody can safely move in the UN area. Sorry… I am so sorry that you have lost your comrade.'

Chapter 22

A Visit to the Shrink

It's almost a month since Rocky's repatriation from Lebanon on medical grounds. It's 8.45am and he peeks out the window of his bedroom in Ormond Square. He hears the gentle hoot of a horn. Parked outside the house is an olive-green Land Rover with the engine running and a uniformed driver behind the wheel. *Bang on time. That looks like Stevie. Jaysus, no, he is so funny. But I am not in the mood for his usual jokes.*

Rocky gulps down the remains of his cup of tea, grabs his keys and pulls the door behind him. Behind the wheel is a much-cherished comrade and experienced senior soldier, Stevie Dawson. They have not met for more than seven months. Stevie jumps out of the car and embraces Rocky in an extended hug.

'Heeeeeyyyy, Rocky, jeez you look feckin' great. Suntanned, healthy. The lads back in the regiment are really worried about you. I was scared that I might be picking up a broken man this morning. But you have not changed a bit. Okay, are you able to hop into the Land Rover or do you need help?'

Rocky slowly climbs into the passenger seat. Stevie notes that the usual beaming smile is missing, with Rocky wearing a somewhat serious, distant expression. He then sits up straight in the passenger seat and forces a smile. 'Stevie, it's great to see you. All is well. I have a few bruises here and there, but I am great. I am even back doing a bit of walking. As soon as I get the all-clear and I'm off the medicine, I am going to drink a gallon of porter with you guys. I am looking forward to a TGIF session and catching up on all of the developments in McKee canteen.'

'Great! Okay, Rocky, the sergeant major says I must bring you to Eccles Street this morning, beside the Mater Private Hospital. I have a sealed envelope for you as well as your LA30 Red Medical Record Book. There is no escaping from the army paperwork. The sergeant major said to tell you that everything must be recorded. Apparently, some consultant is going to meet you. The doctor's name and office number will be in the sealed envelope. Okay, let's go.' Stevie slaps the car into gear, and they are immediately on the move. Rocky suddenly feels slight tension as he hears the familiar sound of the vehicle engine. He realises that this is his first trip in a Land Rover since the day of the accident.

Stevie doesn't notice Rocky's unease and is bubbling away, full of energetic jackeen jokes and small talk. He is one of the regiment's most popular soldiers. 'Ya should have heard the sergeant major this morning… "Now, driver, be there for 0845 hours… *sharp*." Nag! Nag! You know how the major loves to be so feckin' precise. Kissing the adjutant's arse. Anyway, the regiment is the way you like it, Rocky. Very on the ball. I'm sure you know that your brother Lizzy is back with us full-time and he is a great guy. He really enjoyed the Ranger course but, amazingly, they did not keep him. He was a little bit upset about being sent off the course, but we are delighted to have him back anyway. We are short of troops and there's no sign of any new recruits being accepted.' Stevie pauses as they stop at traffic lights. He looks across at Rocky. Then he says quietly, 'Everybody is talking about you, Rocky. They are all worried. So many crazy stories circulating. But you are popular. The lads in the regiment will all be glad to have you back… fit and well of course.'

While they are crawling through the very heavy morning traffic, Rocky opens the envelope and finds a letter of introduction which he must hand in to the office of a Doctor Denis Gibb, Psychiatrist. He is disquieted by the need to visit, what the gunners in the regiment would call, a "shrink". He is worried that the lads back in the barracks might find out. He decides to gently probe Stevie to see if his forthcoming treatment, for possible trauma, is common knowledge.

'Stevie, have you ever been down this way before?'

'Yeah, yeah, Rocky, many times. The guy you are meeting this morning is the "shrink". Ha! Ha!'

Rocky's heart skips a beat. The story of his treatment is out and the lads in the regiment will think he cracked up overseas. What a disgrace. Even the neighbours in Ormond Square might find out that he is mentally ill. This is terrible.

'I know exactly where to drop you. A lot of lads are sent down here after trips to Leb.'

'Were you ever inside, what is it like?'

Stevie is unable to resist a jackeen joke opportunity. 'Oh! Yeah, I went in just once and then I ran back out the door. Oh my God, the place did my head in.'

'What?'

213

'The screaming got to me.'

'Screaming?'

'Oh yeah, the roaring and screaming was terrible. There were all lined up for their shocks.'

'Injections?'

'No shocks with a K. They were all getting their electric shocks. 9.30am every morning.'

'Jaysus, what time is it now?'

'Don't worry, I will have you there on time. The patients are all tied up to stop them running out on the street half naked and screaming at passers-by.'

'Tied up? Naked?'

'They will put you into a straitjacket before the shocks.'

There is a momentary total silence in the car. A minute later, Stevie looks at Rocky's face and they both burst out laughing.

'Ha! Ha! Stevie, you thought you had me there. Ha! Ha! Feck you! I saw that film *One Flew Over the Cuckoo's Nest* too. I am not that bad.'

'I had to get you into good humour somehow. Let's be serious now for a minute...'

'Serious... Stevie, you... not possible. I nearly believed you for a second.'

'Okay, the joke is over. Just listen. You know better than anybody that Leb is becoming a tough mission mentally. Listen, there is no stigma attached to this anymore. No stigma about becoming mentally healthy again. It is vital to get a check-up to be sure you do not have post-traumatic stress disorder. It's called PTSD, Rocky and can be a killer. I am now serious. I have even dropped officers down here.'

Rocky loses his smile and hangs his head slightly. He had wanted his treatment to be kept totally confidential. Stevie notices his distress.

'Rocky, the doc is an ex-army man and he will have you sorted out in pissin' time. Relax, me auld *segotia*.' Stevie uses comforting Dublin slang to indicate to Rocky the warm closeness of their friendship. 'I was picked for the driving detail this morning because the sergeant major knows that I am your friend. Rocky, nobody, I mean nobody, back in the barracks knows what treatment you're getting, and I certainly am not going to tell anybody.' In typical Dublin drawl, Stevie continues with another soft tease and laugh. 'Well, I'll tell nobody until I have a few pints on board. Then I might spill the beans. Ha!'

Rocky, in untypical fashion, now fails to laugh. He is still not well enough to enjoy the usual jackeen banter.

'Ha! Ha! Relax, Rocky, I'm joking again of course.'

Rocky sucks in a deep breath. Now he is becoming increasingly tense as they get closer to the "shrink's" office.

'Okay, we are here.'

In his desire for a few minutes' solitude before the medical appointment, Rocky quickly scrambles out the passenger door as soon as the Land Rover halts. He genuinely fears that the army might send him for treatment to a mental hospital. 'Stevie, no need for you to stay around. You know, I really don't know why they have sent me here. There is nothing wrong with me. I am going for a walk around the shops after my appointment so I can make my own way back home. I am not in any pain and there is no point you being stuck here for hours waiting for me.'

Stevie reads Rocky's "escape" signal and the "I cannot cope with your company. I want to be alone" message. He immediately realises that imposing help or pressurising Rocky in any way is the wrong tack. 'Great stuff, Rocky. I know that there is feck-all wrong with you. You look great. See you soon.' He waves and pulls into a line of traffic. He notices that Rocky turns away from him without saying thanks or goodbye. *He is not himself.*

In the slow traffic, Stevie gradually drifts into deep thought. He admires Rocky and hopes that this morning's banter lifted his mood, even a little. But for other reasons, Stevie is angry. A sick story has somehow quietly circulated among gunners in the regiment. The whisper is that Rocky and Paul Gilmore were in a relationship. The story is gathering momentum. The source appears to be credible: an overheard, loud banter between two lieutenants, travelling in a transit van full of privates. A deliberate act without doubt. Stevie wonders how the traumatised Rocky will cope with this additional scandal. Stevie wonders as to why officers would want to achieve the total destruction of the life of this low-ranking, nineteen-year-old soldier. He guesses that somebody senior needs to discredit Rocky. Stevie has seen this pattern in the army with increasing frequency of late. Perhaps there is a bigger story about the accident waiting to unfold. Perhaps something happened in the officers' mess VIP bar and they might be keen to drive Rocky out, in case it becomes common knowledge. Stevie can now only hope that the sexual speculation melts away by the time Rocky is well enough to join the usual TGIF drinks. If the smear causes Rocky to be ostracised by his friends, Stevie fears that it could have the potential for disastrous consequences.

He is a soft guy behind it all. These bastards are playing with fire.

Meanwhile, Doctor Denis Gibb is preparing for his schedule of appointments. He first has a meeting with a distinguished visitor from the United States. 'Hey, Henry, I am so delighted that we are at last getting to work together on this research project. How was your flight from Logan International?'

'Oh, I took Aer Lingus. The service was magnificent. It was like a magic carpet. Thank you for arranging business class for me. A real treat.'

Doctor Denis Gibb has been collaborating, long distance, for over a year with his US counterpart, Henry Stein, on the many issues relating to trauma. Soon, they will be ready to publish their first joint paper on the subject.

'I am going to send you up to Woodstock Café for an amazing Irish breakfast while I meet my only patient this morning. We can then meet up at 10am for an exchange of our latest research findings. It's great that you are here, Henry, because in America you guys are decades ahead of us on PTSD identification and treatment. I am meeting a soldier in a few minutes so let me pick your brain.'

'Yeah, PTSD, what do you want to know? It's a killer. The death rate is very significant. I have said this to you many times before. Ireland is lucky, Denis. You are fortunate to be behind us because your military role internationally is mostly in peacekeeping situations. For us, it's totally different. We have a massive problem. Young American soldiers are usually in an aggressive role. Sent into harm's way by the rich psychopaths who dominate our country. Now, more US army combat veterans are dying from suicide, after coming home, than we have all-cause deaths in the battlefield. How repatriated young men feel about themselves and the world in general cannot be overstated. Isolation, mental torture, terror, guilt, helplessness. PTSD plays total havoc with their lives. We are seeing self-blame, violence, destroyed relationships, lack of trust, hyper vigilance, destructive actions, extreme fits of anger and rage. Then there is bizarre risk-taking and flashbacks. We frequently find ex-soldiers with a total inability to function in any workplace or in society in general. In some cases, repatriated PTSD victims so much lack trust that they withdraw, seeking total social isolation.'

'But, Henry, you now have various treatments and many soldiers do recover. I understand we are going to look at your finding on this later today.'

'Yeah, what I will be discussing with you later is the need to get to the victim of trauma early. Let's refresh our minds. For a PTSD diagnosis, we are currently saying that symptoms must have manifested themselves for a full four weeks. After that period has elapsed, the sooner the patient gets help, the better. If no treatment is sought, the symptoms can go on for years. The message to the troops must be clear.' He gives the table in front of him an emphatic thump. 'PTSD will not resolve on its own. The words "cracking up" must be eliminated from the military vocabulary and banned as a source of derision. Soldiers must be encouraged not to be ashamed and to seek treatment early. Untreated after twelve months, the symptoms can get worse.'

'But I am a bit unclear on this, Henry. With treatment, is the prognosis good? Are you and I going to be talking about a cure this afternoon?'

Henry shrugs his shoulders. 'What we currently achieve with treatment is the building of post-traumatic resilience and growth. We are not yet able to claim that the victim will totally achieve a return to their old personality. However, they do grow in new areas and come out of the treatment with new strengths.'

'Okay, so it's a challenging situation for both doctor and patient.'

'It is very important to emphasise that the victim must be encouraged to eliminate any feeling of self-blame if they are to heal.'

'Henry, this morning I am meeting a soldier who was involved in a bad traffic accident in Lebanon. Can traffic accident victims fall into the PTSD diagnosis category?'

'Of course, soldiers are not the only ones who can fall victim to trauma. For example, emergency workers or law enforcement personnel witnessing traumatic events are often forgotten about. Transport crash victims, natural disaster victims, people who experience street violence or violent sexual assault are just a few examples of people who can end up with PTSD. Any traumatic event which overwhelms an individual with a feeling of helplessness and hopelessness can leave a person emotionally shattered.'

'Yeah, in the case of assault, accidents or natural disaster, we patch the person up physically while often forgetting about the need to tackle the mental damage. We must keep delivering the message that, in the long-term, PTSD can be a lethal health issue.'

'Henry, thanks for that quick refresher. I will see you in an hour. I must get to my patient.'

Rocky has been with the psychiatrist's nursing assistant for about thirty minutes and has been completing a few questionnaires. Much to his relief, the nurse is good humoured and there is no sign of straitjackets. After a short break for ice-cool water, he is brought to see the doctor.

'Okay, I see that you are Gunner Rockingham from McKee Barracks. I need a less formal name to call you. Paul is your first name, but what do the lads in the canteen call you? I am sure you must have a nickname.'

'Doctor, everybody calls me Rocky, even my father.'

'Great, well it's Rocky then for me as well. Is that okay? I was a peacekeeping lieutenant in Lebanon myself a few years back, so I know it's a tough place. Okay, let's run through this in relaxed fashion. I expect to spend about an hour with you and have all of our business completed fairly quickly.'

Rocky is relieved. He keeps reminding himself that his presence in front of a shrink should be nothing to be ashamed of. It is just a routine day for the doctor, and he probably has seen hundreds of similar people like him before.

Doctor Gibb starts ticking boxes on the page in front of him. 'Yes, I see, like many of us who have been to Leb, you still have a few upsetting memories. That's very normal. Occasional flashbacks with feelings of distress... hmmm, okay... a normal response to abnormal events. Here at home, you often feel detached from conversations, disinterested and sort of mentally numb. This is a very common response and normal. I see here that you have occasional trouble sleeping and have had a few bad nightmares. Also, you mention that there have been outbursts of anger towards your brother and dad. You say that you sometimes act jumpy, and you are constantly on the lookout for any form of trouble or loud noise. Good news is that you have no feelings of self-blame for any incident in Lebanon and, very importantly, you have great plans and are very optimistic. Your accident vehicle was a Land Rover, and you mention here that you were slightly nervous travelling in a similar vehicle this morning. But you see yourself moving on from the stressful events and feel that you will be willing to travel in a Land Rover again. That's just great. All these symptoms we want to see gradually declining in occurrence. You will be coming back to me regularly and we have a few simple treatment strategies to speed up your recovery.'

'Doctor, there is no danger that I am going to be sent to a mental hospital?'

'Absolutely not. That is out of the question. You have mild, normal stress which I will treat in my day clinic. Mostly, we will use a lifestyle approach which you must dedicate yourself to implementing.' He pauses. 'I have not asked you about your physical condition. Any unhealed wounds, and how is your mobility since the accident?'

'Everything is almost back to normal. I had a lot of bruising and a few dislocations but not a single bone-break. All of my stitches are now out, and I am thinking of starting back in the gym fairly soon.'

'Well, that is good news because your instincts are telling you the exact right thing to do. It is now very important to get your body moving once the physical doctors have given you the green light. As soon as you can, we need you to engage in rhythmic physical exercise. Walking is fine, swimming, jogging, dancing – get up to a full thirty minutes of rhythmic movement as soon as possible, every day. What physical exercise does is release what are known as endorphins which make you feel great. It significantly reduces your stress levels.'

'Yeah, sir, I can do that from today.'

'Now, you have written down here that music is a hobby. Do you feel really good about any type of music?'

'I am a musician and singer-songwriter, sir. I had a band which I will try to reform now that I am home. We play a lot of Fleetwood Mac, Thin Lizzy and Gary Moore music. I had a Spanish mother, and I am a fan of Latino music like Santana. I can dance as well.'

Doctor Gibb smiles. 'The perfect patient. We are on a winner here, Rocky. Listening and dancing to music that is uplifting, for you, is a potentially very effective means of getting rid of stress. Sights, sounds, even smells, have the potentiality to transport your mind either positively or negatively. So, Rocky, the music and dance you love can positively and beneficially stimulate your recovery from the traumatic events in Lebanon. Also, playing your musical instrument requires a concentration on rhythm which absorbs your thoughts positively. Singing, similarly, is strongly recommended because it is so uplifting.'

Rocky's eyes are wide open with surprise. 'Wow, Doctor, a winning strategy, right! You are advising me to get back to all the things I adore. This rehabilitation will actually be perfect for me.'

'I think you have enough there to get you started immediately on the right road. Do meet your friends as well. Only people who are supportive and on your side. Avoid negative or critical people as they can seriously set you back. Alcohol and recreational drugs are totally out for now. Eight hours' sleep is important, nine hours even better. But do get up reasonably early and get cracking on your various projects. When I meet you this day next week, we can review your progress and decide if any advanced therapy is necessary. I am very happy with your overall condition. You have some typical traffic accident stress, but that is very normal and common. We have the same all the time with accidents here in Ireland. With the right approach, your symptoms will fade away gradually or even very quickly. If you feel that you need to come back sooner, call us and we will see you immediately without appointment. Now, get stuck into exercise and music and I will see you this time next week.'

'Thank you, Doctor. I have just one question. Is it okay if I have just, say, two pints on a night out?'

'Rocky, the strict medical answer is *no*. Alcohol is a depressant and not good for your condition. However, I do want to hear that you are back socialising, laughing and enjoying the company of your best friends. I stress again, only your positive friends and supportive family members. If you do take a drink, make it one which is alcohol-free. For now, alcohol is out! I really would like to see your rehabilitation kick in first. Let's schedule some appointments over the next month. My medical assistant will do a mutually agreeable schedule.'

Rocky's departure from the consultant's office sees him in a mood of relief and optimism. But, as he bangs the door behind him, there is an unpleasant surprise waiting for him immediately outside in the street 'Oh Jaysus. No! No! Feck, not this total bastard!'

Chapter 23

The Flashback and Shocking Discovery

Rocky's mind is engulfed with panicked thoughts. He awkwardly turns his back to the street, almost falling over on the consultant's doorstep. He scratches on the solid Georgian door like a distressed puppy. He wants to scramble back into the consultant's waiting room, hoping that he can hide there for a few minutes. But the door is now locked. Then he hears an unwanted shout and greeting. 'Hey, Rocky, remember me. Pete Kirwan from Mike Papa Beirut. I met you with Paul Gilmore.'

Rocky looks around with dismay. He tries to smile and gather his thoughts, resolving to make the best of this situation. 'Oh, hello, Corporal.'

'Hey, forget the corporal stuff, it's Pete... some people call me Peatie.' He shakes Rocky's hand. 'Sad about Paul, your very close friend. What a pity. There was real chemistry there. A big loss. So, how was the "shrink" this morning? I always say that it is sad when lads crack up. Mental illness is a terrible thing. No stigma anymore. I keep telling that to my friends. Have no fears, I will not tell the lads in McKee. Anyway, heading into a function there tonight. It's a birthday party for some gunner in the regiment. One of your friends. Did you not get an invite? That's unusual, don't you think? I suppose not. There are so many stories circulating about you and Paul Gilmore.'

'I am not sure what you are talking about, but I am not really ready for parties yet. Are you getting treatment here as well, Corporal?'

'Me? God no. I am totally sane. I just happened to be on patrol in the area and I spotted your Land Rover about an hour ago. I was just curious. As MPs, we like to know everything.'

'You hung around, actually, for more than a full hour, Corporal. Phew! That is an amazing level of curiosity. Who is that across the road with the camera? He seems to be taking a lot of photos… including of us and the consultant's office.'

'Oh, just a plain clothes MP colleague. He is waiting for me and is just bored, I suspect. New telephoto lens. We are trying it out today. It's the beginning of the surveillance society. A changed Defence Forces. Instead of defending the people, we are going to be spying on them. Privacy is soon to become a thing of the past. Everything now is about our politicians obtaining kompromat.'

'Kompromat? I have no idea what you are talking about.'

'Compromising material. Handy for a wee bit of extortion or blackmail. We are starting to gather information on, literally, everybody. It's how our politicians are going to keep control. It's how I found you here at the shrink this morning.'

'Oh! That is a big change for Ireland.'

'Anyway, Rocky, it's amazing to meet you, our much-admired UN entertainer. What a man! Hey, you love weird David Bowie music… I'm sure.'

'Yeah, he is brilliant.'

'What a coincidence because I just bought this album in Phibsborough Shopping Centre. Ha! Ha! Look.' He shows Rocky the cover of the album "Aladdin Sane". 'And now I am meeting you outside the shrink's office. How crazy is that?'

Rocky immediately knows that this is not a chance meeting. Somebody must have leaked the time and date of his appointment with the shrink. Could it be that he is being stalked by Kirwan? Rocky is beginning to form the opinion that Kirwan, for some reason, is on an agenda of soft intimidation and of painting him as being mentally ill. But Rocky is also curious and perhaps this is an opportunity to get an answer to a question that has been bothering him.

'Corporal, one quick business question. Please forgive me, but I am wondering why I was never interviewed about the crash.'

'Oh, it was an open-and-shut case. Gilmore was way over on the wrong side of the road and had a lot of booze on board. You guys must have been drinking all morning. A nice jolly, romantic and boozy picnic in the beautiful north Beirut suburbs.' Kirwan then laughs and imitates the playing of an air-violin. 'I heard that you were even hugging him in a bar in Mingie Street, Naqoura. We are doing you a favour by keeping everything quiet. The decision was made that there was no need to bother a man with PTSD. Your evidence would not be credible.'

'The doctor tells me that I have very normal post-accident stress. Like somebody who was in a traffic accident here in Ireland. I have no PTSD diagnosis. We had no alcohol on the day of the accident, so you are not doing me a favour. I have nothing to hide. Also, to correct you, Gilmore was as sober as a judge.'

Kirwan betrays a sense of agitation as he frowns and glares into Rocky's eyes. 'The case is closed, okay. We are not further investigating it. That is lucky for you. I really mean that. We do not want to open a can of worms now, do we?' Rocky stays silent and calm, causing Kirwan to become more emphatic. 'For your own good, Rockingham, be careful. It was an accident. Everybody is happy to let it go. Get it? An accident. Understood? Right?'

Rocky shrugs his shoulders and raises his palm in a half wave.

'Corporal Kirwan, I must go.'

As Rocky starts to walk away, Kirwan immediately changes his tone and tries to act comradely. They walk rapidly towards the city centre side by side.

'Yeah, let's meet up for a pint some night. I know that you live in Ormond Square.'

'How do you know that?'

'I have just rented a nice apartment near you, over Mary Byrne's fish and chip shop in Capel Street. A funny lady who knows everything about the entire neighbourhood. I am sure we will bump into each other often. By the way, I have an uncle who is very influential in the music industry. I told him about you. Would you like to meet him?'

'We have our own network, thanks anyway.'

'Please think about my offer because you and Lizzy are too musically talented to stay in the army. I know you love the regiment but, after this scandal, life will never be the same again for you in McKee.'

Rocky steps off the pavement as he braves the fast-

moving traffic to cross the insanely busy Dorset Street.
'Goodbye, Corporal.'

Rocky's mind is racing as he walks towards the city centre. After about four hundred metres, he feels too stressed to continue. He enters the deserted small park garden at Mountjoy Square, finds a wooden bench and sits alone.

They are afraid that Gilmore confided in me. But he didn't really tell me much. Now they are after me. Stalking me. Turning my friends against me with sexual smear. Then trying to set me up with fake admirers like that little Kirwan shit. This must be what they constantly put Paul Gilmore through. These are the psychopathic tendencies that he warned me to look out for.

He closes his eyes and grips the park bench seat tightly. Then he is overcome by a vivid flashback. Suddenly, he is back in Lebanon, visualising intensively the events, seconds before the medevac helicopter takes off. Everything again feels so real as he is transported back in time. *Vivid colour. Hands covered in bright red blood. Flapping of the deafening helicopter blades. The smell – aviation fuel. Gilmore's bloodied body being carried. The crushed Land Rover… looking inside. Wow, it's Gilmore's notebook. Wet. Covered in blood. Quick, quick. No time. Snatch the notebook. I have it. Dripping. Pain, head and neck.* Then Rocky again feels the realistic sensation of being hauled, by the Italian medical sergeant, onto the chopper seconds before it takes off.

Rocky takes in a deep breath and opens his eyes. Fortunately, there is nobody in Mountjoy Square Park who might have noticed his distress. Head and shoulders now move in a darting fashion as he looks around in every direction. Is he being followed… watched? Where are Corporal Kirwan and the photographer? All seems clear. He feels the welcome chill of an Irish breeze and is immediately relieved by the realisation that he is on peaceful home soil.

That bastard Kirwan caused this flashback. Why should he want to destabilise my recovery? He wanted to make me feel ashamed of my friendship with Commandant Gilmore. It's soft intimidation and criminal sexual harassment. I am just not ready for this. That sick corporal is a non-entity, moronically following orders, perhaps. He might be a Trojan Horse so I will never trust him as a friend. Gilmore gave me great advice. The more they, suddenly, want to be my friend, the less I should trust them. Immediate red card.

The flashback is a serious source of worry for Rocky. While alone at home in Ormond Square the previous week, he faced an event which was even more gruesome. While unpacking his UN kit, he made a grim discovery. There was a heavily blood-stained item right in the bottom of his big blue UN kit box.

Rocky is deep in thought about the incident as he walks from Mountjoy Square home. He recalls his state of shock. 'Mother of Jeez, what the f… is this? How the hell did this get here? It belongs to Gilmore.'

Rocky ran to the kitchen and violently threw up his entire breakfast. He went into an immediate state of turmoil, began crying and grabbed a stepladder. Despite his pain, he climbed with panicked aggression into the attic, a part of the home directly accessed only through his and his brother's bedroom.

I could get in serious trouble for being found in possession of Gilmore's confidential UN notebook. I can hide it in my big timber kit box and lock it away. Dad or Lizzy never come up here.

He remembers trying, using the light of a torch, to quickly flick through the pages. However, many were congealed with dark, dried blood. He quickly concluded that each page would have to be separated very carefully, one by one. There was a vast amount of handwritten material to read. From the pages that were not blood-stained, he soon discerned that Gilmore was an avid and detailed diarist. For a full year, each entry seemed to have been carefully dated by the officer. Written on the cover, through the thick, dark blood, he could make out the words: "Contemporaneous Notes".

Could it be that Gilmore might have been trying to protect himself by creating a detailed trail of personally handwritten evidence? From crime novels, Rocky knows that keeping contemporaneous notes is often portrayed as being invaluable from a legal perspective.

Rocky sucks in a deep breath.

When I am mentally better, I am sure that this diary will help me understand everything. Was Paul Gilmore in possession of some dark political secret? Then again, perhaps he was just the tragic victim of an accident?

Rocky cannot forget Gilmore's last whisper, which was a definitive statement that their vehicle had been attacked – "they zapped my eyes". Was Gilmore telling the truth? He certainly had jealous, politically powerful and dangerous enemies who wanted him destroyed. Then there is the possibility of suicide. Perhaps Gilmore had a desire to avoid the magnified family distress associated with self-destruction. Rocky is unsure how much pressure Gilmore was under.

It is entirely possible that some bastards just drove Gilmore to suicide. Perhaps the information I gave him about the two culchies in the McKee bar was the last straw. He seemed really upset when he heard that ordinary soldiers like me were being turned against him by means of a malicious political style smear campaign. I should have kept my big mouth shut. I told him too much. I seriously upset him.

Rocky is nearly home and tries to discontinue his psychologically dangerous rumination. *For my recovery, the shrink says that I must not entertain any thoughts of self-blame. I am not to blame. I hope.*

Rocky is certain that he is not yet mentally strong enough to delve into the dead man's privacy. Perhaps, morally, the correct thing to do, and the safest option, is to destroy the document. *Nobody knows of its existence, except me. I will just burn it and go on to live my life like before. Focus on my music and recovery. It's not my fight. Gilmore is gone. Let sleeping dogs lie.*

Rocky wishes that he had a credible adviser with which to share his burden. His trust in Piper Jim has totally evaporated and Lizzy is too innocent to cope with such enormity. If Maria was alive, she would support him. *I have nobody.*

Chapter 24

Big Change at Dino's Bar and Grill

It's the Halloween long weekend and Saturday burgers and beer is the normal order of the day for the brothers. Rocky has found an alcohol-free lager which he likes. He is determined to stick to his recovery regime. They head for Dino's Bar and Grill in Phibsborough where Ping and Lilly are employed. They are assured of special attention and a nice private table.

'So, what's all this about you working on the Monday of the bank holiday, Lizzy?'

'Yeah, I didn't tell you yet. It's a big deal for me and I want you to help me.'

'Lizzy, I am not going into the barracks while I am excused duties. The operations room would have me on explosives escorts at the drop of a hat if they spotted me. I am not ready for that yet and I have my medical certification to prove it.'

Lizzy can see that this might be a tough evening. He has become familiar with many sudden difficult mood swings from Rocky but is gradually learning to cope. He wants, so much, to have the ever-smiling, singing and dancing Rocky back. He has not yet been to a war zone or ever been involved in any type of accident. However, he can see the damage it has done to his brother's morale. If brotherly support can alleviate anguish, then he has the cure. He smiles and gently teases. 'Hey, big bro, UN veteran, you are not going to get sensitive on me now – are ya? Come on. Okay, I'll tell you the story. You know that I did not complete the Ranger course.'

'No. You never told me that. I had to hear it from Stevie.'

'Rocky, it was not important in the light of your far more serious events. I did mean to tell you, at the right time. Anyway, I have some good news on that front. I think the Army Ranger Wing might be thinking about taking me back. I got a phone call yesterday and it seems like they might have an exercise coming up. It was strange. I was sitting at home and the phone rang and at the other end I heard a voice saying… "Agent contact, agent contact".'

'I have no idea what you are talking about, Lizzy.'

'Okay, let me explain. In wartime, special forces often infiltrate behind enemy lines and meet up with friendly resistance soldiers or civilians. So, when the phone rang, I said… "Who is this? It must be a mistake – I am gone. You guys failed me on the ranger selection course."

The voice then said to me that this was my second chance to impress – yes or no? I said, "Yeah, of course, I really want to be a ranger.".'

Rocky, no longer self-absorbed, listens with intense interest and curiosity. 'You said yes, but to who?'

'It sounded like the Rangers' sergeant major using a sort of disguised foreign accent.'

'Well, this sounds like total feckin' bullshit to me.'

Lizzy beckons Rocky to come closer to him and he begins to whisper, 'Rocky, stop being so hard on me. Just listen for a minute. Whoever it was then told me my exercise mission was to be at the polo grounds in Phoenix Park at 0800 on bank holiday Monday. Seems like there will be two small rock climber's rucksacks hidden there. My mission is to find them and deliver them to two city-centre locations. I will get another call telling me where to go. I might only have to walk 3 or 4km. Will you help me? We will be in civilian clothes. It should be good craic. We can take a rucksack each. Then I will buy you breakfast afterwards.'

Rocky responds, also in a whisper, 'A call from a total stranger. I know zilch about special forces, but this is unusual. Did they call just before *Match of the Day* on Saturday night?'

'Yeah, Rocky, just like our gig booking arrangement, I get all of my agent contact phone calls at around 10pm.'

'What do you mean all? Have you had more of these calls? How long has this weird situation being going on for?'

'For a few weeks during the course, but this is the first time since I left the Wing.' Lizzy is basking in excitement and enjoying the experience edge he has, at last, gained over his brother. Rocky has no ranger training. A momentary opportunity for Lizzy to gently engage in a little bravado. 'Rocky, you would not understand. This is typical special forces modus operandi. You can receive calls anytime of the day or night.'

'But you are gone from the Ranger Wing now. Why would they continue to call you?'

'Rocky, my thinking is that I must have done okay on the course after all. I am hoping that they might have reconsidered my suitability. They are bringing me back for an exercise. I was the youngest student on the course. I think they are testing my maturity.'

'Yeah, Lizzy, you know much more about special forces than I do. You are better off not to listen to me. You know, trauma victims like me tend to withdraw into themselves and lack trust. That is where I am at now. I trust nothing or nobody except myself. You have seen that I am still jumpy and watching out everywhere for possible trouble. I am not a good one to give advice now. Look, you will make a super ranger. Sounds like an easy exercise.'

Rocky knows how much this ranger training means to Lizzy. All the letters that Lizzy had sent him to Lebanon were full of descriptions of his action-packed life in the Curragh camp. Tales of jumping out of helicopters, climbing high buildings and then repelling off them, mountain climbing, scuba-diving, bad weather navigation and twenty-mile forced mountain marches through night-time blinding snow. Rocky was delighted that his brother had managed to land this fantastic opportunity so young.

The food arrives and the brothers fall silent as they demolish their favourite monster-sized burgers. The early tension of the evening is easing. What Rocky has not told Lizzy before now is that he has made the big decision. He has deliberately taken charge of his inner self-talk, as advised by that old priest at Notre-Dame du Liban. Every day, he feels that his musical goal is already fulfilled. He imagines Eclectic RRK playing on a big, open-air stage in College Green, Dublin surrounded by thousands of adoring fans. He is constantly affirming his greatness. He reminds himself about the massive power which is inside his head and which no force known to man can diminish.

'Lizzy, what about the band? In my head, we are already

jammin' and doing gigs. The shrink advised me to get back to my music straight away.'

Lizzy smiles widely, delighted to see the first signs of the re-emergence of the familiar dynamic Rocky.

'Sounds great. The girls are dying for us to get going again. It's just that there are so many distractions and diversions. First, there is your health. Second, a possible corporals course for you has been mentioned, not to mention Dad's idea of a cadetship.'

'He has never mentioned a corporals course or cadetship even once since I came home. For some reason, those ideas are dead. I am sure of that.'

'Well, Rocky, for me it's the Rangers and United Nations peacekeeping. But, yeah, of course there is massive musical opportunity. Let's plan a few spare-time gigs at weekends.

Rocky replies with a steady voice and total conviction. 'Lizzy, I am quitting the army. Taking a final bow, exiting stage left, really sorry to part... but it's adios and no tears.'

'Does Dad know this?'

'Yes, I have dropped big hints. Lizzy, in my head, my future has already begun. I totally believe in myself. Wiser people than me have said that "time and tide wait for no man".'

'When is all of this going to happen?'

'This week. In fact, I am not going back. I will buy myself out immediately.'

'What? That soon? Are you sure you know what you are doing?' An unnerved Lizzy is not ready for such a sudden change. He is worried about how all of this might alter his own plans. Nobody he has ever met is as exciting a person to be with as the pre-Lebanon Rocky. High vibration, laughter, dynamism. An authentic person. Brotherly support around the clock. Lizzy is sure that his own decision will seriously set back Rocky's plans. He is staying in the army. He has a great chance of becoming a peacekeeper. Alternatively, he will grab the opportunity of more special forces training. Lizzy loves the comradeship and physicality of his life as a soldier.

'Well then, Rocky, I am out of the band. I am not ready to leave with you. Not until my own Lebanon trip is over. You need to realise that you will be starting off Eclectic RRK without me. In one year or two, I might then join you. Can you not wait so we can both leave together?'

Lizzy finds an excuse to give Rocky silent time to think about this proposal. He stands up and looks towards the toilets. 'Hey, Rocky, it's your round, bro – get that jug filled with beer. It's closing time so the girls will join us. Please stick to that non-alcoholic drink for yourself. I need to make a visit to the loo. Back in a minute.'

Rocky maintains a serious, disappointed look but is not at all dismayed. Had Lizzy decided to leave the army with him, he would have advised against it. Rocky heads up to the bar counter and calls Lilly and Ping.

'Hey, girls, are you ready for the craic? Let's get the jukebox turned up.'

The restaurant is closing so it's a good time for antics. Rocky crouches forward and stays with the girls at the bar counter. He then places his hands over his eyes as if distressed and crying. Lizzy returns and is immediately alarmed.

'Hey, Rocky, are you okay? Girls, is he alright? What has just happened? Rocky, don't be disappointed with me. I will join the band in a year or so…'

Rocky begins to stutter and cry into his hands… 'Ch… ch… ch—'

'Come on, big bro, spit it out. Be calm. Everything is fine.'

Rocky again simulates a stuttering impulse. 'Ch… ch… ch…'

'Are you having a panic attack?'

Rocky swings around to face Lizzy. He adopts an angry face and puts his nose right up against Lizzy's nose. A perturbed Lizzy does not notice that the girls have their hands to their faces, stifling laughter. 'Lizzy, you got to face the future, man!'

'Are you having a breakdown, Rocky? Hey, bro, just keep calm. The whole restaurant is looking at us.'

The jukebox strikes up with the David Bowie song "Changes". To the amazement of Lizzy, the two Chinese girls and Rocky wrap their arms around him and join in the singing.

'I have been had! I'll thump you, Rocky.' Lizzy joins the laughter, putting his brother into a gentle stranglehold. "Changes" is now the new musical chant inwardly driving Rocky's feelings of success.

'Lizzy, I already feel "Hunky Dory".'

Eclectic RRK unite, facing each other in an inspirational circle, singing the entire famous Bowie tribute to change.

'Now, Lizzy, some news we have been keeping from you is that the girls will work full-time with me as soon as we get the bookings flowing again. You must get your United Nations medal. Then, next year, you will be joining a world-class, fully established Eclectic RRK.'

Lizzy is relieved and delighted with the proposal and hugs each of his fellow band members. 'Congratulations, girls, great news. There is no wallowing in the past for you, Rocky. You are still as electrifying for everybody as ever. A feckin' world-class pacesetter! I am so proud of all of you. There's loads of work out there.'

It's closing time in Phibsborough and, true to his

customary romantic form, Lizzy heads to a late-night disco with Lilly and Ping. Rocky must follow doctor's orders and get a full night's sleep while avoiding the temptation of alcohol. He decides to head home to Ormond Square.

'Rocky, before we leave, what about the exercise in Phoenix Park? They said I should have a second person. I dare not arrive alone.'

'It's going to cost you a massive breakfast, bro. It's on bank holiday Monday so tomorrow evening we can finalise the timings. Of course, I will help you.'

Chapter 25

Agent Contact!

Rocky gets home and finds a note from his dad saying that he is visiting his brother in Galway and will not be back until the last train on bank holiday Monday night. Rocky gives a thankful sigh of relief, glad to have the house to himself. He puts on the kettle to make a pot of tea and then notices a copy of the *Irish Independent* newspaper on the dining table.

Typical of Dad of course, the sports supplement is missing. Reading material for the train journey, no doubt. He is so predictable. Never reads current affairs yet is constantly kissing political arse. He is one totally fecked up old man.

Rocky slugs his tea while flicking through the main news pages and spots a large advert with a Dublin map. It's from Dublin City Council.

HALLOWEEN WEEKEND – MONDAY – DUBLIN CITY MARATHON
Dublin city centre from St Stephens Green to Parnell Street will be totally closed to all vehicular traffic from 8am until 3pm on Halloween bank holiday Monday. This restriction is to facilitate the running of the Dublin City Marathon. You are strongly advised not to bring a vehicle into the city and to use public transport. Over twenty thousand runners from forty-seven different countries are expected to participate so your kind co-operation will greatly be appreciated.

Oh great, it's marathon weekend. Should be worth a visit to O'Connell Street on Monday to cheer the runners. Perhaps Lizzy will come as well. We can do his silly job first and then watch part of the race. Twenty thousand runners – massive! Lots of wintergreen smells. Lizzy will surely be excited.

Next morning, as Rocky heads for Sunday Mass, Lizzy has not arrived home. Now increasingly religious, Rocky rarely passes a church without visiting for a few moments of intense meditation. The neighbourhood gossip about his mental state is somewhat magnified by these frequent visits which are seen to consist of mumbled prayers and, always, the lighting of candles.

Rocky today decides to make a return visit and worship at Maria's favourite, the Pro Cathedral in Marlborough Street. Here he can be soothed by the choir music like in the good old days. This is what the shrink has ordered. He will enjoy singing along.

At the Pro Cathedral, he quickly finds his usual favourite pew, kneels and tries saying a few prayers. But he realises that for some reason he is uneasy and tense. His mind flashes from negative memories to bad-tempered exchanges from his past. *Why am I suddenly feeling intense anger? Not good enough. I've got to get back into feelings of success. I have to flood my mind with joy.*

He tries totally blanking his mind and concentrating on the beautiful smell of flowers and incense which fill the cathedral. But his restlessness continues. The pew is, for once, uncomfortable. Now comes a dreadful feeling of foreboding. Midway through Mass, Rocky slips out the side door, feeling queasy. As he walks towards home, he is puzzled.

I cannot cope at all this morning. What the hell? No booze and I was feeling great last night. Now, my mind is dominated by an awful fear of impending doom. Maybe I have PTSD after all. I will have to get a special appointment with the shrink on Tuesday.

As he is walking through O'Connell Street, he notices that crowd control barriers have already been set up for the next day's marathon race. Back in Ormond Square, his condition does not improve as he tries relaxing while lying on the living room sofa. He pulls the curtains to keep out the light and spends hours drifting in and out of sleep. Finally, he is awake and mentally sharp.

The marathon! That's what it is. He clenches his fist as something clicks. He remembers the conversation he overheard when he was hiding in the barman's bolthole in the McKee VIP bar. He is sure there was a mention of the marathon weekend. *I cannot remember what was said but I remember that I did not like it.*

Suddenly, Rocky has total recall of the conversation he heard many months previously. *Got it! Now, where the heck is Lizzy when I really need him most?*

For one hour, he paces up and down the kitchen in a near-panicked state. Finally, the hall phone rings at around 6pm. 'Hey, Lizzy, where are you?'

Lizzy instantly notices a troubled and hurried, aggressive tone in his brother's voice. 'I am staying here in a bed and breakfast on North Circular Road beside Phoenix Park. I have a bed for you as well. You have not forgotten our agent contact exercise. I am afraid I might sleep it out and all the roads around the city centre will be closed for the marathon tomorrow. I want the two of us to be as near to Phoenix Park as possible.'

'Lizzy, I am on my way. Do nothing. Do you hear me? Nothing. Right?'

'Yeah, yeah, I am just watching TV. Relaxing.'

'I'm in a dark depression, not feeling well, bro.'

'Okay, Rocky, I have got us a very nice room and I have coffee and biscuits as well.'

'Yeah, fine.'

Rocky decides to walk, heading uphill through Stoneybatter and onto North Circular Road. After twenty minutes, he spots the bed and breakfast sign. Lizzy is waiting for him at the main door, ready to exchange pleasantries, but Rocky is brusque. 'Let's go to your room. Now! Who knows that you are here?' Rocky, untypically, rudely snaps his fingers as he hurriedly brushes past Lizzy.

'Nobody knows I am here except you and the Rangers, of course. What's going on? Is there something wrong with you, Rocky? You look really tired.'

'Forget that for now, Lizzy. There is nothing wrong with me. Okay? I'm here because I am seriously worried about your agent contact exercise. Please put my mind at ease. Do you really know exactly what you are doing? Have you received any further instructions?'

Lizzy laughs. 'Yeah, no problem. I got a real friendly call here at the B&B about three hours ago. It was that same strange foreign voice. It's an easy test for us. The two small rucksacks are currently hidden in a tree. It is the second tree to the east of the polo grounds spectator stand in Phoenix Park. I will have to climb up about twelve feet to find them. Cushy! I will drop them down to you. A lot of the leaves have already fallen so it will not be a difficult test. I am sure the Ranger Wing want me back and are being nice to me. So, we must pick up the rucksacks at exactly 9am tomorrow morning. We are to walk slowly to the city centre and drop the bags at the pillars of the General Post Office in O'Connell Street between 9.45am and 10am. We have no further task and can go home after that. Seems I will meet no agent and they will monitor my performance covertly. I must wear ordinary civilian clothes as well as a black-and-blue Athlone Town FC hat and scarf. I have a set for you as well.'

'Hold on now a second, Lizzy. Who told you to come here? How did somebody know to call you here?'

'Yeah, yeah, that's part of the exercise. They were very precise. I had to come here to wait for my final instructions.'

'And you registered at reception, did you? In your own name?'

'Yeah, of course I did, Rocky. What would you expect?'

'Lizzy, seriously, have you any idea whatsoever of the identity of the person who called you?'

'Bro, it's the same voice who set up my earlier agent contact exercises in Crossmaglen, in Northern Ireland. He used to call me at home, usually at exactly 10pm on Saturday nights.'

'What? Hold on a minute, Lizzy, you were in South Armagh? Holy Jeez! Did the Rangers send you there on a training exercise? That area was recently referred to as the "Murder Triangle".'

Lizzy shrugs his shoulders, feeling elevated by his brother's exasperation. 'Well, it was the same voice that called me for all of those agent contact exercises. I am sure now it is him who gave me all my instructions. I was sent to Crossmaglen three times, and it never worked out. I think that is why I was sacked from the course. I went there by bus, and I was supposed to meet a friendly agent outside a shop in the village. He never showed up and I was questioned twice by the British army and once by the Royal Ulster Constabulary. Despite everything, it was an exciting experience.'

'This is unbelievable. Are you sure the Rangers sent you? Did somebody from the Rangers personally brief you?'

'No, it was all Saturday night phone calls, in fact... and the mission always had to be performed... yeah... on a Sunday... the next day.' Lizzy's mood was gradually transforming. He was beginning to feel more than a little unnerved by his brother's probing questions. 'Rocky, what do you know that you are not telling me?'

'Lizzy, you are the special forces guy, not me. There is one phrase I need you to explain to me. Have you ever heard of the expression "false flag"? I need to know what it means. Did you learn anything about it on your Ranger course?'

'Yeah, it's when a government or political party carries out an illegal act to frame an innocent group or individual. The Americans do it a lot, or so they told us on the course. The Russians also. For example, political agents arrange for the blowing up of a high-profile building, killing a lot of people. Then the media are persuaded that it was the act of a dissident group. Total propaganda. Then public opinion is encouraged by complicit media to demand retaliation and arrests. The government gets what it desires. That is, to pass oppressive legislation and take, normally unacceptable, harsh military action against opponents. It's a nasty tactic. Innocent people must be killed by their own government. It's horrible! Horrible!'

'Right, that is what I thought. It's the final piece of the jigsaw.'

Rocky now forcefully and aggressively whispers, close to Lizzy's face, 'Did it ever occur to you that it might be extremely important to fully understand the nature of the job you are about to perform for a mysterious voice?'

'Wha—'

'Lizzy, I am not trying to mess up your career. What I am asking you to consider is this. Could somebody be using you as a "patsy"? Perhaps you are planting a real device in O'Connell Street.'

'Hey, bro, come on. That is very far-fetched.'

'Well, Lizzy, I hope it is. But tell me something. Are we going to look inside those rucksacks?'

Lizzy starts nervously laughing. 'Dad is right. You are reading too many novels. Conspiracy bullshit.'

Rocky grinds his teeth and raises his whisper to a level where he is spitting out his words. 'Shut up, Lizzy. *Shut up!* I want to know if you are going to verify exactly what the hell is inside the two rucksacks. It's a simple question.'

'I was clearly and emphatically told that there was a totally sealed private parcel inside the rucksacks which must be delivered unopened. My orders are very clear. You and I are soldiers who obey superiors' orders. So, no, Rocky, I will not be opening the rucksacks.'

'A telephone voice is not a superior. Now, listen. I broadly hinted to you many times that Gilmore was being targeted for some reason. I also told you about that weird conversation I overheard as a barman. There is some kind of power struggle going on. I believe that one or more patsies might be used somewhere in Ireland for false flag operations. That operation might be an attack on the marathon and could be planned for tomorrow. I have been frantic with worry about you, bro, taking instructions from a totally unknown person. Let's look at your situation and mine. I think the possibility exists that you are being set up because you are my brother. Now, I am being set up as well. Because of my friendship with Gilmore, they might think that I know more than I do. Also, a lot of people know that we are close and that you and I discuss everything. Somebody might see you as a threat as well.'

'Come on, Rocky, this is more than a bit far-fetched. Cut the drama. We are all tired of these conspiracy theories. You were in an accident. All the newspapers said it was an accident. You are totally over the top now. It's stress. Remember, you are back in peaceful little Dublin.'

'Okay, well here are a few facts that you should explain to me. Fact! An unknown voice sent you to the Murder Triangle. Fact! You have no indication that it was the Army Rangers that sent you to Crossmaglen. Fact! It would be totally illegal for the Irish army to hold exercises north of the border. Fact! You have not got the foggiest idea what you are doing here today or why.' Rocky pauses to allow his brother to absorb what has been said. Then he forcefully continues. 'Lizzy, here is a scenario I want you to think about. You, a tall, young, coloured soldier is sent to Crossmaglen wearing a conspicuous soccer, Athlone Town FC, blue-and-black hat and scarf. There is no football match on. You hang around and are questioned by the security forces. You had no good reason to go to the Murder Triangle. Your name probably immediately went south to the army and Gardaí and you became listed as a suspicious person. You are easy to identify as there are not too many young, coloured people wearing Athlone hats and scarves anywhere in Ireland. Athlone Town never play in Crossmaglen. I am guessing that the Rangers dumped you when they heard you were a possible security risk. I am not going with you tomorrow. You will be the patsy who will plant a rucksack device to do damage as the marathon passes the GPO at 10am. Think of what the media will say. Links with Northern Ireland dissidents. A disgruntled, failed special forces soldier. Anger about racism. The perfect patsy profile.'

There is silence in the room.

'Now! Lizzy, what do you think of that? You are not laughing at me now.'

Lizzy is expressionless. Could Rocky have been mentally changed so much as to turn him into a total fantasist? His theory is outlandish and totally bizarre.

'Oh, Jaysus, Rocky, I am so sad for you and your state of mind. Is your mental health okay? I know you are suffering from trauma, but you never made up crazy feckin' stories like this before. This is ridiculous. How the hell could you know this information? This is Ireland; things like this don't happen here. Do they? Do they? There has never been a false flag operation in Ireland.'

Lizzy pauses and is visibly perplexed and bewildered. He lies backwards on the bed and stares at the roof. There is a long silence while he takes time to think about the logic of his brother's theory. When he eventually continues the conversation, he adopts a rather melancholy intonation. 'You know, Rocky, I was doing really well on the Ranger course, and everybody liked me until, suddenly, I was dumped.' Lizzy timidly reveals his disappointment at being thrown off the course.

'You know, the other trainee Rangers never even said goodbye to me. I was top of the class, mister popularity on Monday and then dismissed on Tuesday. Shouted at and told to pack my bags. No reason provided. I was given only fifteen minutes to be out of the Ranger complex.'

'I'm sorry it was like that.'

'Yeah. I am sure I was in Crossmaglen the Sunday before I was dumped off the course. There might be something in what you are saying, but why pick me to become a patsy?' After a pause, Lizzy looks suspiciously at Rocky but continues to talk slowly and quietly. 'I am worried now about how you seem to know about all of this. Did Gilmore tell you more that I should know about? Are you involved in something that is going to get the whole family in trouble?'

'Lizzy, all I can tell you is that I have pieces of an unfinished jigsaw puzzle. Gilmore told me that his career had been blighted by smear and character assassination. People wanted him out of the way so they could plant political cronies in key positions. He seemed to be awake to the potential for conversations to be overheard from behind the bar. Then, his last words to me in Lebanon were that his eyes were hit by a laser. Then, bro, I have my own incident in the McKee VIP bar where I personally heard people discussing a very nasty strategy which included a false flag operation.'

'Rocky, you think I could be walking both of us into deep trouble.'

'Both of us? No. I repeat, I am having nothing to do with it. You can walk away from it as well. I hope you do. We, up to now, have done nothing wrong. My advice is not to go to the Polo Grounds tomorrow. If you agree, let's get the hell out of this B&B as well.'

'What about if I agree to open the two rucksacks. Will you then help me?'

'No. If we find explosives and a squad car immediately pulls up and arrests us, what do we do then? How do we explain that away? Who would believe our story? Seven to ten years in Portlaoise Prison? Not for me. I hope I am totally wrong, but we cannot take that chance. You do not know who was contacting you and giving you these outrageous tasks. You cannot take the risk that the entire thing might be a set-up.'

Lizzy needs no further persuasion. His brother is rarely wrong. At the very minimum, the entire agent contact concept is truly bizarre. It might be nothing, but there are strong grounds for suspicion. It is best to err on the side of caution.

'Rocky, what if there really is a bomb and it blows up in Phoenix Park? I think we should tell the Gardaí.'

'No, absolutely not. We do not know who is in on this operation if there is one. Perhaps there are compromised policemen already set up to immediately arrest us after the bombs go off.'

'You are right, Rocky. In false flag operations we studied in the Ranger Wing, the police always seem to be able to announce the name of the suspects within hours of an atrocity.'

Rocky realises that his brother's highly unique appearance would be easily picked up on every single shop CCTV camera as he walks into the city centre with a rucksack on his back. 'You are the perfect patsy profile. Lizzy Harvey Oswald. Ha! Ha!'

'Lay off, Rocky. That's not funny.'

'I will tell you what we are going to do, Lizzy. You and I are jumping on the next train to Athlone from Heuston Station.'

'There is a League of Ireland match on there tomorrow so the hats and scarfs will be perfect for the trip. We will spend tonight and all-day Monday in the company of your friends and will sleep in Custume Barracks. We want to be far away from this city and have an iron-tight alibi. If you are asked why you rented a room here, you can say that you needed a private place to be with your girlfriend. Then, unexpectedly, she could not come so you went boozing down to Athlone and you dragged me along. Pay the bill. Let's get the feck out of here.'

Chapter 26

Waiting for an Alibi

The train journey from Heuston Station to Athlone is uneventful and the brothers hang out for the entire journey exchanging rounds of drinks at the bar. This is Rocky's idea. He wants an Irish Rail staff member to remember them and enhance their alibi. They memorise the barman's name and find out that he is a friendly young lad who lives in Dublin Liberties, not far from their own home.

They reach Athlone around 9pm in good time for a pub crawl. Lizzy is sure that he will meet his friends, and he is right. The first stop is an olde world pub behind the castle on the banks of the River Shannon. Lizzy knows the crowd and, immediately, they are involved in a relaxed social gathering. At midnight, it's off to Miss Elvina nightclub where, again, numerous people seem to know Lizzy.

Rocky is surprised at the vibrancy of the small town.

Lizzy is suddenly relaxed and smiling in the company of good friends.

'Hey, Lizzy, you are one popular man down here. I am surprised you ever came back to Dublin.'

'Yeah, I had a ball. I know so many people.'

At 2am, it's back to the barracks via a stop for burgers and chips in the Italian café. The gate policeman immediately recognises Lizzy and sends the brothers to a billet in the New Block where there are plenty of free bunk beds.

Marathon Monday morning and Lizzy is in the shower at 7am. Despite enjoying his socialising the night before, he is unnerved by the possible events which might occur in Dublin. They have breakfast in the soldiers' dining hall and Lizzy has borrowed a transistor radio which he has left switched on constantly. He is glued to every news programme. It's an early start for the Dublin City Marathon with live commentary on RTE 1 radio. Thousands of people are on the streets of the capital to cheer on the runners. The brothers chill out in the billet and relax, lying on their bunk beds. By lunchtime, Lizzy is becoming relieved by the lack of any devastating developments, but he is also becoming annoyed. There is no consternation whatsoever in Dublin. In fact, the marathon is being described as a brilliant organisational success.

Rocky keeps quiet all day, as would any man facing this lose-lose situation. Involvement in a terrorist incident would be appalling. Yet the absence of any incident would mean that he would have to examine whether he is much more mentally ill than he had admitted to himself up to now. His brother might be slow to ever trust him again. His depression load intensifies all day. He sits slumped on his bed and keeps his area of the billet in total darkness.

Tension is building up between the boys as they travel back to Dublin in silence on the 7pm train. Lizzy continues to listen to every news bulletin on the transistor radio. Suddenly, the frosty silence is broken by Lizzy.

'Oh no! No! Rocky, listen. Hey, listen to this.' Lizzy turns up the volume on his transistor. It's the RTE radio sports summary.

'...and a loud explosion seriously frightened horses and resulted in riders being unseated during a morning polo game in Phoenix Park.'

The news item mentions that three riders were injured and taken to hospital. The Phoenix Park Rangers and Polo Club had to immediately abandon the fixture. A tree had been damaged by "illegal powerful Halloween fireworks". Branches were still blocking the road and polo-playing surface and the Gardaí had to seal off the entire area. In a short interview, the club chairman condemns the use of fireworks in the vicinity of horses. He blames local youths and calls on the government to crack down on the annual problem of, what he called, "Halloween trick or treat vandalism". He says that the Polo Grounds have been damaged repeatedly, recently, and he makes a public call on parents from nearby flats to meet him.

Lizzy takes a deep breath. He hides his face by lowering his head onto his arms on the train dining table. Eventually, he looks up and whispers towards his equally shocked brother, 'Rocky, why? Why? Why me? You saved me. Sorry for doubting you.'

Rocky puts his finger up to his lips, indicating to Lizzy to say no more. He is vindicated but frightened. As they pull into Heuston Railway Station in the city, Lizzy asks Rocky to join him for a pint in a Parkgate Street pub.

'Rocky, there is something else I have to tell you. The

neighbours who Piper Jim used to drink with for decades are shunning him. There has been some kind of smear campaign against him. He has stopped going to his favourite pubs. He drinks alone or goes to tourist pubs.

'I was wondering why he was not going out. I thought it was because of concern for my health. He is so quiet, even encouraging me to talk about music. Now there is no talk either about me becoming an officer. He is a changed man. He must have been involved in something that went badly wrong. But he looks well and is in good shape. I would never have guessed.'

'Naw! Watch carefully and you will see that he seems to be hiding all the time from the neighbours. Avoiding many of them.'

'Wow. I am sickened. We are on the edge of something big and terribly dangerous. We should not breathe a word to him about the false flag. In ways, we should be proud. We actually probably saved many people from injury or death.'

'Rocky, do you think that Dad might possibly have known about the false flag? He has never been one to visit Galway. He and his brother hate each other. It's unusual that he is away from Dublin on this particular weekend. Perhaps, like us, he is creating an alibi. I am horrified to think so badly of our father. But these are strange times. Could he be involved in some political cabal infighting or something?'

'He was certainly involved in something. Political organisations have networks of people spying for them. Also performing dirty tricks, intimidation and setting up compromising situations to eliminate people who question their power.'

'Jaysus! He is not that sick in the head. I hope you are not right, Lizzy. Surely, he would not want you ending up in prison or to have both of us blown to pieces by those bombs.

Did he have any inkling that you were being lured into the Murder Triangle?'

'No, absolutely none. I was careful to conceal everything because secrecy is always part of an agent contact exercise. Sometimes when I spoke, he turned away from me. I was left addressing the side of his head and a cold shoulder. He was deliberately freezing me out at times, not even acknowledging me. Rocky, if he is in trouble, could his enemies be targeting us to punish him? Look, there is a long history to consider. You remember Mother was never happy when he was home. She didn't trust him and even brought us to Spain to avoid his influence.'

'You could be right, Lizzy. So far, we have been lucky. But when is our luck going to run out?'

'You are scaring the shit out of me, Rocky! We are targets… what do you think?'

'We probably are.'

'Whew! Rocky, I never hurt anybody. Why pick me? Why? Why try to destroy me? I am not part of anything illegal. I am just an enthusiastic career soldier. You too, Rocky. A soldier, an entertainer and a barman. What is wrong with that?'

'Lizzy, like me, you obey orders without questioning them. It's easy to make a patsy out of young soldiers like us. Our military training is about obeying orders without question. We are trained to trust our officers and NCOs. That blind faith and obedience lead you, in this case, to fall into a dreadful trap. Then they saw the opportunity to suck me in. Now, together, we luckily avoided horrible consequences. We could both, this evening, be facing a mass murder charge.'

'Luck, just luck, saved us.'

'Okay, Lizzy, let's go home. I am warning you now,

say absolutely nothing at all to Dad. He should be home from Galway by now. I know you are feeling shocked so go directly up to bed and avoid talking to him. I am going to do the same.'

Chapter 27

The End of Carefree Innocence

'Hey, Lizzy, what time is it?'

Rocky knows that Lizzy is awake as he has been disturbed all night by his brother's restless tossing and turning in the top bunk.

'It's 6.30am, I have to get up and head into work shortly. I didn't really sleep at all. My mind is in bleedin' total turmoil. I am a mess. I am in total mental shit. Now I know how you felt after Gilmore's death. I got physically sick three times during the night. I hope I didn't wake you.'

'Oh, I heard you. I wasn't asleep either, but I feel steadier than you seem to be. I am not so anxious. Lizzy, the bastards, whoever they are, failed miserably to trap us.'

'Yeah, you are right, Rocky.'

'Now, Lizzy just go downstairs and ring the orderly sergeant in McKee Barracks. Tell him that you are sick. We can get a doctor's cert. There is no point in you going to the barracks all worked up and ill at ease. Just chill out today.'

'Yeah, I will ring in sick. I have never done it before. You know, Rocky, I am not malingering. I am really feeling very broken.'

'Shussssh! Keep your voice down so Dad can't hear us in the next room. Let's stay in bed until he has gone to work. I don't want us talking to him in our present condition. He might start asking too many questions. I have no desire to be interrogated and give him any information. I am totally scared of that man. Who is he? Who the hell is our father?'

'Rocky, unfortunately, all night I was asking myself the same question. I really suspect him.'

'Okay, Lizzy, let's go to a coffee shop where we can have a late breakfast and talk in privacy.'

By 10am, the boys are in Bewley's café in Grafton Street in possession of three Dublin daily newspapers. The coverage of the events at the Polo Grounds is scant and relegated in all the newspapers to the inside pages. It seems that the media are unanimous in accepting the proposition that the explosion was a Halloween fireworks prank. They all quote a Garda Press Office source. One newspaper has a photograph of the damaged tree branches blocking the polo ground pitch. Another picture shows a badly injured horse lying on the ground and being attended to by a vet. Another paper leads with the story that the noise of the explosions caused a false security alert at Áras an Uachtaráin, the nearby residence of the president of Ireland.

The boys are pale-faced and unsmiling. Lizzy disappears to the bathroom and declines to eat breakfast. Though Rocky is less traumatised, he is still anxious. He closes his eyes and tries to turn the conversation towards positivity. 'You know, I am still trying to sing "Changes" in my head.'

Lizzy is staring at his cold, trembling fingers. His mind is elsewhere. He is not listening.

'Come on, Lizzy, chill out.' Rocky is clearly the calmer of the two, bolstered by a firm conviction that he knows what direction his future is taking. 'Lizzy, I told you already what I am going to do. Now, after this, I am totally driven to escape this mess.'

'Oh, come on! Please shut up, bro! I am not ready to talk about the future. Rocky, those were big enough bombs to kill or injure a lot of people.'

'Worse, Lizzy, much worse. Listen. This newspaper article says that the explosion occurred at 9.45am. The rucksacks could still have been on our backs and we both would have been blown to pieces. I can see the media story now. Two disgruntled suicide bombers, one, a newly returned Lebanon veteran, a psychiatrist's patient for PTSD. The coloured soldier, ex-special forces, easily identified due to his football hat. Links to the South Armagh Murder Triangle. Already flagged by the RUC and British army. Failure of the Irish government to crack down on terrorists. Lizzy, if you survived the blast, the media would have had you convicted before any trial. Probably me too. Our family would have been destroyed by the hatred of the victims' loved ones. The real perpetrators would have got away, literally, with murder. If we were not killed, and planted the bombs, absolutely nobody would believe our version of events. This was a very cleverly planned trap. A professional cabal network with spy involvement. Somebody wanted to use us to cause political and security turmoil.'

'More and more of Dad's behaviour worries me.'

'I have the same suspicion. Why did he put me in the officers' mess VIP bar? Why was he always looking for information about Gilmore? Why did he go to his hated brother in Galway for the weekend? Why did he tell me that the Devil's Breath drug is childish Enid-Blyton-style fiction? Then he advised me not to alert Gilmore about the trap that was being set to destroy the officer. That was wrong. Very wrong, but I took his advice.'

'Yeah and, Rocky, why was I sent to Athlone? Then he seemed so upset that I was coming back to Dublin. Does he hate me enough to kill me or to set me up for a murder rap? He loves you, Rocky. He probably would not have known that I was bringing you on the agent contact exercise. Surely he could not be that depraved?'

'No, Lizzy, often, I have overheard petty jibes from officers and senior NCOs. There is a lot of questioning as to how the famous Piper Jim could have landed so many financially lucrative overseas posts. Time after time, he managed somehow to jump the queue. In what way did he prostitute his integrity to be rewarded so nicely? Perhaps it was payback time. He didn't deliver.'

'Yeah, I have often heard the saying about the sins of the father being bestowed on the sons.'

'I, for one, have no interest in becoming more involved. I want out! Out! Out! I want away! Away! Away! Dad's influence is toxic. It could be that we are living with a total nutcase. Everybody's friend, joking, smiling, entertaining, socialising, shaking hands, telling traditional stories, playing music... the proverbial great guy.'

'The professional Trojan Horse.'

'Exactly. False love, fake admiration and phoney friendship. He is always listening, plotting and is dangerously manipulative. For me, it's over. This has become far too dangerous.'

'We can no longer take the risk of giving him the benefit of the doubt.'

'Exactly, I am not waiting for the next frame-up. I am not waiting for my brother to be blown to pieces before I act. Criminals and spies making up these cabals always ensure that their guilt can never be proven.'

'I think that I am going to live in the barracks for a while. I know that if I move out, Dad will never even bother to look me up. We both will be rid of each other for good. I will miss our home and the great memories of Ormond Square with Mam. I will still have you and the band as my closest friends. Then, in a few months, I will be off peacekeeping to Lebanon and will leave all this crap behind me… forever.'

'Let's hope your Lebanon trip is still okay. Lizzy, if they find out about this incident and know about the trips to the Murder Triangle, it might screw everything up. You want to be sure that nothing else happens that will cast you in a bad light.'

'So, a clean break from Piper Jim is essential. I will tell him nothing. Let him think that I am living with my Chinese girlfriend. What about you, Rocky?'

Rocky takes in a deep breath, feeling that the incident has totally freed him from any doubts he might have had about leaving the army. 'My future in music now is clearer than ever before. Sometimes, Lizzy, there is luck hidden even in a dreadful set of circumstances.'

'Good for you, Rocky.' But Lizzy mournfully shakes his head. 'Rocky, something inside me has died, gone forever. My innocence. My youth is finally over. Somebody has taken away my bright, optimistic spirit and crushed it. I am in mourning because all of the decency and morality that I believed about life has been destroyed.'

'Yeah, Lizzy, I understand. What a horrendous underbelly! When you discover what is really going on, it changes your attitude forever.'

'Rocky, it's true. I now have woken up to see Piper Jim and his pals as dependent, selfish old men. Slaves to a system of underhand political self-serving corruption. Give me time for my sorrow, Rocky. You might be ready for bright, optimistic ideas, but I am not. You should worry, Rocky.'

'What do you mean?'

'Could they be watching us, Rocky? I am afraid. I trust nobody anymore. Come on, let's go; I am shaking and feel weak. I need some alone time because I do not want to be spotted crying here publicly in the café. I need to go back to bed. I have a severe headache and I barely know where I am or what I am doing. Don't worry, I know that we did nothing wrong. I will be okay in a few days.'

Rocky can see that Lizzy is in a bad place mentally. A broken young man who now has no clear direction in life, no safe family home, doubts about his selection for overseas service and fear that he might continue to be targeted by evil people.

Chapter 28

Mr Antoon Chamoon

The brothers are back in Ormond Square by noon. Lizzy immediately retires to his top bunk. In contrast, Rocky clamours to maintain his calmness and emerges with a far different attitude. He is energised by the fact that, somehow, he accurately predicted the patsy trap his brother was walking them into. He begins endorsing himself.

Somehow, I have beaten all that has been thrown at me. I am flooding my mind with thoughts of success now. I see the band on stage with thousands watching us. We have so much to offer.

This morning, Rocky has an opportunity to privately use the home phone in the absence of his prying father. He pulls out his pack of business cards and wastes no time. He knows exactly the first call he will make.

'Hello, sir, I am Rocky from the band Eclectic RRK… yeah… you might remember us from a gig we did in Dalkey.

Yes, you got it… yes it's in Ireland. Do you remember? You suggested I call you after my trip to Lebanon. Yeah! Yeah! The Chinese girls and the coloured guitarist. Yes, that is us. Correct. You do remember. Oh! That's great! You cannot talk to me now. I see. You will ring me back shortly. Thanks for accepting my call anyway.'

Rocky is "shaking the bushes" and immediately searching for work in the music industry. He stands in the hall of his home and paces up and down, fist still clenched, affirming himself.

'Look, I see the band on the cover of the *Rolling Stone*. Yes, what an achievement.'

Rocky sorts through his crumpled pack of old business cards. He decides to leave the phone free for the possible call back. He is certain that the first person he has just called, a Mr Antoon Chamoon, is a particularly hot prospect. He has guarded that card particularly carefully and kept it in his wallet throughout his trip to Lebanon. He received the card nine months earlier at the end of an all-night gig in a magnificent house in the wealthy suburb of Dalkey. He sits down on the living room sofa while he vividly recalls that night.

The rest of the band had gone home, but Rocky talked all night, slowly sipping beer, networking and generally mingling with this small, select gathering. At first light, all of those still present moved to an outside patio to enjoy the emerging spectacular dawn view, breaking over Dalkey Island. Golden sunlight then highlighted Killiney Hill and the Vico Road. In the distance was the summit of Sugarloaf Mountain covered in a beautiful white, cotton-wool-shaped cloud. Rocky fell silent while he soaked in the magnificence of all that was around him. He was deep in thought when he heard a voice coming from behind him.

'Wow. This part of Dublin is beautiful. You are Rocky?'

Rocky looked around and found that he was being addressed by a distinguished-looking, grey-haired, elderly businessman. He nodded and smiled as the man extended his hand.

'I am Antoon Chamoon. I didn't realise that you were still here. I was planning to contact you.' The man spoke slowly with a heavily toned Middle Eastern accent as he lit up an expensive Cuban Cohiba cigar. 'You know, Rocky, that was a really smooth, tight performance tonight. I really like your band.'

'Thanks, sir, the audience feedback was very positive. I am guessing from your accent, Mr Chamoon, that you are not Irish… and not British either.'

'Ha! Ha! Good guess. I have been based in London for many years now, but I am originally Lebanese. I left Beirut more than a decade ago. Things were bad at the time. I had to get my family out for safety reasons. We left our home while under intense fire. A lucky escape but sad times for my country. My wife and I had some savings, ended up as refugees in London and, eventually, I set up a business there. We worked hard and made a success of our new life.'

Rocky laughed. 'Wow, that's a coincidence, Mr Chamoon. Believe it or not, I am going to your country in May. I am putting my music career on hold for a while to allow me to become part of the Irish peacekeeping battalion. I am sure you know where Tibnin is. That will be the location of our headquarters. I will be living a few kilometres from there in a small, hilltop village called Ayta Zutt.'

'Tibnin! Yes, yes, of course.' He slowly puffed his Cohiba in a perfectly relaxed fashion, looked into the distance, then continued the conversation. 'So, you are actually a soldier. Except for the short hair, I never would have guessed.'

Rocky detected a tone of disappointment in the elderly man's voice.

'But it's so sad that you are breaking up such a fantastic band. You know, tonight's performance was as good as some of the best bands I have seen on the London West End circuit. I actually knew about you guys in advance of tonight.'

'You did?'

'I read a very positive article about you in the *New Musical Express*. I think that might be why you were invited to perform. I am sure you know that this is a gathering of nightclub owners from England, Scotland and Wales. We are over here in Dublin for a few days of golf, entertainment and some of us are doing a little bit of business as well. For me, it's talent scouting, and I must say that your band has great potential. I am just a little bit disappointed to hear that you are taking a sabbatical. Some of my nightclubs get a sizeable young Asian crowd so your "eclectic" make-up would have been a big attraction for me. Those Chinese girls are wonderful. I was going to talk to you about a contract. What a pity.'

Rocky's mouth fell open. 'Wow, I am shocked and delighted. What can I say?'

'Rocky, Eclectic RRK is a new and exciting sound. It's fresh and the coloured guitar player is immense. How do you hold onto a musician as good as that? He could have his pick of top bands in London and be taking in a six-figure salary.'

'Well, he is my brother, that is how I keep him.'

'Ah! I see. Could he possibly be looking for work after your band breaks up? I have lots of contacts who would jump at a chance to sign him.'

Rocky now needed to go on the defensive in the nicest possible way. 'Sir, he also has a military enlistment contract.'

'Oh dear. What a pity. By the way, I should not fail to mention that your own lead vocals possess impressive clarity. I can see that you have a professionally trained voice. You do not seem to realise how good you guys are. Special, in fact. Being different and authentic is so important.'

'You are giving me a swelled head, Mr Chamoon.'

'So, Rocky, for now you are going to become a peacekeeper. That is a fantastic direction to take as well. A brave soldier trying to bring calm back to my sad little country. I admire your efforts. It will be a difficult task. Be careful.'

'I certainly will, sir.'

'I still have family there in the heart of the northern suburbs of Beirut. Have you a pen and I will give you a few phone numbers. I will write them here on the back of my business card. You will find, in Lebanon, that hospitality is still our biggest cultural strength. Even war cannot take that away from my people. No traveller will ever be left hungry or without a bed in a Lebanese village. For sure, my family will be genuinely overjoyed to welcome an Irish peacekeeping soldier.'

'Wow, thank you, Mr Chamoon.'

'You will be treated as a VIP. In Lebanon, our tradition is to serve a fresh, delicious meze of warm naan bread, tabbouleh, hummus and fattoush. Then, a glass of our Chateau Ksara wine is not to be missed. You should try to visit the underground caves in our Bekaa Valley vineyards.'

Mr Chamoon continued, waxing enthusiastically about his tragic but magnificent homeland, 'Then, don't forget that you must try to see Cedrus Libani, two-thousand-year-old cedar trees in the northern village of Bsharri. We call it the forest of the "Cedars of God". A sublime mountain location sometimes blanketed in snow. Our cedar trees are the proud national symbol of Lebanon.'

'Wow, you are making me feel really excited about my trip. I think my opportunity to visit Beirut will be very limited. I am not even sure if we are allowed to spend our free time there. I know that security is very tight. Kidnap is a big fear.'

'My family will show you around and keep you safe. Now, don't be shy. I will tell them to expect a talented young musician, singer-songwriter called Rocky. They might even ask you to do your party piece. In our household, there are three beautiful unattached daughters who must be about your age. One of them is a great amateur singer. She also has a fully trained voice.'

Rocky looked at the businessman's card, greatly appreciating the invitation. He was gobsmacked that he was already making valuable social contacts in Beirut. 'I will be down in South Lebanon all of the time, I think. It's a long shot. But you know, Mr Chamoon, if I get to Beirut for a couple of days I will certainly look up your family. That's guaranteed. It will be a great experience to break bread in Beirut in a real Lebanese household.'

'Well, young Rockingham, either way, do give me a call in London when you get back to Ireland. All my nightclubs have live music. We are open six nights per week. We are always looking for new talent to freshen up the offering. I am over to look at four more Irish bands this week, so tonight is actually business for me.'

'Oh, right!'

'You did not know that you were actually being auditioned tonight. Ha! Ha! Did you?'

Rocky blushed and nearly ate his words. 'Jeez, I… I…I … you're right, I did not realise… wow! Tonight was an audition! I am glad that I did not know in advance, or we would all have been petrified. Wait until I tell the band.'

'Yeah. I always want to see bands at their relaxed best. We know that there is massive, untapped, musical talent here in Dublin. Johnny Logan was fantastic in winning the Eurovision Song Contest… and I love Rory Gallagher and Thin Lizzy. The talent here is massive, and that is why there is a gang of us here from UK. This time, you and I will not do business. Perhaps another time. Now, young man, I must head back to my hotel. My wife will be worried.

'It was nice to meet you, sir, and thanks for all the advice and contacts.'

Nine months later, Rocky is waiting for his call to be returned, praying that Mr Chamoon might still want to hire the band. The telephone rings and, immediately, Rocky grabs the handset. After less than a minute of conversation, Rocky feels like he is talking to an old friend.

'Yes, Mr Chamoon, I did look up your relations in Beirut. We had a great time. You have a lovely family and it's a great city… ha! Ha! Yeah! I got to perform in The Blue Note. Yeah! A special venue. It was awesome. You remember me now. Well, I have reorganised my band and I know… oh! Okay… yes, you still have the six live music venues? Oh, I see. Four in London and one each in Manchester and Barcelona. Do you think I could come over and have a chat? Yeah… tomorrow? Oh! Wow! I will see if I can get a flight that soon. I will call your secretary then and make an appointment for the late afternoon.'

Rocky hangs up the phone and rushes upstairs to give Lizzy the news. Lizzy is already sitting up in the bed and looking healthier.

'Hey, Rocky, it sounds really promising. Did you really meet his family in Beirut?'

'You bet I did and had a ball! It was me who got them tickets for the gig in The Blue Note.'

'Now that was a really nice thing to do.'

'Lizzy, I think, with Mr Chamoon, I might be pushing an already open door. I am sure he was ready to make us an offer after the Dalkey gig last year.'

'Fair play, Rocky. You and the girls will do well. I am sure. I will miss you. It will be sad for me to be left behind. Good luck in the interview tomorrow.'

Rocky is on the 7am Aer Lingus flight from Dublin to London Heathrow the following morning. The meeting with Mr Chamoon is short, businesslike and friendly.

'Okay, Rocky, based on your audition in Dalkey last year, I am now making you a serious offer. Four live late-night gigs per week in London and Saturday nights in Manchester. You will be off Sunday and Monday. You speak Spanish so I want to include in your contract an eight-week stint in Barcelona in the summer. The commitment will be twenty-four months and includes you releasing three singles with your time in the recording studio paid for by my company. I advertise my nightclubs heavily on 208 Radio Luxembourg so I can arrange plenty of airplay for your singles as well. Now, the first three months will be probationary, which is normal. I will arrange and pay for the visas for the Chinese girls. Included in your package will be a rent-free, two-bedroom apartment in Fitzrovia, near the Post Office Tower, with underground parking. You will have full-time use of one of my fleet of vans. How does that sound, Rocky?'

Rocky tries hard to conceal his shock and delight with the arrangement, but he is unable to hold back a smile. 'For me it sounds perfect. I need a little bit of time to wind up some business in Dublin. When would you need us to start?'

'I was about to sign another band when you called. You fully understand, I charge my customers premium entry prices so I must always have live bands in my clubs. Never piped disco music. It is important that you decide immediately. The band must be ready to go on stage here in London in five weeks. I need to get all of you over straight away to sign contracts, next week in fact.'

'Oh! Wow! Okay! That soon, I see. I am going to talk to the band. Please give me a few days to pull it all together.'

'Just to clarify, Rocky, I assume that the band will have the same personnel as seen in Dalkey. Yourself, the two Chinese girls Ping and Lilly and your brother Lizzy, the coloured guitar player. Right?'

Rocky stalls for time, knowing that Lizzy is a doubtful starter. 'Mr Chamoon, I will show all of the band members what is on offer and confirm everything with you in the next few days.'

'Rocky, I must be straight with you – it's the "eclectic" part of your name that is very attractive for my audience. Diversity is the name of the game. I do not want you to pull together a new band that I have not seen or heard. I want Eclectic RRK as auditioned in Dalkey. So, Rocky, no subs, okay? The offer is strictly for the four-piece band. Now, if you cannot pull that together and there will be a delay persuading people, you need to tell me immediately. That is why I want all four members here to sign contracts by Friday of next week. I will talk to all four of you to ensure that you are all fully committed.'

'Look, it's a really nice deal, Mr Chamoon. I will not mess and if there is a problem, I will call you straight away.'

'Great. That is business talk over for now.' He frowns, looking suddenly serious. 'How was Lebanon? I heard that you had a narrow escape yourself. The accident was widely covered in the Lebanese newspapers. I knew immediately it was you because Adeline called me. She was devastated by the news.'

'Oh, wow, I did not know she had heard. I have not been in contact with her since the night in The Blue Note.'

'You know, I give our Beirut family phone number to many people, but very few actually make the call. Fair play for making the effort. Adeline was delighted with the music and dance coaching you gave both her and the band. You made a big impression there. She told me that you performed together and there was hours and hours... ha! ha!... of soundchecks apparently. Very professional and that is the standard I want from my club bands.'

'Thank you, sir. The Blue Note gig went really well, and the time spent in rehearsal was well worth it.'

Mr Chamoon continues with a more relaxed expression on his face. 'Then I heard also about that famous very long stage kiss... I hear everything. Adeline is coming here to London soon to complete some courses in the London School of Economics. You will probably bump into her. Your apartment is in the same part of the city.'

Rocky leaves Mr Chamoon's office smiling from ear-to-ear. As he heads to Heathrow Airport, his thoughts are dominated by memories of the fantastic Blue Note gig.

'Notre-Dame du Liban... you must be coming to my aid. At last, things are beginning to go my way. I have not felt so calm and relaxed since all those wonderful musical days in Ormond Square with mother. I feel elated, just like the old days.'

As Rocky boards the Aer Lingus plane for Dublin, he wonders if he can pull everything together fast. Most worrying is that he must, somehow, get Lizzy's signature on the contract. Rocky debates in his mind the fairness of asking him to abandon his United Nations opportunity. The London option is, by far, the more lucrative, particularly with the record deal. Lizzy, in his current stressed-out mood, will now be presented with the additional pressure of having to make a massive career choice. Rocky realises that he will have to pose the question straight away. The future for the entire band hangs on Lizzy's decision.

Chapter 29

Cold Sweat

By landing time at Dublin Airport, Rocky has his plans fully formulated. He has had time to study the written copy of the draft contract provided by Mr Chamoon's secretary. He is satisfied that the terms are excellent and, in fact, way beyond his wildest hopes. The news that he is sure to be reunited with Adeline is a further massive incentive. It's the clincher. Past turmoil fades into irrelevance as Rocky walks through Dublin Airport possessed by an overwhelming feeling of success. Rocky realises that there is an onus on him to make things happen and quickly. He has glory within his grasp, and he is confident that all probable barriers are surmountable.

'First, I have to get out of the army. I will ask for leave of absence, but buying myself out is also a possibility. Second, Lizzy must be sold on the deal. He will miss his peacekeeping trip and will also have to quit the army. Ping and Lilly are already on board, willing and enthusiastic, but they will need to give notice at Dino's Bar and Grill.

Rocky arrives home to Ormond Square just after midnight. The house is in darkness and the sound of snoring indicates that Piper Jim has consumed a few pints and has already retired for the night. Lizzy is nowhere to be found and Rocky immediately becomes alarmed. All of Lizzy's clothes and gear are missing from the bedroom wardrobe.

'Wow, he has either moved permanently into McKee Barracks or has gone to the girls' apartment. I hope he is okay.'

Rocky feels that his young brother is in poor mental health after the false flag incident. Rocky knows that he will not rest tonight unless he knows that Lizzy is in a safe place. He decides to go to McKee Barracks first, to see if the planned move into the second regiment F Block billet has taken place. His first port of call is the military police hut at the entrance gate of the barracks.

'Hi, Corporal, do you know if my brother came into the barracks this evening?'

'Your brother is Lizzy, the guitar player, right? I have just come on duty but let me check the list here on the gate. Hmmm, he is not mentioned anywhere. Sorry, Rocky. Look, he might have come in on the back of a truck or Land Rover, so I suggest you take a look in the second regiment billets. The canteen is closed so there is no point going there.'

Rocky starts to explore the two floors of second regiment accommodation. It is quiet and most of the bunk beds are empty. There is no trace of Lizzy. Without delay, it is time to move on immediately to Ping and Lilly's apartment in Marlborough Street. Rocky is increasingly concerned, but he is still composed as he knocks on the girls' door well after

1am. Ping immediately answers and there are tears in her eyes.

'Oh, Lizzy was in a desperate state. He was really drunk when he dumped his luggage here about three hours ago. He told us that he is homeless but will be moving into army accommodation. Then he started bawling like a baby and we could not calm him down. Then, while we were making some food for him, he suddenly left the apartment. We called him back and he told us that he needs to be alone. He told us that he was going to Temple Bar for a few more late-night drinks.'

Rocky knows exactly how to calm Lizzy down and immediately moves his search to Temple Bar. He walks through pub after pub, but his brother is nowhere to be found. With most of the establishments closed at 3am, he gives up the search and heads home.

He will show up tomorrow, I am sure of that. I have such good news for him, but I am sick with worry.

Next day by lunchtime, Lizzy is still missing. Rocky checks the second regiment orderly room and discovers that he failed to renew his sick cert. Now he is AWOL, absent without leave. Rocky decides to ask Stevie Dawson for help. The sergeant major must be told nothing for fear that he will alert Piper Jim. Stevie has a Land Rover out on requisition and available for all general duties. Without delay, he commences a search with Rocky.

'I have to ask the hard question, Rocky, are you guys in some kind of shit? Lizzy is a model soldier, and so are you, but there have been stories circulating.'

'Stories about who? Lizzy? Me?'

'Okay, forget it, Rocky. It is the usual tabloid-type smear. I am personally sure that neither of you did anything wrong. But Lizzy is missing.'

'Stevie, he told the Chinese girls that he is homeless. Let's go to the homeless hostels and see if they have taken in a young, coloured lad.'

The search of hostels and rough, open-air sleeping places continues fruitlessly all day and Stevie must return the Land Rover to McKee Barracks by 6pm. Both Stevie and Rocky worry about a more serious scenario.

'Hey, Rocky, he is a solid guy and will show up. What do you think? There is no reason to consider self-harm or anything like that? Is there? Be straight with me now, Rocky.'

Oh my God! Jaysus, Stevie, I hope not. Not self-harm. He has been under a lot of pressure. I am going to keep quiet about it for now but, yes, I am extremely worried. He always seems calm and solid but, behind it all, he takes even little things very hard. The poor guy. I am so sorry for him. He's never disappeared like this before.'

'So, there is something you are not telling me, Rocky.'

'Okay, Stevie, you are right, but I cannot go into it right now. Trust me, I have good news as well which could solve everything. Let's keep everything quiet for just one more day.'

'Yeah, but if we do not find him by tomorrow evening, we must tell your dad, the Gardaí and the sergeant major. Lizzy becomes a missing person and that's serious.'

Rocky heads for home intent on minding the hall phone for the evening in the hope that Lizzy will call. He dozes off on the living room sofa until his shoulder is shaken by an aggressive and drunk Piper Jim. His fist is clenched, and he smells of whiskey.

'Rocky, where the hell is Lizzy? The sergeant major called me today to say that he is AWOL. What the hell do you know about this?'

Rocky has his answers well prepared. 'No idea, Dad.

Have not seen the man in a few days. He is probably off shagging his Chinese girlfriend. Watch for a baby from that direction soon. Ha! Ha! You will be a stepgrandad.'

Piper Jim glares, teeth clenched, body movements momentarily frozen. He knows that Rocky is holding back the truth. Two years earlier, he would have shouted aggressively at a more obedient, younger Rocky. Then it might have worked. But not anymore. He stumbles out of the room, deciding not to pursue the matter further.

He is drinking alone far too much lately. His political friends and our neighbours have deserted him for some reason. I hope that this is not going to add to our problems.

At 10pm, the phone rings. Rocky rushes from the living room to the hall and grabs the receiver. 'Hello, this is the Rockingham family.'

'Rocky, this is Lizzy. I'm sorry.'

Chapter 30

Playa de Santa Maria del Mar, Cadiz

'Where the feck have you been? Are you okay?'

Lizzy sounds a little drunk. '*Estoy en Cádiz con mi abuelita.*' Lizzy is in Cadiz, with his grandma.

'*Estoy encantado.*' Rocky is delighted. 'Lizzy, that's a gorgeous place to go but you should have kept your brother posted. I have been so worried. Dad is going around the house like he has bees up his kilt. You didn't apply for leave. You know that you are AWOL.'

'*No podría dar dos mierdas.*' Lizzy could not give two shits. 'Granny and I have had a few vino tintos. After what happened, I needed my granny for support. I had to escape to a friendly atmosphere to wind down. Don't be hard on me, bro. I am not coming back. I am finished in Dublin for good. Granny is our biggest fan. I am so happy being back here talking in Spanish to somebody who I can trust. I will start busking and looking for work tomorrow. I know I can be a success and happy here in Spain.

'Look, Lizzy, that is perfect. Just relax and stay with Granny. Don't do anything crazy. I will fly down to Seville on the charter and take the train to Cadiz. I have good news. I will tell you everything when I get there.'

Granny interrupts, talking in Spanish, sounding relaxed and in command. 'Rocky, your brother is fine. Have no worries. He is in my total care. Seems like you both had a little shock. Come on down. I am dying to see the two of you. It will be like old times.'

'Okay, Granny, I love you. Tell Lizzy I am going to get a new doctor's certificate for him, to cover a full week, so that he is not AWOL. I will hand it in to the sergeant major.'

A couple of days later, Rocky has joined Lizzy and they are both basking in the warmth of a spotless golden Cadiz beach. Automatically, they revert to their second native tongue, Spanish. The change of language signals a massive improvement in both of their moods. Lizzy is surprisingly happy, and they both feel reborn and like kids again. They know every street. The staff in many of the shops recognise them and make them feel welcome. It's like old times. Now they are enjoying sunbathing and listening to the waves on Playa de Santa Maria del Mar, one of the most magnificent beaches in all of Spain.

'So, Lizzy, somebody wants to drive us out of Ireland. Hurray! Ha! Ha! I have good news for them. They are winners. I'm out, for sure. I had a superb meeting with Mr Chamoon.' Rocky pulls out the contract document from his backpack. 'Look carefully at what is on offer. Personally, I think it's a great package. Ping and Lilly are overjoyed and giving their notice as soon as we sort out your decision. We are being asked to sign the contracts for a four-piece band next week.

Lizzy, we need you. Eclectic RRK is your musical home. It's a whole new beginning. What we have always dreamed of.'

'London with you guys would be great. My options in Dublin are terrible. I am not going to have a home in Ormond Square anymore. You guys are leaving. I feel unsafe. I do not know who to trust. Then, Rocky, the names for peacekeeping in Lebanon are not yet out. Though I am high on the list, I am not certain that I will be selected.'

'It's your decision, Lizzy. We want you to come to London. In fact, you are vital to our success. Be clear. Mr Chamoon is offering the contract only to the four-piece band he saw in Dalkey.'

'Rocky, you know that I have had enough. I cannot take any more.'

Both brothers smile simultaneously as this decision is increasingly looking like the proverbial slam dunk.

'Here is a printout so you can write on it. I am going for a swim. Read every word. In summary, there is excellent pay, free accommodation, guaranteed performances in huge nightclubs and a recording opportunity. A brilliant package. But there is something even more important.'

'What's that?'

'All four of us get to stick together. I don't want to be worrying about you and the possible shenanigans that might be going on back in Dublin.'

'Yeah, you are right. We get along really well. This looks like a massive opportunity. Just give me a half hour to read, understand and confirm everything.'

'Then join me for a swim. Lizzy, remember, all going well, I must get all four of us to London next week. I need to go to the travel agent this evening and book the flights.'

'Enjoy your swim, bro, and relax. I think we will be having a celebratory party tonight with Granny.

Chapter 31

"Con Te Partirò"

The move to London happens with far less hassle than any of them had expected. Lizzy, faced with the ugly situation in Dublin as well as the departure of his brother and girlfriend to London, is left with the easiest of decisions. Then, both brothers find that their military "discharge by purchase" application is processed in less than a week. With financial allowance given for unused holidays, the amount they need to pay is insignificant.

As luck would have it, Piper Jim is on a week-long West of Ireland tour with the band. He knows instinctively that big moves are afoot and is saddened that he is neither being consulted or informed. It therefore suits him to be away and play dumb. Sadly, he is facing an "empty nest" situation, living alone and coming into his senior years at Ormond Square.

At lunchtime, on their last day in the regiment, Rocky and Lizzy visit McKee dining hall to say farewell to their treasured soldier comrades. It is difficult. Lots of handshakes, hugs, a few farewell cards and many promises of unlikely future rendezvous. They both quietly shed tears as they walk out through the gates of McKee Barracks for the last time.

The next day, Eclectic RRK are on the 7am Aer Lingus flight to Heathrow. A new challenge begins, and nervous smiles are the order of the day.

Life in Dublin is quickly forgotten. Rocky, with typical efficiency and enthusiasm, has the band in rehearsal well before the contract is due to commence. Their apartment in Fitzrovia is old, elegant and large. It is warm and clean with an underground space for their new Mercedes travelling van. The location, in the heart of central London, is awesome and very convenient to their nightclub venues. It is also close to the London School of Economics where a Lebanese girl called Adeline Chamoon, unsurprisingly, pops up. Their entire life focus changes as they leave their troubles behind. Time quickly moves on as they rapidly come to flourish in their new cosmopolitan environment.

'I cannot believe we are here in London more than a year already, Rocky.'

'Yeah, time has flown but we have made immense progress. We are packing them in. Full houses almost every night for Mr Chamoon. He told me last week that he is experiencing his best business numbers in many years.'

'Yeah, our two singles moving up the charts is a great help. BBC Radio 1 and Radio Luxembourg seem to really love us. Then there are the Asian party nights, which are a total sell-out every week.'

'I give Ping and Lilly full credit for that. Singing many top hits in the Chinese language has been a massive success.

Your Chinese is excellent as well. No other top London band has comparable language skills. We are even attracting interest all the way from Hong Kong. When we have enough "dosh" I think we should look at a short tour of Asia. The girls already have ideas, and their family members will help us. China is surely a country where we could make millions on our record sales.'

'Well, here is another offer. Have a look at this. It's a letter from Dublin City Council asking us to play at the New Year open-air celebrations in College Green. It's for charity. Cancer. If we agree, we will be the main band.'

'Have we time off?'

'We work right through Christmas here in London but are off from the 30th. Mr Chamoon is doing renovations in all venues during the first week of January. What do you think?'

'Rocky, I am not sure I am ready to go back. You know I still have those bad dreams. You do too. Adeline said you were shouting in your sleep last night something about "Rainbow One" and "medevac".'

Rocky flushes red. By day, he sees himself as a calm, joyful and in control bandleader. He hates being told about how night-time still exposes a very sensitive side of his psychology. He feels a little bit guilty that he did not finish his treatment with that friendly shrink back in Dublin. He quickly dismisses Lizzy's revelation with a change of subject. 'Right, well here is another nightmare. Piper Jim's latest letter asks if we are coming home for Christmas or the New Year.'

'Why do I get no letters from him?'

'Lizzy, the letter was addressed to both of us. Here, take a look. Reading between the lines, I tell myself to try to understand that he is suffering. It must be tough on him to be alone, abandoned in his old age, knowing how well we are doing. I think he is mortified that he is not being invited to be a part of our success story. He backed the wrong horse. I always knew we were going to be a success. All we needed from Dad was honesty and support.'

'Rocky, he is old-school. Always dependant. We are totally self-reliant here in London. Independently making our own success.'

'Yeah, Lizzy. You are right. No sneaky stuff. Every day I think about how we can be even more successful and different as a band.'

'Exactly.'

'Well, bro, now an exciting change of subject. Take a look at this little box and it will put you in good form. Diamonds are forever.'

'A ring? Wow!'

'You bet, Lizzy. I am about to pop the question to Adeline. We have had a wonderful year together and I have had all the indications that something more permanent would be welcome.'

Lizzy springs up from his seat, punches the air and hugs Rocky. 'Hurray. Fantastic. I knew everything was going very well there. She kept signing on for more and more courses in London School of Economics. The longest master's degree in history, or is it a PhD? Ha! Ha! I am overjoyed. When will it be official?'

Rocky whispers, 'Shhh. Okay, bro, brace yourself. If we go to Dublin, I want to pop the question there on New Year's Day. New beginnings. Then I will introduce my fiancée to Dad at Ormond Square. I might even pop the question in our old home.'

Lizzy suddenly disengages from the conversation. He looks towards the floor with his thoughts captivated by past trauma. Rocky immediately knows why his brother has become so quiet but he says nothing. Finally, Lizzy comes around, bringing his thoughts back to the present moment. 'Rocky, I am not sure I will travel back to Dublin. God only knows what they might try to do to us this time.'

'Look, we are going to be in the public eye for the entire visit and RTE will televise the concert live. I have my worries too. My idea is that we fly in early on New Year's Eve and be back here on an evening flight on New Year's Day. I think our new-found celebrity status makes us less vulnerable. If anything happens, it will make big headlines all over Europe.'

'I'm not sure.'

'Lizzy, I have a fair idea as to what was behind our problems.'

'Rocky, how do you know? You never told me this before.'

Rocky has never revealed the continued existence of Paul Gilmore's contemporaneous notes to anybody, even Lizzy. 'I am saying no more, Lizzy.'

'Tell me, Rocky.'

'I might write a book in the future.'

'Perhaps it's best, for me, that I never know.'

'You are probably right.'

Rocky immediately changes the subject. 'Okay, back to the gig in Dublin. If the girls agree, please, Lizzy, do come with us. The engagement will be a very special event.'

'Okay, if everybody wants to go, I will too. I will be jumpy but what the heck. We cannot allow ourselves to be bullied forever.'

'Exactly.'

'Now, Rocky, I am only saying yes because of the engagement. It will be incredible to see the look on everybody's faces, particularly Piper Jim's. It's really nice to do it in front of your dad.'

'Oh, he will be so happy. It's an opportunity as well to carefully improve relationships. I think he will be quite proud.'

'Now, the deal, Rocky, is that it will be a one-night visit, no more. You and the girls can stay longer if you wish, but I will fly back on New Year's Day. You are a great man to forgive all that has happened. I think you should be proud of that trait. You never hold anger inside you for long.'

'Yes, but we are going to be very careful. Piper Jim will be all smiles and hugs. But none of the five of us will tell him anything sensitive. We can never let our guard down. We must continue to keep Dad and his dangerous contacts out of our lives. But anyway, I think they have rejected him. The warriors of smear have done their job. I have heard that he has no close friends left.'

'Yeah, well if he was like Mr Chamoon, everything would be different. To me, Mr Chamoon is the dad that I never had. Always caring, advising and supporting me. Rocky, that is why I am so happy here in London. The last time I felt so good about myself was when Mother was alive.'

'Yeah, Mr Chamoon, dishes out really tough love. Like Gilmore, he can be hard and demanding, but you always know that he is authentic and on your side. No sneaky stuff.'

* * *

The weeks pass quickly. It's a mild New Year's Eve on College Green, Dublin, and around fifteen thousand revellers pack the historic square. Eclectic RRK come on stage at 10.45pm to a warm welcome from their Irish fans. Standing on the stage, they spot soldiers from McKee Barracks and Athlone, as well as neighbours from Smithfield, Stoneybatter and Ormond Square. There are more than two hundred young Chinese fans all together with flags. Lilly and Ping are delighted. The music for the night consists of the Eclectic RRK repertoire of chart hits sung mostly in English. They also include a few top chart singles sung in Chinese.

Midway through the gig, the live television coverage begins. Rocky does a special address to the fans. 'Hello, Dublin, and welcome to people from all around Ireland watching on RTE.'

There is a big cheer from the crowd.

'It's great to be back. Just over a year ago, we were all living and working here in this great city, less than fifteen minutes' walk from this stage. Things have happened very fast. Eclectic RRK have had a fantastic year and our latest single, "Serendipity", is up ten places to number three today in the Irish Top 20. I want to say that nobody in the band has forgotten that Dublin is where it all began.' Sustained cheering. 'I want to start the build-up to the new year by thanking a special elite group who are here tonight wearing blue berets and flying flags of the United Nations and Lebanon. A special round of applause for the peacekeepers. Yeah, here they are right in front of the stage.'

More cheering. 'For a little nation like Ireland, it is in peacekeeping that we can make our biggest contribution to the world. It's the season of goodwill, so let's quietly think for a moment of the people suffering in the war-torn Middle East. I have a special treat. Ladies and gentlemen, I want to invite onto the stage a beautiful girl from Beirut who will sing a seasonal song in Arabic. Your quietness will be much appreciated because she will sing acapella, without any backing music. Please put your hands together for Adeline Chamoon from Lebanon.'

A flushed Adeline arrives on stage to sing for the first time in front of such a large audience. Her choice is a Lebanese Christmas carol. She has been rehearsing "*Sawt el Eid*", meaning "Silent Night", for nearly two weeks under the guidance of Rocky. Whatever stage fear Adeline might have been experiencing quickly disappears as the Irish UN peacekeeping veterans wave the Lebanese flag exuberantly in front of her. A haunting moment follows as her powerful, clear voice echoes all around College Green. The audience become totally silent, as if hypnotised by both her performance and the call for peace.

After this special carol, Rocky suddenly increases the vibration, tempo and volume as Eclectic RRK launch into a performance of their recent high-flying chart singles. The show continues with Eclectic RRK due to play until ten minutes before midnight. Then, a giant screen located behind the band is scheduled to beam in "Hogmanay" celebrations from Edinburgh Castle in Scotland. At exactly midnight, a firework display over College Green will welcome in the New Year.

Ten minutes before midnight, Rocky gets the signal to stop playing. Magnificently dressed bandsmen flash onto the big screen. The master of ceremonies rushes onto the stage and snatches the microphone from Rocky. 'Ladies and gentlemen, we have a surprise for you. Make way for our own Dublin Hogmanay. Coming on stage are the pipes and drums of the Irish Defence Forces Band under the command of Company Sergeant Jim Rockingham.'

Rocky and Lizzy initially look startled but then begin to laugh as they spot Piper Jim on the big screen. 'What the f… Jaysus, Lizzy, he looks ten years younger.'

Now the pipe band emerges, through the Trinity College archway and out the gates, marching towards the stage, led by a slim Piper Jim. They proceed flawlessly through a pathway in the crowd to the, almost deafening but atmospheric, sound of "Mull of Kintyre". There is a tense expression on Piper Jim's face as his band joins Eclectic RRK up on stage. However, a wide smile from Rocky immediately sets a positive tone. It's a great moment as Rocky and Lizzy embrace the newly promoted Piper Jim. Rocky grins, wondering how the promotion was achieved. He winks at Lizzy while pointing out the company sergeant rank markings.

Then the countdown to midnight begins as the trials and tribulations of the old year are left behind. The crowd watch the clock and shout out the countdown, 'Five, four, three, two, one.'

At midnight exactly, to the backdrop of fireworks and champagne, all on stage open up with a glorious rendition of "Auld Lang Syne". The pipers provide the music, and Eclectic RRK bellow out the words. There is much handholding, hugging, kissing and even some emotional crying in the audience. A year with fresh opportunity and challenge has arrived. The pipe band repertoire continues and what follows is a specially extended performance of "Amazing Grace". First, there is a haunting pipe solo played by Piper Jim himself. Then, his entire pipe band join in, with the four members of Eclectic RRK providing backup vocals.

The master of ceremonies keeps the concert momentum moving. 'Ladies and gentlemen, a big round of applause for our pipe band who will leave us playing "*Fainne Geal an Lae*" or "The Dawning of the Day". We want you all to enjoy the dawning of a brand-new year.'

Before Piper Jim leaves the stage, he reminds Rocky of breakfast for all at Ormond Square in the morning. Then, Eclectic RRK play on for a further thirty minutes, giving the audience a taste of their forthcoming new music, including the Bowie hit title "China Girl" sung by Lizzy in Chinese.

The next morning, New Year's Day at Ormond Square, and, as predicted, the new slimline Piper Jim is beaming from ear-to-ear. With the help of two army chefs, he provides a massive Irish breakfast for all and is introduced to Adeline for the first time. After breakfast, Rocky produces the ring and, down on one knee, in front of all present, he asks the big question. It is a joyous yes and multiple bottles of champagne are popped open. Rocky does a round of the neighbours' houses in Ormond Square with a tray of champagne and introduces his new fiancée. He learns from his old neighbours that he is now considered a celebrity due to the performance of the band in the singles charts and on Radio Luxembourg. He is surprised at how well the neighbours already know the newly released singles. As Ping, Lilly and Lizzy come out onto Ormond Square with their glasses of champagne, they are besieged by locals wanting to get photos and record sleeves autographed. Adeline is shocked as Ormond Square is gradually becoming mobbed.

'Hey, Rocky, is the band that famous over here already? I never knew.'

'I never realised either. There are hundreds of people here. But it's great. We might make number one in the Irish Charts next week.'

* * *

A week later, back in Fitzrovia, Rocky and Lizzy relax, reflecting on how successful the trip to Dublin was.

'You know, Lizzy, that pipe band music could really be successfully integrated into a whole range of pop tunes. I mean, Paul McCartney and Wings have done it. We have a father who is one of the best pipers in Europe. I think I will write a tune which includes a pipe and drum solo. It would be very new, authentic…'

Lizzy finishes the sentence, '…and eclectic. Rocky, it seems that Dad has turned over a new leaf. Ha! Ha! He looked slim and fit and so did his entire band. The uniforms seemed to be brand new.'

'Yeah, you are right. The new president has taken a big interest in the pipe band. He has them at every ceremonial event in Árus an Uachtaráin. Pipe music is being reborn into the mainstream in Ireland. Dad's pipe solo at the beginning of "Amazing Grace" stole the entire show. For that magical minute, despite all the celebrations, you could hear a pin drop in College Green. He had everybody spellbound. What a musician. What a superb way to start the new year.

'Oh. Absolutely. It was fab. Look, we have had our difficulties. You know, it's a pity for all of us that everything went so wrong with our relationship.'

'Hmmm. Yeah, it is sad. But there are creative routes we could now take, Lizzy. How do you feel about us recording a single in Dublin? I will write it and include a bagpipe solo. It will be totally unique and should, at least, sell well in Ireland and Scotland. I will include Chinese, Spanish, South American and African voices singing in the background to celebrate Dublin's increasing diversity.'

'I love the idea.'

'Yeah, it will be a great morale booster for him. He can brag to whatever friends he has left that he is on Radio Luxembourg every night. Then, we can bring him over here to do an occasional live cameo performance with us in the clubs.'

'Yeah, Rocky, it's time to get rid of the bad blood. You'll want him also to play at your wedding reception in Ashford Castle in County Mayo. That will be another great moment. From being an almost broken man, he made a tremendous comeback, losing weight and getting promoted. He could not stop talking to Adeline, telling her about all his experiences in Lebanon. He was like an excited little boy. Getting engaged in Ormond Square was a brilliant idea. I am so glad that everything worked out so well. On the wedding day, he will be beaming from ear-to-ear.'

The hall phone rings and Rocky picks it up. 'This is the orderly officer in Cathal Brugha Army Barracks, Dublin here. I am looking to speak to a son of Company Sergeant Jim Rockingham.'

'Hello, sir, Piper Jim is my dad.'

'I am sorry to tell you that he passed away in St James Hospital an hour ago.'

'What?'

'He was having an operation to have his aortic heart valve replaced and unfortunately, the hospital has informed us, the procedure was not successful. He died peacefully in the operating theatre at 5.05pm this evening. Please accept my condolences. He will be a huge loss to the community of army pipers and to everybody here in Cathal Brugha Barracks.'

Rocky puts down the phone and Lizzy immediately knows that there has been bad news.

'Oh my God. It's all too late, Lizzy. Dad is dead.'

* * *

It's four days later. The army have arranged a full military funeral at Glasnevin Cemetery. A salute is fired over the grave to render military honours. Company Sergeant Jim Rockingham's pipe band plays his favourite piece, "Con Te Partirò". Many mourners accompany the band, singing the English language version, "Time to Say Goodbye."

This book is printed on paper from sustainable sources managed under the Forest Stewardship Council (FSC) scheme.

It has been printed in the UK to reduce transportation miles and their impact upon the environment.

For every new title that Matador publishes, we plant a tree to offset CO_2, partnering with the More Trees scheme.

For more about how Matador offsets its environmental impact, see www.troubador.co.uk/about/